THOUGH HEAVEN FALL

Though Heaven Fall

A Medieval Parable

JERI WESTERSON

Old London Press

Crispin Guest Mysteries by Jeri Westerson
available from Minotaur Books

Veil of Lies

Serpent in the Thorns

The Demon's Parchment

Troubled Bones

Blood Lance

Shadow of the Alchemist

Crispin Guest Mysteries available from Old London Press

Cup of Blood

 Printed in the United States of America. For information, address Old London Press PO Box 799, Menifee, CA 92586

www.JeriWesterson.com

Cover design by Jeri Westerson

ISBN-10: 1502466287
ISBN-13: 978-1502466280

First Edition: October 2014

To Craig, always

"Let justice be done though heaven fall..."—Proverbs

CHAPTER ONE

Worcestershire, 1225

Edric listened testily. He'd heard it before. It was almost the same speech word for word at the last monastery, only this one wanted to preach: how he was urged to devote his life to charity, how he looked upon each soul that came to the door as another opportunity to befriend a lost man in Christ, and on and on.

Bollocks.

Because the monk was still holding the loaf and wedge of cheese, Edric settled in and pasted on an expression of bland regard, a familiar transformation of relaxed brows, loosened jaw, and vacant eyes.

I need no reminding I'm poor, Edric reasoned, patience wearing thin. *I'm standing here at this sarding monastery, aren't I?*

The cleric's voice resonated under a stick-built covering that shivered with each strong gust. The covering must have once been a proud structure clad in tiles, but the years and the weather had taken their toll and now it hung careworn, gray, and as forgotten as Edric.

The monk eyed Edric not with the charity he preached but with a certain level of suspicion Edric had come to know well. Those eyes were red, perhaps from the cold or from long hours of reading. He wore a well kempt cassock, black for the Benedictines.

Edric's own tunic was not quite black, though it was dirty. Threadbare enough to be transparent, he layered it over several shirts to keep warm. A sooty, patched cloak hung loosely about his shoulders, with the ends of his dark, stringy hair just touching them. His stockings were bound at the calves with cloth gaiters and were checkered with holes like a nuthatch's tree.

But it wasn't his clothes exactly that kept attracting the monk's attention, though he tried to look at Edric's eyes, with little success. It was his feet he kept staring at. A worn, leather shoe covered one foot. But the other was wrapped in a leather sack, no shoe able to cover the unholy flesh beneath.

Edric sighed once more, passing a dry hand over a face weathered beyond its twenty-five years. He eyed the food and sucked his teeth. It had been a full day since his last meal, and the bread in the monk's stiff embrace, though perhaps a day old, smelled fresher than the fare he was used to. There were times he felt the pains of hunger all the way through to his spine. There was nothing akin to that pain. Nothing drove a man to such desperate actions except the groaning of one's belly. Even after it was meagerly filled there was always the sharp fear that such hunger would return with longer patches between the meals. It was that fear that made begging a stark necessity.

Impatiently, he changed the weight from one foot to the other and back again.

At last, and with breath reeking of onions, the monk handed the bread and cheese to Edric. "God's eyes be praised," Edric murmured. He swung his clubbed foot away from the shadowed archway and limped down the steps. Moving briskly, his mind fell void of thought or emotion except that of relief. He simply put the one good foot forward, hitched up his hip, and swung the other in front of him in a rolling stride, pleased to be getting quickly away from the monk's unsettling scrutiny.

He tore into the dry loaf with blunted teeth, stuffing a good fourth of it in his mouth. He bit the yellow wedge and wadded bread and cheese into one solid lump in his widened cheeks.

But before he got very far along the muddy road, before he could entirely escape the monastery's stark influence, he slowed to a disjointed amble and finally stopped completely, listening.

A chanted song from beyond the wall rose gently above the monastery's blossom-littered rooftop. Light and boundless, the tones blended harmoniously, shimmering through the heavy morning iciness.

The music filled him, smoothing his ruddy face into childlike wonder. He closed his eyes and stopped chewing. He swayed dazedly with the rhythm, forgetting the bread, forgetting the monk, and mostly forgetting himself.

Oh to make music like that! It sang in his head, dancing from heart to mind, stroking his senses. *If only I could sing.* He had tried, but he made do instead with the carved reed he used for a pipe. How could the world be so gray and lifeless, he wondered, while there were sounds such as this in it? He liked monasteries best for that. The alms were inconsistent and never filling, but often he could settle outside against a church wall and just listen while such sounds flowed from a lofty bell tower. The male voices rose like incense and filled him with its intoxicating rhythms. It was as close to being fully alive as he could come.

The tones died swiftly.

Coming back to the reality of the cold morning, Edric looked back at the monk still standing in the doorway. He assumed an air of indifference and leaned forward on his good foot. He chewed and swallowed the large wad sticking to the roof of his mouth. "What's that they're singing?"

The monk, who had watched his slow progress with a familiar mix of pity and disgust, raised his head. "That? That is the song of the Good Samaritan."

"The 'good what'?"

Sighing, the brother moved reluctantly into the courtyard. His worn shoes crunched the gravel. He carefully picked his way over the damp ground, lifting his cassock above his feet to avoid the deeper puddles. "The Good Samaritan," he said disdainfully, impatient breath fogging his face. "Surely you have heard this parable?"

The chanting melody suddenly rose again, rolled along the wall and cascaded down, spilling into the courtyard and spread outward.

Edric licked his lips. "I'm not one for Scripture, Brother."

"Our Lord Jesus told the parable of the Good Samaritan, of a man who stopped to help another in need, even though they were enemies. It is a message of charity."

Edric scowled. The music abruptly fled, leaving him again in the isolation of mist and damp early spring. He glared at the monk's fleshy cheeks. Only a shadow of a beard shrouded the pale complexion, unlike Edric's sprinkling of patchy stubble. "Charity, eh? 'Love thy neighbor'? I see." Casting his glance up and down the well-fed monk one last time, he turned and hobbled up the road.

Sarding monks! He wanted to stay at the outskirts of the monastery to listen to the music… *Bah! What does it matter?* He lumbered along, dismissing the event and grimaced when his bad foot hit the stony road. He ate the stale bread slowly, knowing it would have to last.

The road followed a swell and rose above a creek, widening to a smooth pool. Above, a heron winged, circling the nearby marshes before lighting on the water. It picked slowly along the shore, dipping its long beak in search of frogs. Cowslips bobbed along the bank, ducking from the fluttering marsh grass. Wet breezes skimmed the water, scooped the honeyed fragrance of blossoms, and carried it to Edric.

He inhaled the spring bitterly and then sat on a log, watching the heron while he finished the last of the bread and brushed the crumbs from his lap. Where would the next meal come from? "The beggin's better in a town," he muttered to the birds. "I'll not eat frogs like your lot," and he kicked at the water, sending a cockerel's tail over the still pond, frightening the birds into flight. He watched them wing in circles before they lit again on the other shore, eyeing him warily.

What *of* the next town? He remembered the face of the monk, like a thousand other expressions of pity and loathing he saw before. It was all the same. It was not that he possessed so unpleasant a face. It was a face of any ordinary young man, with its careless swath of dark brows sheltering darker expressive eyes, and a sharp nose planted solidly over full lips and square chin. On any other shoulders he would have caught the eye of many a maiden. But because these features were situated on heaping, uneven shoulders and legs of two lengths with a twisted foot at the end of the shorter one, there was little hope of an endearing look. He told himself he was used to it, even benefited. "Charity," he murmured unpleasantly.

With a sigh, he rose and journeyed onward, staying at the outskirts of town, getting his bearings. At twilight, he watched the light go out at a farmhouse from his hiding place at the edge of the woods. In the moonlight he could make out the leaning henhouse but saw no dog. He rubbed his hands together and made his stealthy way across the meadow.

A simple wattle fence separated the courtyard from the wilderness. The house itself was small and made of stone with a thatch roof. The tenant farmer who lived there might even own the modest dwelling. Which meant there would be no workmen living near the henhouse to spoil his intent.

Carefully, he unlatched the little gate and crept across the quiet yard. He stopped, listening. The inhabitants made no sound and the smoke gently huffing from the chimney hole diminished, which meant that the coals had been covered with ash for the night.

Edric stood halfway between the house and the shed that housed the chickens and he cocked his head toward the warm shadows and loose shutters of the dwelling. Inside, there was probably a family lying cozy on a straw covered pallet, each child tucked up against a parent to keep them warm. Supper had been finished and the wooden bowls stored away on a shelf for the morning meal of pottage and bread. Perhaps they sang songs before retiring, and perhaps they laughed together, the little daughter clutching a straw doll the father had fashioned, and the boy setting aside his bow made of a yew branch and arrows made of reeds.

For a moment, Edric felt the urge to peek through the shutters to see if his musings were correct, until he suddenly scowled and shook out his head. *What difference does it make?* he thought sourly. *It don't make the pullets taste any better.*

Cautiously, he slid into the shadow of the cobbled henhouse and rested against it, smelling the sharp stench of chicken droppings. Looking through the spaces between the sticks, he saw the chickens sitting in fluffy clumps on their roosts, clucking dreamily. Moonlight scored the darkness with shafts of gray light, just enough for Edric to make out ten little bodies, most of them huddled together. But there was one alone, and as luck would have it, it was the closest to Edric.

Now if I can only find the damn door! His fingers ran over the bundled sticks that made up the walls and at last found a latch. Gritting his teeth, he pulled the door open slowly and took his time reaching for the nearest hen. He knew he would have to obtain it on the first grab or they would all awaken. One hand grasped the henhouse for balance, while he snaked the other forward to close on the neck.

His stomach suddenly growled its annoyance, and he froze.

Eyes darting to each sleeping bird, he reached again, fingertips just touching the downy feathers puffed up at the neck.

Edric held his breath and did not move for several heartbeats.

The roost creaked under their rumps, but the chickens did not stir nor did the night with its noise of crickets and mice rustling in the brush cause them to awaken.

Edric darted his hand forward and closed on the neck. At the same time the bird startled he squeezed with all his might. No sound issued from the bird's constricted throat, but it thrashed and flapped until he pulled it free of the henhouse. The others complained sleepily, but never fully roused and Edric quieted the bird with a quick twist to its neck.

He smiled, licking his lips. "Easily done," he whispered to himself and chuckled. He wanted to laugh out loud.

Until he heard the low growl.

Slowly he swiveled his head and saw a dog's muzzle bearing its canines. "There's a nice pup," he cooed. The dark dog stood stiffly, snarling. Edric measured the distance between the henhouse and fence against the size of the dog, and suddenly doubted he could make it. He looked quickly at the chicken and wondered if he should not sacrifice it to the dog. His belly churned again and he scowled. "This is mine," he said, but the dog only growled again in answer.

Edric tore from the henhouse and raced across the yard. "Don't look back, don't look back…" But he could not take his own advice and looked in time to feel the air whoosh as the dog snapped for his trailing cloak.

Edric doubled his speed, using his shoulders to assist his rolling gait, but it did no good. The dog was gaining. Edric's lungs were bursting, and just as he turned again, the dog jerked upward and halted with a choking yip. It had reached the end of its tether.

Edric stopped, too, and caught his breath. The dog tried to bark, but the rope tied about its throat constricted. Edric stood three feet from the struggling dog and beamed. "Well now. Looks like your job's done, me lad. Now don't feel bad about it. You done your best. It's just that your best wasn't good enough for old Edric." He chuckled and thrust the dead chicken at the struggling dog. "This is what you're after, innit?" He shook it and the dog reached for it, nipping. Edric snatched it back with a laugh. "Don't fret. You've got nine others." He dangled the chicken before the distraught dog's face again and the dog yanked wildly on his tether, squealing with rage. "It's me what wins this time and you what loses."

The tether snapped.

"Holy Virgin!" Edric scrambled for the fence but this time the dog snagged his teeth on the hem of his cloak and yanked. With a final burst of flagging energy, Edric leapt for the fence and tumbled over it with the dog still clinging to its quarry. Struggling to disentangle himself, Edric wrestled with the cloak. "You can have the damn thing, if only I can get it loose!"

He heard a ripping sound and he was suddenly cut free. The dog shook the piece of cloak wildly as if he were breaking the neck of a rat. Edric rose, the chicken miraculously still clutched in his hand.

A light was lit in the farmhouse and Edric sprinted for the woods. He ran a long way, but after stopping to listen to the path behind him, he was finally convinced that no one followed. Once the moon lowered in the sky and lengthened the shadows to tangles and mazes, he felt secure enough to set a cooking fire in a ring of gathered stones.

He prepared the bird and suspended it over the flames on a leaning stick. He picked at the pin-feathered skin while it cooked, pressing the seared juices to his mouth with dirty fingertips. Laughing, he eyed the smoking fowl, inhaling the succulent aroma. He pulled the breast meat off the bird, happily burning his fingers on the hot flesh. Satisfied, he chewed and sat back, gnawing on the bones.

When he could eat no more, he wiped greasy hands down his tunic front and settled against a tree, tucking his feet near the warm stones by the fire. His tongue found the last of the meat, sucking it from between his teeth.

Looking up at the starry sky he felt cold on his cheeks, but its clean crispness rejuvenated. A choir of crickets began their song and an owl hooted from the dark hollows. Edric smiled. It was easier to appreciate the solitude with a full belly.

He wiped his hand again before reaching into his shirt, and pulled forth a reed pipe. Licking his lips, he pressed the reed to his mouth and blew softly. A high-pitched tone issued from the tiny reed, clear, resonant, and pure. Edric's greasy fingers played over the holes, coaxing the monastery's tune from the instrument, hearing each note in his mind. He closed his eyes and the song spilled into the night and billowed into the star-filled sky, dancing on flickering firelight.

Edric played a long time, perfecting the new tune and giving it a permanent home in his memory. Afterwards, he played other songs, merry strains that filled the night with solitary piping, until weariness told him to sleep.

In the morning and frosted with dew, Edric shook the rotting leaves aside and wiped the slugs from his cloak. There was a little left of the pullet blackening over the smoldering fire, and he pulled it off and chewed the lukewarm flesh. He decided to tramp through the woods for a while before returning to the road, just in case that farmer went searching for him. With those thoughts, he buried what was left of the carcass, scattered the fire ring, and moved hurriedly through the long morning shadows.

Coppiced alders and thickets of bracken soon gave way to the open road, and Edric stood at the verge, looking up one way and down the other. Not a soul appeared along the gently rolling plains of green.

With crooked steps he moved into the open and trudged southward, hoping to remain unmolested. His luck held, for only once did he move aside for a man with a cart of barley sacks. It lumbered over the rise, and the man gave Edric only one mistrustful glance before moving onward.

Sunshine wore a musty yellow throughout the afternoon until gray clouds blended to a dusky overcast sheet. Rain sprinkled down, lightly at first, until the streams fell harder, muddying the road to a slurry.

Edric kept to the verges, wrestling his uncooperative leg over the slick grass. He brooded again over the beautiful music, mourning his inability to sing, and hummed the tune softly instead.

"Good Samaritan," he grumbled, thinking of the monk and others like him. How many times had he stood at an almshouse with bowed head, waiting for scraps? Some monks preached to the beggars at the door while others eyed them with open contempt. Was it his fault he was born a misshapen heap of a man? Was it sin that did this to him? It must be so.

Sneering at the raining sky, he yanked the hood over his soggy brows and shook out his cloak. He patted the reed pipe kept dry and safe next to his skin. His friend.

Struggling over a root, he pondered his empty belly. If the weather cleared, he might be able to steal something from some grange. He knew of a woodsman's lodge nearby. If he could steal another hen...

His foot lurched on the slick grass and he slid down the long incline, coming to a jolt at the soft bottom of a ditch. Slowly, he lifted his head from the slurry and spit the mud from his mouth. "God's teeth and bones," he grumbled and wiped his face. He flicked the mud out of his eyes with his fingers but it continued to dribble from his lashes. Struggling to rise he slipped again.

"Christ!" Bracing himself, he propped his hand on something soft and unfamiliar. When he looked down and fixed his eyes on it, it still made no sense.

It was a hand. A white, lifeless hand.

Edric let out a hoarse scream and jerked away, scrambling backwards up the slope, staring at the lifeless form with a grimace of disgust.

The man—a tall man by the look of him—lay on his face, arms up over his head. Edric expected the putrid odor of death, but the body apparently had not yet bloated with decay.

And then it lifted an arm.

Edric sprang back again with heart pounding. "I don't want no trouble!" Edric clambered up the rest of the way and hurried a few unsteady paces away before he stopped to pant.

The tune from the monastery tickled the edge of his senses and he suddenly remembered what the monk said. The monk called it the song of the Good Samaritan, the man who stopped to help his enemy.

Edric looked back over his shoulder at the ditch. What was it to him? Some drunken fool drowning in a ditch. Maybe he was a murderer and getting his just deserts. Edric rolled his uneven shoulders. "What's it to me?" he said to the empty road.

Wet, skunky bracken swayed noiselessly with a gust, but there was no other movement, no one along the road.

"He's just some fool." In a moment, the ditch would fill with water and the man would soon drown. Edric looked up the road again, the melody of the monastery song throbbing in his skull.

The rain fell harder, thickening his lashes. Edric did not know this man. No one would care if the stranger died, least of all himself. He had his own concerns.

Walking forward a few paces Edric stopped again. Another piece of human refuse. *That'll be me someday*. Dying alone, no one to care about it. That was what he expected, after all.

Again he walked forward but again he stopped. An unfamiliar emotion tugged at his senses and he threw his head back in frustration. Gradually, his mouth formed a tight-lipped line until his face folded into a scowl and he expelled an exasperated, "Christ's bollocks!"

Swinging his bad foot forward, he half-slid, half-limped down the slope and stood over the hapless man. "Good sarding Samaritan!" he hissed. "Come, lackwit! Out of the mud with you." Grasping the man's shoulders, Edric yanked him, but he was unable to lift the man, so he clumsily rolled the limp body up the side of the ditch.

Once laid on his back, the rain peeled away the mud, revealing the stranger's extraordinary features. Only a bruising cut on one side of his forehead and mud plastering the hair to the other side of his temple marred the intriguing face. The jaw hung loosely and the eyes remained closed.

"Oi!" Edric nudged him with his foot, then harder when his prompting received no response. "Awake, me lad. I've saved your stinking hide. I'm your Good sarding Samaritan. Get up, dammit!"

The man groaned again and writhed but did not open his eyes. Edric looked about and saw a sheltered spot under a granite outcropping. With a curse, he lifted the man's shoulders and dragged him the rest of the way, leaning him against the stone while he went in search of dry wood and tinder.

At last he achieved a smoky fire. Huddling over it, Edric eyed the man coming slowly to his senses. "There now," he urged.

The man opened his eyes and glanced dazedly at his surroundings. He stared at the growing flames uncomprehendingly and raised his head toward the leafy canopy dripping with silvered droplets. Raising a hand to his temple he gingerly felt the wound.

"That's a right nasty bump you got there. Someone hit you? Rob you, did he?"

The man did not acknowledge Edric and instead studied his own lowered hand a long time. He stretched out his arm, wiggled the fingers and observed the effect. Then he pressed both hands to his temples. He ran his fingers over his nose, feeling each nostril, and then his cheeks and neck.

Edric watched amused while the man took inventory of his entire body, even running his hands down his torso.

"I didn't take naught," Edric said, and cursed under his breath for not thinking of it himself, though from his place across the fire he could well see the man wore no money pouch, no scrip of any kind.

Finally, the stranger raised his head and stared at Edric. The stranger was a handsome man, looking more like some nobleman than a beggar like Edric. His face was clean-shaven and his eyes were a piercing blue. Rusty blond hair, though disarrayed and muddy, sprouted from his head and curled about his ears. The thought occurred to Edric that if this man were a lord, there might be a reward for saving him. "Here now. Back to yourself yet?"

Somewhat amazed, the man only stared at him. The fire seemed to entrance him far more than Edric did, and he glared into the flames again, eyes barely blinking.

Cocking his head, Edric inspected the man's odd contemplation of the flames. "Did you hear me, man? Are your senses back? Who did this to you?"

Again the man glanced at Edric, glaring at him from head to foot. Slowly, he leaned against the stone and pushed himself unsteadily to his feet.

"Oh, I wouldn't do that. You've got a nasty bump. You're liable to sick up."

The stranger grasped the stone with his dirty fingernails and held on while he panted. Again he looked down at himself and then at Edric.

"Well? Can you tell me who you are? Do you know?"

The man licked his lips and upon tasting them, lifted his fingers to run them over teeth and mouth.

"I'm Edric," he said, losing patience. *And you, my man, are a halfwit, lord or no.*

"Yes," said the man weakly. "Yes, I know who I am."

"Well, now. That's an improvement." He certainly possessed the voice of a lord. Anxious, Edric rubbed his hands. He could almost taste the reward.

The man straightened and angled his head imperiously on his shoulders. Looking down his long nose at Edric, his voice grew with the intensity of authority. "Do not be afraid!" he said. "I am Azriel, an Angel of the Lord!"

CHAPTER TWO

Startled, Edric backed away from the ragged man. "What's that?"

"I said, I am Azriel, an Angel of the Lord God. You need not kneel." Azriel postured unsteadily against the stormy sky, wet tunic rippling.

Edric blinked. "You're a what?"

"An Angel. Have you never heard of Angels?" Brushing sticky leaves from his shirt, Azriel examined his torn stockings.

It should have been humorous, except for the manner of the man. It reminded too much of the monk back at the monastery. "A lunatic!" Edric cried to the woods. "I saved the life of a sarding lunatic!"

Azriel blinked, snapping up his head. "Whose life?"

"Yours, you sarding fool. They hit you harder than you thought."

"You saved my *life*?" He rested his hand on his chest then looked down curiously at the white fingers. "But I do not have a *life*."

Edric planted his fists at his hips and laughed. "Well begging your pardon, Master Angel, but if I left you back there in that ditch we would not be arguing the point now."

Alarmed, Azriel touched his face and body again, hands exploring anew. When his fingers reached his wounded temple he drew his hand away in shock. "No! O Almighty Lord, no! Not this!"

Edric looked for a heavy stick and got to his feet. Cautiously he backed from the fire. "I'll be going, then."

Azriel's blue eyes widened. "Don't go. I need your help."

"Not mine, friend." He waved his hands in dismissal and hobbled over the wet bracken.

"Wait!"

A hand darted forward and closed over Edric's wrist. Edric cowered down and yelled. "Get off! Leave me be, curse you!"

Azriel released him immediately, clasping his fluttering hands together. "But I *am* cursed. I am being punished by the Divine Father."

Edric rubbed his wrist, eyes darting furiously into the lonely woods. "Just leave me be, do you hear? Cursed you are, friend, that's a certainty. And cursed I be for ever saving you. Now let me be off!" Eyeing the madman fearfully, Edric backed away, but Azriel moved with him.

"As strange as it sounds, I need your help, Little Creature."

Edric jerked to a stop and frowned. "Here! Who the hell do you call 'little creature'? I'm Edric, and that's that!" He thumped his own breast in emphasis. "I'm nobody's little sarding creature."

"But we are all God's creatures. It is just that I am His Angel."

"You don't look like an angel. You look like a lackwit, to me."

Azriel raised his hands to his chest and buried his fingers in the wet cloth of his shirt. "I know," he muttered. "It seems…I have been sent to earth in this guise…" he blinked tremulously, "as punishment."

"Punishment? I thought if an angel needed punishment he'd just be sent to Hell."

"Never say that! God forbid!" Clapping his hands to his ears Azriel stumbled in a nervous circle, licking his trembling lips.

"Never speak of it again!"

"As you will," Edric muttered. He saw his chance and turned, walking briskly. But soon footfalls approached from behind. Over his shoulder he cried, "Go away, you madman!"

"I am not a madman," the voice called from behind. "I am an Angel! Truly!"

"Angel, madman, you're trouble, that's all I know."

"But I need your help. Stop! I command you!"

Edric half-heartedly laughed but kept going. "Command me? Tell me another. I'm just a crippled beggar. I can't do naught for you."

"I am being punished, yet I do not know what I am to do for recompense. This…this world is strange to me and this body…I do not understand it. It is so…heavy."

Azriel slowed and teetered before sitting abruptly on a nearby rock. He dropped his face into open palms. "My head…it hurts," he said through muffling fingers.

Edric paused to eye him. He was never this close to a madman before. Might he become violent? "Punishment for what?"

"I do not know."

Edric laughed at that, but sobered when Azriel jerked up his head with a scowl.

"Why do you laugh? You are just a miserable little creature. I could smite you with a mere look."

Edric laughed again. "Could you, now? I'd like to see that!"

Azriel rose up, his face reddening.

Suddenly thinking better of it, Edric backed away, but the "angel" did nothing more than fiercely glower.

Azriel's face collapsed into a deep frown. "I do not understand. I have no powers at all. Oh, this is dreadful!"

Laughing nervously, Edric leaned on his good foot and searched the countryside for a scapegoat. "Go back up the road. There's a monastery there. They'll help you."

Azriel clutched his hands, shaking his head. "No, no. Not a monastery." He sat again, staring at his worn shoes. He lifted one foot, then the other, looking sideways at the worn leather.

Edric regarded the forlorn man with irritation. He thought to make a run for the woods, lose him in the shadows and dark hollows. He knew well how to lay low, to be part of the forest to hide himself.

While he considered, he noticed the shadows of evening closing in and the fire flickering weakly behind Azriel. Perhaps it might be better to spend the night, make certain the man was well enough to travel, and then leave him by first light. He glanced up into the drizzling sky and beyond to the Heaven he never understood. "It's late," Edric said cautiously. "Let's go back to the fire and warm ourselves."

"And why would that help?" Azriel moaned into his hands, wet hair falling over his knuckles.

"Because I'm freezing me bollocks off here." Without waiting, Edric moved back to the fire and crouched by the flames, holding out curled fingers to the warmth.

For a long moment, Azriel stayed immobile except to sway forlornly, his face buried in his hands. A soft murmuring lament escaped his enclosing fingers while he prayed or wept.

Edric glanced once in Azriel's direction and spit into the fire. *Good. Stay there. Freeze to death.*

A few moments passed before Azriel slowly raised his head. With a melodramatic sigh and a petulant tilt to his shoulders, he dragged himself to the fire and lowered heavily to a rock. Edric scooted away, putting the flames between them. For a long time they sat in silence while the landscape darkened and crickets called over the crackle of licking fire.

"What sort of fool name is Azriel, anyway? Is it Welsh?"

The stranger glanced up at Edric, blinking. "No. It means 'God helps'."

Edric laughed again. "He didn't help you, did He? Abandoned you."

Azriel blanched. "You are a strange creature. An Angel of the Lord appears to you and you are completely unconcerned."

"Two things about that, *Master* Angel. One: you're not an angel; and two: I don't believe in them. In Heaven neither, for that matter."

Azriel jerked to his feet. "I have never heard such blasphemy! How could you *not* believe?" Azriel shook his head. "I do not understand Man at all. You sin, you help no one, you love no one, and then you do not understand your own lives. It is a wonder any of you get to Heaven."

Edric readjusted his layers of tunics. "No more of that talk, now. You make me skittery." He hugged himself for warmth, eyes following the amber flicker.

After a time, his glance irresistibly rose again to the forlorn expression of the self-styled angel. Did the man believe this nonsense *before* he was struck, or only *after*? "Do you remember who hit you? Was it robbers?"

Azriel raised a hand to his head but did not touch the growing bump. He dropped down by the fire again. "No one hit me. It must have been…when I…fell."

"Fell? Into the ditch?"

"No," he said miserably. "When I…*fell*." Slowly his eyes inched upward and Edric followed the glance into the heavens.

Edric puffed a snort of disgust. "Ha! More like you was pushed."

Horror thinned Azriel's features and he mumbled an indecipherable lament for several minutes. He shook his head and finally fell silent.

Relieved, Edric settled back. Walking was wearying, especially with his irregular gait. With lids drooping, he thought of sleep, hoping the "angel" would succumb first, but his tired eyes snapped open when Azriel heaved a distraught sigh.

"This is *such* a feeble body! I do not know how you stand it. I was an amazing being. Much greater than this. Brighter than even these flames."

Edric sat up again with a weary sigh, rubbed his chapped hands near the fire, and tossed another broken branch onto it. He eyed

Azriel critically. "I thought angels had wings."

"Something like wings. But we are fire and power. Mighty."

"'How the mighty are brought low', eh?"

Azriel darted a barbed glance. "That is not funny."

"Isn't it? I think you're being punished for pride. It sounds like you've a lot to learn."

The smoke curled, lofting into the air above their heads in white puffs. Azriel did not move. His voice lowered in warning. "You would never dream of saying such to me if I were in my full raiment."

"You mean motley?"

"You are a particularly insolent creature!"

Edric did not like that tone. It reminded too well of all the arrogant faces on perfect shoulders, two perfect feet striding forward to tell him to shove off. And that grating term "creature."

Edric popped angrily to his feet and jabbed a finger at Azriel. "I told you not to call me a 'creature'!"

Mildly aroused, Azriel glanced up. "Do you actually intend to strike me? How interesting."

The anger that drove Edric dissipated. He lowered his arms and examined the lofty stranger anew. A blue bruise formed on the side of Azriel's face where the crusted blood dried, and mud still flattened the hair to his scalp. A hole was torn through on the knee of his stocking, and the sole of one shoe flapped from the rest of the leather. He did not even have a cloak.

Shrugging, Edric limped back to his place. "Bah. Only a fool would bother to strike a lackwit, and I'll be damned if I'm ever called a fool." He sat heavily, hunched over his knees, and scowled at Azriel from under brooding brows. *Little sleep I'll get this night.*

"You talk of…damnation…a great deal," said Azriel gravely. "I wonder if you truly know what you are saying."

"What? Do you mean Hell?" He said it with particular delight, watching Azriel cringe.

"Yes," Azriel whispered. "Surely you do not understand, or you would not speak so."

"Suppose you tell me." Edric settled back indifferently, closing his eyes.

"Shall I?"

Edric's eyes snapped open when he heard Azriel rise and move toward him. Fully awake, Edric scooted to a sitting position, his hand reaching for the hilt of his knife.

"When you creatures die, there comes a judgment," said Azriel. "The Divine Father shows you what you have done with your miserable little lives. For some, it is Heaven. But for many more, the cleansing fires of Purgatory are mete. But for still others, it is Hell. Do you think you can imagine the Pit with your puny little minds? Do you think it is serpents and demons with pitchforks? Is that your view? How paltry. You have no idea."

Azriel's voice softened. "Do you understand that the presence of the Divine Father is light and love eternal? That it is so powerful and encompassing in its glory that it is unimaginable to such small creatures like yourselves?" Breathing rapidly, eyes afire, Azriel moved closer. Edric crept backwards, regretting for the hundredth time saving the man's life. "At the moment of judgment," Azriel went on, "you are shown the most fleeting vision of this splendor, and then…the light, the love, the immense knowledge is suddenly snuffed out like a candle flame. And through all eternity in unceasing regret, you know the tremendous loneliness under which you are now yoked! A loneliness you yourself chose."

Edric grimaced, shrinking back. "That's enough of that."

Azriel drew closer, features more menacing in the uncertain fire glow. "To know you could have possessed all, but lost it for all time through your own neglect and apathy—that is the very essence of damnation!"

"I said that's enough!"

"Your soul pleads, it screams, it writhes in the agony of eternal darkness and solitude, but there is no reprieve!"

"Stop it!"

"So," Azriel said calmly. "It *does* frighten you."

"*You* frighten me! Off with you! I don't give a damn if you freeze to death! I'll not have you nigh me tonight. Get out, you hear?" The blade hissed from its makeshift scabbard. Its nicked steel gleamed dully in the campfire's light.

Azriel stared down at the short knife. "Is that a weapon? You show yourself in your true light. Mark what I said of Hell. It is your very next destination."

The blade slashed outward and Azriel reeled back with a gasp, clutching the cut to his arm. Amazed, he watched the blood flow and then raised his eyes. "I *felt* that!" he said incredulously. "You meant to hurt me!"

Edric rolled to his feet, still holding the knife forward. "Damned right! And so did you with your words!"

Clutching the wound, Azriel slowly sat. Blood flowed over his fingers. "Look how it flows. Red. Red. The pain so sharp!"

"So were your words. Don't I hear enough hurtful words in me life? I don't need the same from a madman! Be off, or I'll kill you!"

Mildly, Azriel raised his face. "Would you add that to your sins?"

"Off with you!"

"You are right, of course. I did mean to hurt you. Words are all I have left."

"Then off! I've no use for words."

"I shall be on my way and trouble you no more. Except..."

"Except what?"

Sweat speckled Azriel's pale face. "I...I suddenly do not feel well."

Edric watched helplessly as Azriel fell face down in the rotting leaves, breath raising his shoulder blades. Edric stared a moment and prodded the unconscious Azriel with his foot before nodding in satisfaction with a jerk of his head.

Sleeping on and off, Edric finally sat up and watched the day lighten. The rain had stopped hours ago, laying a blanket of glistening droplets and the musty scent of damp leaves over the woods. The pale silk of spiders' webs among the grass became visible with dew.

Azriel breathed but did not awaken. *Maybe the sleep will do him good*, Edric thought. Who was this madman? Was it dangerous to be in his company? Edric snorted. He just wanted to be on his way with no further mishaps. Perhaps he should leave now before the man awoke. That idea aroused Edric to his feet.

Then Azriel stirred.

Edric stood back and reached for his knife. "Oi! Lackwit!"

Gingerly, Azriel sat up. He examined the cloth binding his arm and then discovered it came from his own tunic hem.

Edric gestured with his knife. "Off you go, then, do you hear? Go back to wherever you came from."

For a moment Azriel merely sat cradling his arm in the other, staring at Edric with an unreadable expression. Then he laughed. White, even teeth spread his cracked lips. The laughter soon ripened to hysterics. But as suddenly as it began, the laughter stopped, and Azriel ducked his head, rocking and clutching his upraised knees. "Go back? Why Little Creature, I want nothing more than that. I want no more of this place. This is not my home. It is cold and dark and lonely…and filled with *your* kind, fleshy shells encasing shriveled souls. I do not like it here. I do not like *you*. And I would leave if only I could."

An unfamiliar coldness seeped up Edric's chest. "I should have slashed your throat when I had the chance."

"Yes," whispered Azriel. "I almost wish you had."

Rolling his eyes, Edric waved a dismissal and limped forward. "I'm off. Good luck to you."

"You are leaving me, then?"

"I told you where the monastery is. If you're troubled, you'd best go there."

"No! I said no monasteries!"

"Suit yourself." Edric did not look back.

He parted the brush and Azriel disappeared from view. Edric trudged forward, back in his element. Wet clusters of spindle soaked his stockings and pulled on the ragged hem of the knee-length outer tunic. He bunched his cloak about him.

Yet even while he struggled over a fallen log, he wondered what would become of the man who thought himself an angel. "Of all the fool things…" Chuckling, he landed on the other side of the log, catching his cloak momentarily on a twig before pulling it free, and limped swiftly into the foliage.

Deep in the woods and feeling safe at last, Edric was stopped by a sound. It rose out of the distance, strange and haunting. It pierced the unyielding tangle of woodland and absorbed the dense echoes.

A solitary voice. Its mournful song raised gooseflesh up Edric's neck. It rose clearly into the rising sunlight like ascending motes of dust with such resonant beauty that it threatened to overwhelm his senses

Edric turned, and without another clear thought, he quickly strode back through the woods, pushing aside brakes of yew and buckthorn until he parted the undergrowth and reached the little clearing where he and Azriel spent the night.

Azriel had not moved except to throw back his head. His dirty blond hair rested upon his cloak-less back. Eyes closed, neck rising and rolling with music, he sang his lament into the dappled canopy.

Edric leaned against a tree. So beautiful. Only his pipe could make those sounds. The beauty of it ached his heart, so tangible and yet so unreachable.

Breathless, he listened until the song came to its end and then he summoned the courage to stagger forward. "You sing like a…like a…"

"Like an Angel?" Azriel's mouth formed a rueful curve. "Yes."

Edric licked his lips and brought out the pipe. Slowly and precisely, he played the best imitation of Azriel's song, even finishing in a long, solemn note like the stranger had done. He lowered the pipe. They regarded one another.

"To use your words," said Azriel, "'what is it to me?'"

"You may be a madman but you have a talent, friend. One I can use…I mean…that can be turned to a good end." He crouched, tucking the pipe away. "I learned m'self how to make music. It's a small gift, but one owed me for so many miseries. I play in the towns and they throw coins. Sometimes. It's what I'm good at. But along with your singing, we'd eat well. What you think?"

"Do I understand you correctly? You want *me* to sing and play for the other Little Creatures in order to make a living?"

Frowning, Edric rose and attempted to square his shoulders. "Aye. What's wrong with that? It's better than begging."

With one graceful movement, Azriel stood. He regarded Edric down his nose. "I am an Angel. A Divine Spirit. I have no need to 'make a living'."

"Well down here you do." Snorting, Edric threw up his hands. "Go on, then. You've got better things to do, haven't you? Flit about in the meadow and all. Looking for your halo. Meantime, the rest of us have to eat. That's *our* lot, Master Angel." He forked an obscene gesture with his fingers before he turned. "A little humble living is what's needed to learn a thing or two about pride, but don't let me stop your moping." Cursing, he stomped into the undergrowth.

"Wait!" Wind lifted Azriel's golden hair gently from his shoulders. A rusty stain colored the cloth binding the slashed arm. Even hurt and dirty, Azriel appeared formidable, but Edric's fear dampened. He knew what this man was.

"There is…*something* to what you say," Azriel admitted, ducking his head. "I do not know the reason the Divine Father sent me here to be one of you, but perhaps it is to learn a lesson in humility." He swallowed. His eyes darted past Edric, seeking deeper into the woods. "It is indeed a humbling experience to be deprived of all that I was."

"Right. Does that mean you'll go with me, then?"

Grudgingly, Azriel nodded. Edric smiled, but just as quickly sobered. Was this a victory won…or lost?

CHAPTER THREE

Brother Latimer strode briskly through the shadow-striped cloister, wishing he had worn another under tunic to keep the wind at bay. Its lament howled through the arcade every spring, urging the monk to glance over his shoulder with a shiver. He looked down the long row of arched carrels with their smoky braziers, past the rain-glittered cloister grass, and finally up toward the two-story dwelling, the monk's dorter. It rose above the stone walls and hugged their gray planes like a loose mantle. Dark arched windows gouged a bright exterior shining from an early morning drizzle.

He reached the last empty carrel, eyes examining the tight nook of desk and worn seat, before he paused at the stone arch, fingering the scabrous limestone. Stark coldness emanated from deep within the rock. He thought it strange that there was no warmth to be found in its permanence.

The high corner window in the dorter caught his attention again and he sighed. His customary carrel was this last one, but Brother Peter's was the one directly behind. Now some other young monk sat shivering on the wooden seat studying a rat-gnawed book.

Latimer rested his angular cheek against the stone. His dark eyes blinked in languid remembrance before they lowered.

What was cannot be again. But he did miss those days, the early ones at the monastery, when it was all fresh and new and terrifying. Who but Brother Peter with his irreverence could bring a smile to his face, even when a solemn expression was more to the point? How many times did they both get into trouble for it?

Latimer chuckled, causing the young monk in the carrel to glance up.

Latimer moved away from the arch and flopped the cowl over his dark ring of hair. It was streaked with silver now. When had time tinted his hair and creased the flesh at his eyes? Slowly it had happened. Everything at a monastery by necessity happened slowly. Was that a blessing or a curse?

With measured steps, he walked along the greensward in the center of the cloister, resting his hands within his scapular. It was best to forget. The mourning was over, or should be by now. Life went on in that slow, precise manner.

He wanted to see the abbot and then the rector about the meals. The stores were scarce on lentils and the rector asked if they could not substitute the pickled oxtails or should simply go without. Since the consumption of flesh was only allowed certain days of the week he did not know how he could allow the substitution, yet to cut the rations even more during the spring with so much to do seemed counterproductive.

He shrugged to himself. If it were up to him, he would allow it. But he was not the abbot. Just the sub prior, the overseer. He turned on his heel, shaking off the odor of resentment, and headed for the warming house.

Friendly vapors from an ash-log hearth fire greeted him while he ascended the short steps. The cool skin of his face immediately felt a splash of warmth. The door to the abbot's lodge was open, and so Latimer merely stood in the archway a brief moment until acknowledged. "My Lord Abbot," he said with a bow, before tossing his cowl back onto his shoulders.

Abbot Gervase nodded. A younger monk standing before him twisted round. Latimer guessed the monk was seventeen or eighteen—at least some twenty-odd years younger than himself. A pug nose protruded over pink, trembling lips, and ginger hair flamed over the bone white of a tonsured scalp. Latimer squinted mildly at him without recognition.

"Brother," said the abbot to Latimer. "Come. Meet our newest monk, Brother Herbert."

"*Benedicti*," Latimer said with a brief nod.

"*Deo Gratias*."

"Brother Herbert comes from Evesham. We have so few young brothers here that my dear brother abbot offered him to us. At least during reconstruction."

"Good. The work in the fields has begun in earnest as well. More hands are needed."

"I knew you could find suitable tasks for him, Brother Latimer. Will you show him about the grounds?"

"Yes, my Lord Abbot. Of course. But the rector asks again about the oxtails…"

"Tell him no, Brother. Lentils or nothing, I am afraid."

"As you will," he said, ducking his face. It was so small a thing. Surely St. Benedict himself would not insist… Catching the eye of the young monk, Latimer flattened his expression. "Come along, then."

The nervous monk's footfalls scratched the chalky pavement behind him. The noise persisted across the courtyard a long way before Latimer angled his face over his shoulder with barely concealed annoyance. "You need not walk behind me as if I were a lord."

"Forgive me." Herbert scurried to catch up and fell into timid step beside Latimer. "It was different at Evesham. The newer monks were required to defer to the older."

"It is so at all monasteries, Brother, only we at Pershore do not insist on so obvious a display." Brother Herbert said no more and lowered his head. They passed the wounded church with its scorched walls and broken roof, and Herbert lifted his smooth chin. Latimer watched the younger man's eyes widen.

Gesturing toward the cracked walls of the presbytery, Latimer said only, "This is one of the many projects set for us, Brother. As you see, laborers are few. Masonry like this is best left to experts, but some of our brothers are allowed to help." Dark cassocks moved along the catwalks while Latimer spoke. The monks hoisted buckets burdened with stone to a higher scaffold where masons chipped the set blocks into place between the wooden beams.

"A fire," was all Latimer offered in explanation, yet he saw Herbert glance worriedly toward the monk's quarters. "The fields have been planted, but always, there is much weeding to be done."

Reaching the wooden gate, Latimer rested his chapped hands on the stone posts and leaned over. Latimer inhaled the sweet scent of turned soil touched by the mustiness of last year's rotted stalks.

Herbert joined him, and followed his glance up the slope to the fields. Dark soil speckled with puddled water followed the lee side of the monastery wall. A few monks hacked dispiritedly against the invading weeds. A young oblate fanned away ravens with a ragged cloth.

"Which of these tasks suit your mood, Brother?" asked Latimer with only a breath of a smile.

Herbert vigorously shook his head. "It is not for me to decide, Brother. Surely that is your task."

"Quite right." He watched the fieldworkers a silent moment before jerking his head toward the church. "Then it is the church."

"Brother!"

Herbert's strained cry drew Latimer back. He frowned. Was this young creature going to be trouble? "Yes, Brother Herbert?"

"It is just that…perhaps I *am* better suited to the fields. I do not know if I would be comfortable…that is, the church… It burned, did it not? *Someone*…burned it."

Latimer scrutinized the young monk's smooth, white face. He suspected the reason for Herbert's discomfort, but refused to help. Latimer stood instead with a blank face and hands folded loosely in front of him.

"That is," Herbert went on, "I heard tell it so. Someone *here* burned it." His voice fell to a husky whisper, "The Mad Monk."

Latimer's jaw tightened. He expected it, yet it still grated. "His *name* is Brother Peter," he said in a controlled tenor. "We do not call him the 'Mad Monk'."

"Oh...forgive me, Brother. It is just that I have heard—"

"What you have heard and what is the truth are two different matters, no doubt." The boy was a chittering squirrel. He was no one. Why should it vex him? He blinked at Herbert instead, inhaling deeply. "It is true that Brother Peter did cause the St. Urban's Day fire that damaged the church, but it was an accident."

"He is not insane, then?"

Resisting a strong urge to tell the boy to mind his own business, Latimer smoothed his expression to complete blandness. But his eyes could not help but glance toward the upper corner window of the dorter. "He...well...Brother Peter is not able to..." He sighed, checking the anger that was unfairly directed to the innocent monk, no matter how rude he was. "He is not quite sane, no. But there was a time when he was," he quickly added. "Quite extraordinarily adept at his work here."

"What did he do here? Before..."

"He was the librarian. A true scholar. He was well acquainted with many of the greatest written works. He knew many languages. Brother Peter was...*is* a rare man."

"But...you said..."

Latimer turned toward the dorter, following Herbert's gaze. "He lives in that upper room. You obviously know this because you keep looking there. He never leaves it."

"Oh. Is he not...is the door not...bolted?"

"He is locked in, Brother, if that is your query. He has to be. The night of the fire...that terrible night..." He raised a hand to his face, almost feeling the heat still radiating from the blaze. Sweat-scorched skin and the smell of old timbers and burning pitch still plagued his memories. "It was two years ago. Best forgotten."

"But what happened to him?" Growing bolder, Herbert pressed closer.

"No one knows. He was an unusual man, full of energy and spirit. Perhaps he was too intelligent, too full of information with little outlet. I do not know."

"Were you close to him?"

"He was my dearest friend." Galled suddenly by so intimate a confession to a stranger, Latimer drew himself up and turned a scrolled nostril toward the younger monk. "He is my very dear brother in Christ…as are you."

"Is he dangerous? I feared to come here when they told me, but I could not object. And I must confess," he said, his fingers dancing together, "I still fear to be here."

"Why should you fear him? Brother Peter is locked in his room." Latimer turned toward the church again in an attempt to redirect the conversation. There was no more to say. He walked several paces instead to show by example, but the fool young monk would not take the hint.

"But is he dangerous, Brother? If you must keep him locked away—"

"He is 'locked away' as you call it, to protect *him*. He…he cannot care for himself any longer."

"Who cares for him, then?"

"We all do. We take our turn. You will as well, when the time comes."

Abruptly, Herbert stopped and lifted his face again toward the dorter. "Me?" he gasped. "I do not think I shall be able to do it."

"Come, Brother," Latimer answered sharply. "Let us move quickly to the church and to your duties. We have wasted much time on useless chatter."

It was simple to shut his mind to Herbert. Latimer set his senses instead to the rhythm of the masons' hammers, mirroring the faint sounds of the hoes in the fields. His mind filled with lists again, of his rounds to check on his many spheres of duty within the monastery: the rectory, the hostelry, the almonry. So many duties to look after, so few capable of performing their tasks with any skill. Latimer would dispatch this one to work on the church.

Herbert would get used to the idea of Brother Peter just like all the rest did. It was only a matter of time, and did they not have that in abundance?

Fleetingly, Latimer wondered what his life would have been like outside the protection of abbey walls. He might have been a scribe for a lord, perhaps moving up into the position of steward.

An airless chuckle escaped his lips. He was steward now, and very safe within the hive of the monastery. The world outside could be a bitter place, undignified in its demands. Here was a community of like minds…well, at least like temperaments. After twenty years of cloistered life, he was settled and content. If only Peter could have continued to be a part of it. In the back of his mind, he harbored the hope that Peter would recover his senses, return to the camaraderie they once shared. Intellectually, he knew this to be impossible, but in the innocence of his heart and in the underlying fervency of his prayers, he continued to hope.

Latimer stopped before the open archway of the church and planted his hands within the wide cuffs of his sleeves. Herbert stopped with him, raised his face, and heaved a trembling sigh. Latimer scowled. *Lord preserve us from timid monks*!

Resigned, Herbert took a step forward. The church's shadow washed the pale of his skin to gray tones. He would have disappeared into its charcoal depths completely had the shouts not echoed down the cloister. Herbert cringed at the incongruous noise and then fell back against the doorposts.

The cries came first from the direction of the fields, but then the agitated alarm soon rippled from man to man. Frenzied becassocked figures appeared, running across the courtyards and down the colonnades. Amazed, Latimer stepped back against the wall.

The frantic sound of shoes slapped the stone cloister walk. A monk, terrified and distressed, careered through the shadows, but upon recognizing Latimer he swung toward him and clutched his arms. "Brother Latimer! May Almighty God help us!"

"Brother Gavin, what is it?"

Gavin lowered his head and rested his weight upon Latimer. He drew in a long, labored breath before raising his face again. "It is Brother Peter!" he gasped. "He is gone!"

CHAPTER FOUR

Edric stole glances at the tall man. Azriel seemed to observe the landscape with curiosity, but after a while he appeared to lose interest and turned his sober gaze toward the road ahead.

Lonely copses and tinted headlands gave way to a gentle swell of hills. A scattered mixture of leaning houses shouldering a long, low wall of stone finally revealed a village.

Edric braced himself for the expected reaction to his appearance, and when it came in its grimaces and shudders he did not follow with anger. After all, he needed to beg money from these people. It didn't do to enrage them. Coins came after pity not anger.

He made his way over the muddy gutter and through milling folk to the stone cross standing in the center of the village. The cross itself was ancient, crumbled and veined with mossy cracks. Edric clambered up its steps and settled against it before taking out his pipe.

When the music lifted into the air and the village folk began to gather, Edric winked at Azriel standing nervously aloof. Azriel stared back uncomprehendingly, even looking back over his shoulder at whoever it was Edric was gesturing to. Grimacing over the pipe, Edric gestured again and with more urgency.

Finally realizing what Edric wanted, Azriel sighed heavily and moved to the foot of the cross. Taking a deep breath, he opened his mouth.

The amazingly fluid sounds of Azriel's voice filled the square and Edric caught himself to keep from missing a note. He played the song through to the end and Azriel sang every verse, every refrain to perfection.

When the song ended at last, cold silence followed.

Edric held his breath and lowered the pipe. Why were they staring like that, he wondered? Did he misread Azriel's voice? Was it not amazingly beautiful? Was it only his imagination that fashioned it so? Or perhaps… was it witchery? Maybe only *he* heard it that way.

Edric limped to the edge of the step. He readied to hurl himself forward out of harm's way.

But then, the first tentative cheers began. To Edric's surprise, modest showers of silver coins were flung forward, rolling and spiraling toward their feet.

Edric stared at the coins gleaming in the sunshine. Never before did he see this much generosity. Slowly, he lifted his stubbled face to Azriel and smiled, but Azriel glanced back without emotion and made no move toward the bounty.

Dismissing him, Edric hobbled forward, scooped up the scattered coins, and hurriedly stuffed them into his pouch. "Would you have another song, good masters?" he asked excitedly, rubbing sweaty palms down his shirtfront. When a few mumbled their assent Edric raised the pipe and licked his lips. "You ready, Azriel?"

"From your manner, I expected this to be difficult."

Without answering, Edric began to play again. Three more songs they sang, and half a sausage, a loaf of bread, and a wedge of cheese were left at their feet. Edric prepared another song, but while he wiped the pipe down his tunic front he found himself glancing up at the face of the village priest. Instantly, he popped the pipe clumsily within his shirt and bowed. "God keep you, m'lord."

The priest glared at the two while the village folk scattered. "What is this revelry during the working day? Who are you?"

"We are only humble men, m'lord," said Edric. Carefully, he made his way down the steps. He bent further to make his back appear more hunched, and gazed upward at the priest through stringy hair. "Only humble men, m'lord. Earning a wage through song."

"There are far more industrious ways to earn a wage. But…I see you are afflicted."

"Aye, m'lord."

Turning his frowning countenance to Azriel, the priest examined him from head to foot. "Although this one looks hale enough."

Azriel eyed the priest critically. "Who are you?"

"Who am *I*? I am the parish priest. Who are *you*?"

"I am Azriel, an Ang—"

"We were just leaving," said Edric, hastily taking Azriel's wrist and yanking him away.

Angling toward them, the priest raised a hand. "Just one moment."

Edric blanched. He squeezed Azriel's arm desperately.

"This one has the manner of a lord," said the priest, "yet he does not look as a lord should."

"I am not a lord," Azriel answered. "I am a servant, like yourself."

"I serve God."

"As do I."

The priest and Azriel locked eyes in a fierce appraisal of the other. If the priest made complaint, they could lose all the fine coins they gained. Edric tried to mutter a prayer but it came out as a curse.

The priest opened his lips to speak but nothing came out. The priest blinked, rubbed his chin with a finger, and slowly stepped back, frowning.

"Let's be off, Azriel!" urged Edric, pulling on him. "M'lord, we will sing no more today, if that is your will." With a tight hold of Azriel's arm, Edric yanked, sending Azriel stumbling backward and suddenly out of the priest's sphere.

Edric looked back over his shoulder. The priest had not moved and continued to stare at them in puzzlement.

Edric kept Azriel close, hissing into his side, "What you want to go and do that for? You can't tell nobody your lunatic tale of being an angel. It don't make sense to folk, see?"

"He thought what we did was without value," he said looking back.

"It had plenty, if you ask me." Edric shook the pouch and listened to the jingle of coins with a satisfied grin. The sausage was tucked into his belt, the bread under his arm, and the cheese in his pouch. "Let's sit over here and eat."

They sat in the shade of a blacksmith's paddock, nestling on the grass. The sun warmed, lofting the sweet scent of thatch into the air. Edric stretched his legs out with a sigh and pulled out the pungent sausage and the round loaf. He dug his teeth into the sausage, tearing off a chunk in his mouth before handing the sausage to Azriel.

Azriel watched Edric chew for a moment while he examined the greasy meat in his hands. "Do you not give thanks?"

Cheeks bulging with food, Edric merely chuckled. "To who?" he said, spitting bits of food upon his lap while he spoke. He wiped the spittle from his chin with the back of his hand.

"To the Divine Father, of course!"

"Why?" Edric stuffed in more food until his mouth could barely hold it all, exhaling through flared nostrils. "He didn't give it to me. These fools did," and he waved his hand toward the town.

"But without the Divine Father's intervention there would be nothing."

"And there's many a time I've thanked Him for naught," he chuckled. "Go on. Eat."

Azriel shook his head in disdain and mumbled a prayer. Only then did he take a bite, grimacing while he chewed the sausage.

Edric hummed while he ate, pleased his belly would be full and his purse as well. It was a long time since he owned a decent amount of coin, and even the madman's annoyed expression could not spoil it. He tore into the bread and swallowed, feeling thirsty from the salty meat and dry bread. Edric looked up and noted an unattended wineskin hanging on a peg near the blacksmith's archway. Licking his lips, he realized he had not tasted spirits for many days.

Rising, Edric dropped the bread and sausage into Azriel's lap. "I'll be back," he said and hobbled to the post and stood quietly until his presence was no longer noticed. Smoothly, he lifted the skin from its peg, stuffed it within his cloak, and sauntered back toward Azriel. "Come along, Azriel. We can't tarry all the day."

Azriel followed for several paces before Edric pulled forth the skin and drank from it, spilling its scarlet contents in rivulets on either side of his mouth. "Want some?" he asked, holding it forth.

Azriel eyed it and shook his head. "It looks to be very poor wine. Why did you waste the money?"

Edric rumbled a chuckle. "I didn't," he said and took another swig.

For a moment, Azriel's face remained impassive until the implication of Edric's smile sunk in. "Did you *steal* that?"

Edric spit the wine across his chest, catching the droplets at his chin with a cupped hand. "Be still, you whoreson!"

"You *did* steal it! Edric, that is a *sin*! Do you know *nothing*?"

Eyes darting, Edric motioned plaintively with his free hand even while he tried to hide the skin beneath the cloak. "Keep still!"

Azriel threw up his hands and raised his face heavenward. "First you blaspheme—the greatest sin—and now you steal!"

Fearfully, Edric eyed the passing villagers who began to slow and harken to Azriel's loud admonishment. Two burly men halted deliberately before Edric and pointed fat fingers at the bulge in his cloak.

Oi!" said one. "What you got there?"

"Naught, good master," said Edric with a tense bow.

Beside himself with wrath, Azriel bristled. "And now you lie!"

Edric's eyes rounded with disbelief and then with horror when the crowds moved in. Desperately, he scanned the street. Alleys cut through on either side. An alehouse blew smoke and drunken men into the muddied lane, joining the disgruntled townsfolk already approaching.

"What's the cripple done?" someone asked.

"Stole something," came the reply.

"But there's a mistake," Edric pleaded, eyes darting.

Someone yelled, "Get him!" and they all converged.

Without hesitation, Edric shoved Azriel at them, and took off at a run.

CHAPTER FIVE

Brother Gavin spoke quickly. They hurried toward the warming house and Latimer, barely able to catch his breath, listened to each gasped word. It was not until they burst in upon the abbot that Latimer realized Herbert was still with them, cowering within the shadows of the wall and well out of the way.

Before the abbot could object to their unannounced arrival, Gavin lurched forward. "Brother Peter has escaped!"

Gervase paled and fell back into his chair. "Blessed Virgin!"

"One of the fieldworkers saw it, my Lord Abbot," Gavin went on. "He had tied his cassock together with the bed sheets to make a rope and lowered it out the window. But it was still a good ten feet to the ground. He must have taken a terrible fall."

"Was the room checked?" asked the abbot.

"Yes, my lord. I did so myself. Not a soul, and the door was still tightly bolted. Last night's supper was still there. He must have done it in the middle of the night."

"What of his mixtum?"

"Brother Peter never ate a morning repast," said Latimer flatly. It was as if his head were encased in wool. Sounds were muffled and movements blurred. It was unbelievable. Unbelievable!

"Did...did you search the grounds?"

"The brothers are doing so now. But he must be long gone, with all night and all morning..."

Latimer stared at the abbot. Neither one breathed. "You know him best, Brother Latimer. What would he do? I fear for the church—"

"No, no," Latimer heard himself mutter. "He would not do that again. He would flee. Yes, I think he would flee. To where…I do not know."

"Oh brothers," said the abbot shaking his head. "We must find him. His violent and unpredictable nature would surely wreak havoc upon the innocent. We cannot allow that."

Gavin rested his trembling hands within his scapular. "What do you propose we do, my Lord Abbot?"

"We go in search. Brother Latimer, you, of course, must go."

Breathing at last, Latimer lowered his head in a nod of compliance. "Yes, my lord."

"But not alone. Oh, I cannot spare anyone!" His glance darted toward Herbert cringing in the corner. "Take this brother with you."

"My lord!" cried Herbert.

"Now Brother Herbert, comport yourself. Obedience."

"But my Lord Abbot…I…I…"

Latimer rested his hand on the young monk's shoulder. Herbert's pale face turned to his. "Trust in God," he said softly. "And in me."

Herbert fell silent while the abbot explained Latimer's duties. No one was to know except the knight Hugh Varney whose lands lay directly outside the abbey demesne. A message would be sent, but in the meantime, the two monks were to go in search secretly. "You must not alarm the community. My brothers, go in haste and go with God."

Latimer advanced to the stables with measured and careful steps. It was a nightmare, echoing so many other nightmares before it. Oh Brother Peter. Why did God choose to slay his mind, a mind so nimble and shrewd? Was it some flaw in his character? In Latimer's? Were they both being punished for some forgotten sin?

He shook his head subtly, chasing the unwholesome thoughts. He told himself to calm and then mounted the awaiting horse.

They passed under the gatehouse arch and onto the road. There they paused and Latimer glanced up the road one way and then down the other. Which way did Peter go? To choose wrongly would waste much time. How was Latimer to know? "This way," he said after a quick prayer for guidance.

With horses plodding heavily over the muddy lane, Latimer sat back, allowing the beast to carry him along. What would poor Peter be doing now? Cold and without his cassock, he would be wearing only a tunic and stockings. He would be at the mercy of the elements, without food and without shelter. How would he survive? How much of a head start did he have? It was impossible to tell. His last meal would have been brought sometime after the prayers of None and he could have escaped any time after that. Latimer had wanted to see Peter last night, too, but talked himself out of it. Now he cursed himself for a cowardly fool. If he only he had gone he might have discovered Peter's plot, might have stopped him.

Shoulders limp, he raised his chin dispiritedly to the sky. If only Time could be turned back and they could both relive their moments of youth before madness intruded and spoilt everything. How could all have gone so wrong? Sometimes even prayers did not seem enough—but no. The Lord's plan was not for him to fathom. Surely there was a reason. But it was miserable not knowing

Out of the corner of his eye, Latimer spied Herbert cowering on his saddle. Poor Herbert. Already in mortal fear of the "Mad Monk," here he was in pursuit of him. Latimer knew he should offer some words of comfort, but he had taken a dislike to the graceless youth and so said nothing.

"Brother Latimer." The timorous voice arose between the heavy thuds of hooves and the chatter of crows crowding into the beeches along the road. "If we find him…we are not in any danger, are we?"

Latimer's horse whinnied apprehensively before the monk let go of his taut hold of the reins. He pulled his cowl up and settled himself on the saddle. "You have quite an imagination, Brother."

"I need no such gift when the abbot shows fear himself. Tell me. I beg of you."

Latimer considered. "Perhaps…I was not being entirely honest with you before, Brother. You see, Brother Peter..." Sighing, he drooped in the saddle. "When…when Peter and I were novices, we spent much time together. I sensed he was a smart lad, and he was. He taught me much, on what to read and how to interpret it, what questions to ask and how to put the answers into practice. Not only was he a fine scholar but also an exemplary monk. He possessed eccentricities but no one took much notice of them until they became more pronounced. We were in our tenth year as monks when he seemed to reach a breaking point. I do not know what sparked it. It matters little. All I know is that he was not himself from then on. He muttered to himself, even argued. He became enraged. That was when the abbot made the decision to lock him up. Jesus mercy, we even tried to exorcise him, but to no avail."

Herbert crossed himself, stealthily searching the hedgerows and afternoon shadows. "And the church? What happened there?"

"The church," Latimer said with flat resignation. "It was my turn to bring him food and offer prayers. Oft times he was gentle and quiet. He took to the prayers readily, reciting with each brother who brought him that blessing. Yet other times it was impossible to hear one's own words over his shouting. But this time he was calm, deceptively so. I should have known. I should have been prepared. Alas, I was not. I closed my eyes to chant the Psalms and did not see him creep upon me. I was struck down and he escaped into the church. I do not think he intended to cause mischief. Perhaps he accidentally toppled a cresset. I refuse to entertain the notion he did it intentionally! But there are those who do not share my view."

"Brother! He tried to kill you!"

"No," he said softly. "No. He only wanted escape and I stood in the way of it."

"But you were friends."

Slowly, he shook his head, rippling the cowl. "How could he see me as a friend when I was also his gaoler?"

Silence fell between them, with only the sounds of birds and the rhythmic tread of horses. Latimer fell into an anxious reverie until startled by Herbert's unexpected, "If we find him, what are we to do with him?"

Latimer blinked. "I…I suppose we must subdue him."

"How are we to do that?"

Irritated, Latimer pulled at his cloak to hide a shiver. "With the grace of God! Now for the love of Saint Eadburga, please be still!"

Herbert reddened and pulled his cowl to cover his face. Latimer sighed with relief. Why did he have to endure this on top of everything else? What did this young monk know of the world? He could tell by his accent and turn of phrase that he came from poor stock. Probably could not even read. Latimer and Peter were from gentry. They spoke the same language, thought the same thoughts. Peter was practically the only one at the monastery with whom he could carry on a proper conversation.

A small flush of heat suffused Latimer's face. These very thoughts caused him to do much penance. Why should he feel this way about Herbert and those like him? Surely this was not the intent of Benedict's Rule. These were his brothers, souls like himself. Even Brother Peter—though of similar sentiments—tried to curb them both from these bad habits with logic and rhetoric. And who knew more of Heaven and Hell than Brother Peter, except for *Saint* Peter himself?

Despite Peter's admonishments there seemed so much to resent, from the monks' refusal to elect Latimer abbot, to their questioning his authority and decisions as overseer. If Peter was in his right mind he would have suggested Latimer not take it as a slight, yet how could Latimer see it any other way?

He watched the young monk bob on his horse, his white and freckled face shadowed by the cowl. Sometimes Latimer spent hours with Peter. The more time he spent with him, the more the ramblings of his madness took on a logic of their own, a puzzle to be figured out. What was he to learn from it? Peter seemed to be searching for something, for reasons for his presence on earth, for God's plan in his life, for ways to use his gifts. These were valid questions, such Latimer often pondered himself.

Since the day Latimer devoted his life to God he foolishly thought life in a monastery would be simpler, the company of men less confusing than that of women, and courts, and managing estates. It was harder than he imagined. Men with whom he would never have exchanged two words were now enclosed with him. Though they slept in individual cells in the monk's quarters—and he thanked God for that relief, for many monasteries still clung to the open dormitory—there was little privacy, and it was the small annoyances that grew to be the greatest challenges, as when some young monk harangued him with endless questions.

Stealing a glance at Herbert he settled back on his mount. Latimer was expected to reply to his gibberish with a respectful tone. Yet how *could* he when Herbert's indecipherable queries made even the mules in the stable seem like philosophers?

He supposed that wasn't a very charitable thought.

Latimer wondered about his own purpose on earth. At one time he thought it was to serve God as an abbot, but when his brothers declined to elect him, he was devastated. He learned his Scripture well, knew every nuance of running an abbey, and was well prepared for the responsibilities awaiting him as the representative of Christ to his flock of monks. When the new abbot made him sub prior instead, he fumed at first. This was no better than being a steward when he expected to be lord of the manor. Eventually, he accepted his new role, even enjoyed it to a small extent. It did allow for a certain amount of autonomy. Brother Peter had been proud of his accomplishments, helping him adjust.

But had that been enough?

Looking back over his years now rolling into one continuous scroll with no beginning and no end, he could not decide if any of it was enough. No wonder Peter went mad. Peter could not find his place in the scroll any more than Latimer could, and it destroyed him. Peter replaced his shriveling life with a fantasy that fluctuated from day to day. What was it now? Who was Peter today and how long would he remain in this fantasy? Where *was* Brother Peter?

"Who is Hugh Varney?"

Startled, Latimer tried to adjust to the new sound of Herbert's intrusive voice. "He is the bailiff of these lands and a respected knight. Very generous to the abbey."

"Yes. You are fortunate. I mean…*we* are fortunate. Will he go in search, too?"

"Most likely. I hope he shall be discreet. As discreet as we plan to be," Latimer said, staring at his companion over his shoulder.

"Oh yes, Brother! I would prefer to be silent."

That is also my preference. I only pray you would do it now! But that was not a very charitable thought either. Instead of feeling guilty, Latimer closed himself inward, thinking of Peter and their lost friendship. These melancholy recollections diffused at last to a drowsy recitation of a prayer.

CHAPTER SIX

Madelina. Hugh Varney watched her sleep. Time did not mar the inherent beauty that first attracted him almost twenty years and three children ago. Chestnut hair, now streaked with strands of silver, lay across the pillow. A curled wisp covered her eyes, but she did not seem to mind. Wine had flowed freely the night before, and so he knew she would sleep for many hours.

Unable to sleep himself, he rose long before the sun blushed the horizon. Striding into the solar, he carefully sat in the deep window seat. The ache in his gut twinged again and he doubled momentarily, free in his solitude to indulge in the pain. Sucking the cold air through his teeth and clutching the spot, he eventually straightened and then sat back against the stone, breathing deeply. She caught him once. He pleaded indigestion though she gave him a look with a raised brow, signifying dissatisfaction, yet she did not pursue it. Madelina. A wife in a thousand. She knew if he cared to discuss it, he would. And if he did not, the subject would disappear. Ideal to a fault. Yes, he was blessed.

He rose halfway to his feet. Maybe if he drank a little wine.

Pain jabbed again and he sat, collapsing into the cushion. There was no doubt. It was getting worse, just like the physicians said it would. Many times he wanted to tell Madelina, to find comfort in the warm depth of her eyes, but he knew he would encounter her fear there instead, and that he could not bear.

He leaned his temple against the plaster and raised his hooded lids to peer through a crack in the shutter. The garden lay below in shades of undistinguished gray. Only the different shapes of coifed hedges, empty trellis arcades, and benches defined the space and made it real. How Madelina loved her garden. The children, too. No doubt Teffania would be courting there soon, though the thought made him frown. And Rauf—a hellion already at twelve—made armies of the hedgerows. Henry, too, though only eight, tried to be like his older brother and felt the gardener's switch often when he was caught hacking at a sapling with a wooden sword. Hugh often watched them, especially when they did not know he watched, and secretly puffed with parental pride.

Who would see to them once he died? How long did he have? "How I hate dying," he whispered to the wall, watching his breath cloud.

Once the aching wave subsided, he was certain it would not return for some time. At least this was the pattern he became accustomed to. Settling back, he pulled his heavy mantle about him and nuzzled his gaunt cheek and sharp nose securely into the fur collar.

Slowly, the day grew lighter, taking its time, waiting for him. Tints crept into the garden hedgerows, first as dull light on the topmost edges like a dim halo, until more gold was thrown into the mix, enlivening the greens and deep blues of the shadows. He appreciated the beauty of a sunrise, knowing how fortunate he was to experience one more.

Why did God choose to do this to him? Was he such a sinner? Did he not pray enough?

Snorting, he knew the answer to that. He blasphemed without regret often and found very little time to pray when some other amusement suited better. He supposed he was like most men, thinking his mortality was for later, always later. How did his dying now fit into God's plan? How would leaving his children in the hands of strangers—or worse, the king—suit the Almighty's mysterious scheme? Heaven, Hell. What did he truly know of it all? Was he to go on ahead and clear a path for the rest of them? He doubted it. Madelina was better suited for that than he.

Though more colors arose out of the vista below, his eyes were drawn to the dark shape of the bed in the other room. He was glad to be going first. He did not think he could endure without her. *What a foolish, selfish thought*, he sighed. *Poor Madelina*. There was not yet enough light for him to see her face, but he knew it; each rounded, rosy plane, the vague dimples at the edges of her mouth, the laugh lines at her eyes.

An unmanly tear threatened, but he rubbed a knuckle into his eye and softly cleared his throat before rising. Quietly, he left the chamber and stepped over sleeping servants while he descended the stairs. A hinge whined only slightly when he opened the door to the garden and he slid a derisive glance over his shoulder to the man who continued to sleep. He would have something to say about that later. But for now, he only wanted to be alone.

Stepping onto the wet gravel, he startled a red squirrel that scampered up the side of an elm and disappeared into the new foliage. He walked a few quiet paces, inhaling musty dampness and timid scents of nectar, before he tired. He settled on a wooden bench.

Peering upward into the indefinite clouds, he tried vainly to see beyond the ethers, past the stars disappearing with the day, and into Heaven itself. "I do not know if I am bound for there, Lord," he said softly. "I do not know if I will ever see it. Where is it exactly, I wonder? Can one sail there on a great flying ship, or is death the only ferry? Why are Your most important secrets such mysteries, Lord?" He squinted, but his eyes could not see further than the rosy tint and a white swath of cloud. "I wish I knew for certain. I suppose if I were a more godly man I would know, eh?" He snorted ruefully. "Every man is more godly at the moment of death. Oh, he *is* fervent." Emotion clogged his throat and, angry with himself, he dropped his head. But the anger soon gave way to fear again. "Holy Jesus, help me to understand. Help me come to terms. Help me...die in peace."

The gravel crunched. Hugh jerked up his head and glared, hastily wiping his wet face. "Sebastian! Damn you! Why are you creeping about at this hour?"

The squire's dark brows hovered over sympathetic eyes. "Forgive me, my lord. I had the feeling you might be abroad."

Hugh relaxed back onto the seat. The squire remained tentatively in the archway, shadowed by the ancient stone. His pale complexion was a washed-out blue in the spare light, a striking contrast to close cropped black hair framing his face like a cap.

Hugh resettled himself, tightening the mantle over his chest. "You need not stand there, Sebastian. Come. Sit beside me."

Trotting forward, the squire first bowed to Hugh before he sat.

Both chiseled noses faced ahead in their silence until Sebastian cleared his throat. "Are you in pain again, my lord?"

"No. Not now. But I could not get back to sleep."

"Is my lady still abed?"

"Yes. I did not want to disturb her."

Sebastian rubbed his cold fingers along his wool-clad thigh. "Have you given any further thought to telling her, my lord?"

"No." Hugh glanced upward toward the still dark window. "I do not wish to discuss it now. Please leave it alone, Sebastian."

"As you will, my lord."

Hugh regarded the young profile fondly. It was a harsh secret to lie in his lap, but he knew Sebastian was mature enough at eighteen to shoulder the burden, and he needed someone other than some physician in which to confide.

"Will the hunt go on today, then?" asked Sebastian.

"Yes. There is no need to disappoint everyone. I will find some convenient excuse at the last minute to beg out of it." Sebastian nodded, pressing his lips tightly together. Hugh smiled. "Why are you so solemn today, my friend? Just because I do not go on the hunt does not mean you must remain with me. Go. That daughter of the steward will no doubt be riding and I know well you have an eye for her." Hugh warmed at the brief smile he managed to tease out of the squire.

"It is not that, my lord. It is..."

"You have made no commitment to her, have you, lad?"

"No, no." His head drooped forward and the straight locks swayed over his cheeks. "It is...you, my lord. These past few years...you have been like...like a father to me..."

Hugh leaned forward and rested his hand upon the squire's shoulder, feeling him tremble. "Let us not do this. We have been over it before."

"I only wanted you to know—"

"I know your feelings." Hugh watched the swaying boughs above, and the golden light glitter among the leaves while Sebastian composed himself. If nothing else, he knew Sebastian would remain after him to see to his family. There was no man more loyal. "It could happen to anyone. By the grace of God, I was allowed to live this long. I should have been killed in battle many times before this. You know I am not that clever with a sword, no matter how much I boast."

Sebastian chuckled. "Pure luck, my lord."

"Angels smile on fools," he said, relieved their emotions were once more out of the way, tucked back into the folds of their lives. "I wish I knew an angel. Then I might ask him all I need to know."

"Perhaps...there are a few things of which *I* can enlighten you. The steward's daughter, as you know, is a terrible trifler. I have only looked, my lord. I have never touched."

"Good. I thought you had better taste."

"I do. That is...I certainly did not mean...I would never dream...Blessed Mary! How am I to say this?"

"Sebastian? You are blushing! I have never seen you wear that color before." Hugh's elbow playfully jostled him. "Tell me."

"My lord, naturally I would have taken more time telling you. But I fear that time—"

"—is no longer on our side." Hugh tried and failed to keep the sardonic tone from his words. He shrugged, attempting to lighten the mood. "Tell me anyway."

Sebastian inhaled deeply. "Well…it is my Lady Teffania."

Like a spark igniting in his head, Hugh's eyes suddenly lit with comprehension. And then his eyes narrowed. "You and Teffania?"

The squire shifted to face him. "All very honorably, my lord. I had not meant to draw close to her. We have exchanged tokens only, but vowed to abide by your word…whatever that word was."

Hugh let the anxious squire fret for a moment while inside he beamed. There was certainly no one he would approve of more than Sebastian. The boy possessed enviable affiliations. An alliance with his family would certainly get Hugh's over the bad times to come. He would like to see his daughter betrothed before he died, at any rate. Why had he failed to consider Sebastian before? A broad grin widened his face when he slapped Sebastian's back, sending the unsuspecting youth jerking forward. "You wily fox! Sebastian! Of course I will approve. How did you keep it such a secret?"

"I am good at secrets, my lord."

"Yes. Yes, you are. Well, well. Let the steward's daughter pine, eh? We will announce it before the hunt, and have the hunt to celebrate. Bless me, I will even go myself! Sebastian!" He grabbed the squire, who endured the bear hug with even darker red spots on his cheeks.

"I am glad the news pleases you, my lord," he said after extricating himself. He straightened his tunic, brushing it out over his lap. "I was afraid what you might think."

"Nonsense. You know me better than that. And I know you. You would never lay a finger on her. Would you?"

"Oh no, my lord. She is a lady of deep personal honor. I would never suggest anything and she would never agree to such."

Hugh grinned judiciously. "Well said," he muttered. "We will post the banns right after Lent, then."

Sebastian sighed with relief. "Thank you, my lord. I…I love her."

Hugh could not stop smiling at him. "My son-in-law. I never suspected. What a fool, eh?" Reaching forward, he mussed Sebastian's hair. The squire submitted with a bleat. Hugh withdrew with a satisfied exhalation. "What of Lady Madelina?"

"I think she knows, my lord."

"Women. They always know. Like a wolf smelling the weakest in the flock." Sebastian only raised his brows, uncertain. "We will have a glorious hunt and then a fine banquet tonight. I hope I acquire an appetite. I should very much like to gorge myself. We will have a lot to do afterward. We must send messages to everyone. Lady Madelina will no doubt have a list—"

"Lord! I almost forgot!" Rummaging in the scrip at his belt, Sebastian pulled forth a sealed missive. "This arrived early this morning from Pershore Abbey."

Hugh frowned and broke the seal with his thumbnail. He unfolded the stiff parchment and read quietly for several seconds. "What the devil—?"

"What is it, my lord?"

Hugh laid the missive in his lap. "I am to go on a hunt, right enough; not to search for deer, but for some damned mad monk!"

CHAPTER SEVEN

"You whoreson!" cried Edric over his shoulder. It had been difficult eluding the villagers, but Edric was adept at it, ducking inside a stable and out the other side through a chink in the wall. Alone, he made his way into the twilight of the woods, but Azriel managed to follow and hovered precariously close to his back. With a howl, Edric swung his arm out, but Azriel sidestepped it, a stupid expression painted on his face. "You nearly got me killed!" Edric snarled. "What the hell's the matter with you, you sarding lunatic? Off with you! I don't have any more use for you—voice or no! Lunatic!"

"I am not a lunatic," Azriel said calmly. "I am an—"

"Enough of that, do you hear!" Edric spat, jabbing a finger at Azriel with each word. "You're not a sarding angel! You're a lunatic; off your head; a jibbering idiot! And you're dangerous to me! Now out with you!" He shoved Azriel hard in the chest.

Azriel's face clouded with puzzlement. "You want me to go?"

Edric laughed, hysteria tinting the edges. "Aren't you a piece of work? Aye! I want you to go!"

"Alone?"

"Oh not alone," said Edric acerbically. "God is with you."

Turning, Edric stomped up the road.

"But…I speak to Him, every moment of every hour, and hear nothing in reply."

Squinting over his shoulder, Edric studied Azriel's desolate face. "Now you know how the rest of us feel."

"Edric. I think…I am truly frightened. I am afraid I am cut off from Him. All my experience, all the thousands of years of my existence, I have never heard of such a thing. Edric, I do not know what to do."

"Then maybe there's something you haven't considered."

"What is that?"

"Maybe you *are* in Hell."

He expected the madman to burst into tears, waited gleefully for it, in fact. But instead, Azriel's glazed eyes grew large and round. He reached up to his hair and grabbed great fistfuls of it, and his voice suddenly welled up to a scream, lips mouthing unintelligible words.

"Christ!" Edric twisted quickly and limped quickly away. *Good Samaritan! That was the foolest thing I ever done!* Swinging his arm, he cast low-lying branches out of the way drawing long red scratches along his forearms. Wet duff sprayed aside from his desperate strides. Then he heard pursuing footfalls. He gasped, moving quicker and dared not look back.

Hands seized him and he tumbled backward, landing hard on the uneven ground. Edric struggled, vainly pushing and kicking. But Azriel flipped him and forcibly pinned his shoulders to the ground, grinding them downward with a maniacal glint in his eyes. Azriel laughed into the wind. "Ha! Just like Jacob, but this time *I* win!"

"Leave me be," Edric squealed. "In the name of God, get off!"

Azriel's expression changed again, and abruptly he rose. "In the name of God, I shall."

Edric studied him before he slowly rose, ducking. He slid his knife from its sheath and backed away.

"Edric," pleaded Azriel, "I do not want to be alone. You do not know what it is like, this loneliness. Before, I was a part of a community of angels and saints, like a hive, it was all-abuzz with ideas and the excitement of shared thoughts! But here, my mind echoes with the dreadful sovereignty of isolation. My thoughts…are alone. *I* am alone."

"Take one step closer and you'll *be* with the angels!" His blade quivered in his hand.

Azriel never looked at the dagger. Slowly he approached. "You do not know what it is like."

"Are you senseless *and* mad? Of *course* I know what it is to be alone, you dull-witted, miserable, son-of-a-whore!"

Azriel frowned. He cocked his head, listening to something far away. "I know you think me a lunatic, but Edric…think. What if I were an angel? Would it not be better with me than without me?"

Edric faltered. The voice soothed. Edric's grip on the knife loosened. The terror of only a moment ago faded with just a lingering fetor of apprehension. "I've been without angels a long time," he grunted, uncertain.

"Oh, but you are wrong." Azriel grinned. The transformation was spellbinding. Edric lowered the knife. "One is with you even now. And I am not merely speaking of myself."

The blade lay against Edric's thigh. "What sort of nonsense is that?"

Azriel's face darkened again, and he lurched forward with fists tightly clenched. "It is not nonsense!"

Cowering back, Edric raised the blade waist high until Azriel's rage diminished.

Azriel took a deep breath, closed his eyes, and said more smoothly, "What I mean to say is, each one of you Little Creatures has a Guardian Angel."

"I wish I had one guarding me from you!"

Azriel offered a smile. "Do not be absurd. You do not need guarding from me. I *am* an Angel, remember?"

"What does he need to guard me from, then? I have no food, no shelter—"

"Guarding you from sin."

Edric laughed. He sheathed the knife with one swift gesture. "From sin, eh? Then there's a lot of angels out there doing a piss-poor job of it."

"Angels cannot work miracles alone, Edric," he said. "All we have to work with is your soul. The more stained it is by sin the harder it is to keep you from it."

Edric folded his arms over his chest. "All right, then. Where is he?"

"He is here."

"But where? Show me."

So certain before, Azriel's face shadowed. "I…I cannot see him. If I could I would ask him…talk to him…"

Edric rocked on his heels. "I see."

"I cannot see him while I am a mortal creature," Azriel quickly amended. "I could before."

"Of course."

Azriel frowned. "Your lack of faith astounds me!"

"You are an arrogant bastard, aren't you?" Azriel was a sight in his rags and dirt, but standing like a lord waiting for his horse. Edric snorted. He should take the knife to him again. That would serve him right! Azriel's sudden violence terrified, yet it did not seem so threatening a thing when it ebbed so swiftly. The man appeared like a lost boy. And all alone. *Little wonder!*

Edric sighed. Why should he give a damn? It was easier traveling alone, laying his head where he liked, and not worrying about some fool giving him away if he lifted something for himself. He was used to it. It suited. If he were with someone, he would have to listen to their chattering and moaning. Is that what he wanted?

He looked Azriel over again; bandaged arm, bruised head, and a blond moss of hair beginning to cover his jaw, hollowed eyes pleading. *Poor bastard*, he thought, actually feeling sorrier for Azriel than himself. It might be good to have company, someone to watch his back if trouble threatened. Someone to talk to… "I must be a lunatic too," Edric grumbled, rubbing his hand across the back of his neck. "Very well, Master Angel. You stay with me and see for yourself how grateful I am for this miserable life. You see what it's like. I'll wager by the end of it, you lose faith, too."

A wry smile brightened Azriel's face. "I warn you, I have an infinite advantage."

"Just see that you control yourself and make us some coin with your voice. Then I'll tutor you about humility. Is that a bargain?"

"You? Teach me about humility?"

Edric grimaced a smile before drawing back his fist. It slammed it into Azriel's jaw with a blunt thud.

Azriel stumbled backward and fell, grasping his bruised chin in astonishment. "Why did you do that?"

Edric rubbed the sore knuckles. "You been asking for it. You'll get more of the same when I think it time."

"*This* is your lesson on humility?"

"You feel humbled, don't you?"

"I feel pain!"

"Well…one's like another."

Azriel got to his feet and touched his face, his former madness seemingly forgotten. He probed his teeth with a finger.

"And you'll have to stop all that ranting," said Edric. "It makes a body skittery."

"Ranting?"

"You grabbed me, sat atop me, and nearly made me soil me braies! Remember that?"

"Oh, that. My apologies."

"Well don't do it again, you hear? Or I'll give you a lesson in humility you won't soon forget!"

For a full day, the brooding madman quietly followed Edric over the road. Edric looked back at him now and again. *It takes a lunatic to want to be my friend, I reckon.* But the notion was not very amusing. Did he become so desperate for human companionship that he was willing to risk life and limb for it?

Edric glimpsed Azriel picking at a thread on his shirt and contemplating it with all the seriousness of a knight at a battle plan.

Azriel was not so bad most of the time, he decided. Only when he got his blood up. If he could behave himself, they could make a pouch or two of coins together, perhaps even stay in a real bed at an inn.

Azriel glanced his way briefly, eyes smiling. A strange flare grew in Edric's chest. Azriel actually seemed to like him. This in itself was an unusual notion. "I been thinking. How'd you get away back there, when I run off?"

"You mean when you stole that wine?"

"Aye. I know how slippery I can be, but you were right in the thick of it."

"No thanks to you."

"Well, that's as may be but…how'd you do it?"

Azriel raised a smug shoulder. "I simply walked away."

"Go on! They had you surrounded. But…they didn't lay a finger on you. How'd you do it?"

"I told you. I walked away. I *am* an Angel, after all."

"Now look, Azriel—"

"Why do you persist in believing I speak an untruth? I am a Divine Spirit. I cannot lie like you creatures seem to do so easily. When I tell you I walked away, that is the truth."

Edric scrutinized Azriel and shook his head. He knew it could not have happened that way, but the man was stubborn about his fantasy. Yet if he did not simply walk away how *did* he escape unscathed? "We'll be coming to a town soon," Edric grunted. "Remember what I said about behaving yourself."

"I remember." Azriel sighed. "If only I could show you a small portion of what I was before. Then you would know. You would understand—"

"That don't mean much now, does it? You got to act more sensible. More human."

Azriel made a face. "I am *not* human. I may be in this guise now, but I am an Angel! Perhaps not *all* my powers are gone. If I concentrated I might be able to fly."

"What nonsense. Don't you need wings to fly?"

"I told you. We do not have wings. I will show you."

"But you aren't no angel now, remember? You're a human—Ah! Harken to me, will you? I'm talking like you!"

"I will show you. My faith will uplift me." Azriel shrugged off Edric's pleas and left the road, scrambled up the side of a boulder, and perched himself atop.

"Azriel, get your fool carcass down from there!"

"Oh you of little faith, you Little Creatures who need signs and wonders to believe. Believe in this!" Poised six feet above the ground, Azriel arched his back and spread out his arms. With eyes closed he leaned into the wind.

For a breathless few seconds, Azriel teetered on the edge. A gust of wind lifted his tunic, billowing the cloth like the belly of a sail. He seemed to hover between heaven and earth for several breaths…until he fell like a sack of barley to the turf below.

Edric cringed. "It looks like you need wings to me."

Azriel shook himself and rose to a sitting position, his face completely devoid of life and color. "I do not understand."

"It's a good thing you didn't try that off a cliff."

"Why is every one of my miseries amusing to you?"

"Does it look like I'm laughing?" Ambling forward, Edric looked the man over. He did not seem to have broken any bones. "This is just the sort of thing I mean. You can't go telling folk you can fly and all. They'll run us off."

"Is that all you care about? Your purse?"

"What else is there to care about? I'm hungry most of the time and fill me belly less often. But with you…well. It might happen more often, see? I'd like to eat regular, maybe sleep in a bed under a roof. Is that too much to ask?"

Brushing his stained tunic, Azriel sniffed the marsh-tinged air. "No, it is not. Your wants are few. You are very simple to unravel."

"What you mean by that?"

"You are human. You only need a little food, a little bit of shelter out of the rain, and a place to wipe your bum in peace. Anything beyond that is superfluous."

Edric postured, considering the knife at his side. "You don't know naught about me!"

"Do I not? Let me see…" Running his fingers over his stubbled chin he eyed Edric from head to foot. "Your mother died in childbed, and your father hated you for it, making your life a misery."

Edric's jaw dropped. Blinking away a wave of fear, he stepped closer. "It's…it's a trick!"

"No trick," Azriel said indifferently, peering up the road. "It is obvious. You hate everything. If your parents were kind and loving there would be very little reason for you to hate so much, even as misshapen as you are. Only sin and hate breed such sin and hate."

With drawn brows, Edric drew up to a rock and plopped down. "I need to rest."

Azriel's mood shifted again and his eyes warmed with concern. "Does your foot hurt you?"

Edric laughed huskily. "Only to look at."

Slowly, Azriel sat beside him. He looked Edric over and, intrigued, Edric coolly regarded Azriel's expression. Gently, like a parent to a child, Azriel said, "If you had faith, the Divine Father would heal you now. 'Ask and it shall be given you.'"

Edric gave a derisive grunt. "Like He let you fly?" He spat at Azriel's feet, delighted by the hurt in his eyes. "You don't know how much horseshit that is. Don't you think I had faith once?"

Azriel blinked, but Edric shook his head, weary of Azriel's innocent demeanor. He wanted to shake him, to slap him. "When I was a lad, I was mostly bruised and beaten because the others didn't like a cripple in their midst. There was many a night I prayed m'self to sleep, weeping my eyes out. You didn't know *that*, did you, Angel? I prayed. Prayed to be healed of all this. If there was anyone to do it, it was Jesus Himself, wasn't it? Heal a poor, beaten boy, like me. I prayed so hard that in the morning I was certain He heard. So certain, I threw back the covers with joy in me heart." A sharp breath inflicted the same hurt in his chest of that long ago day. "Did I see a healed foot?" he snorted. "No. Only that disgusting mass of flesh. Then I saw me sire's face, just as disgusted as my own. You were right, you know. Me father beat me, hated me for killing my mother. I never knew her. I did kill her, just by being born."

He gazed at a distant point in the road. It helped keep his eyes dry. "I ran away. Had to, to stay alive. And I'm still wondering *why* I'm alive. So by the blessed saints, don't talk to me of faith. I've had me belly full of it." A burning in his eyes only made him angrier, but he masked it by running his sleeve over his forehead to wipe the sweat. "My faith is in the rain soaking my bed of straw, and that in each town I'll be run out of it. My faith is that I'll be dead before another winter, maybe cudgeled clean in my sleep instead of starving to death. I haven't heard no God talking to me neither. I did my praying a long time ago and it got me naught. That only means there isn't nobody listening. But I tell you what I *don't* need. I don't need a whoreson like you telling me that faith will heal me. To hell with your faith!"

Azriel shook his head. "Your suffering has made you bitter."

Edric barked a laugh. "Aye. You might say that!"

"But your suffering should bring you closer to our Lord. He suffered for you, so that you may endure, but not when you wallow in your sin."

"If I haven't me sin, then what else have I?"

Azriel blinked his disbelief. "The promise of everlasting life."

Edric chuckled with genuine amusement, and looked up at Azriel's sincere face. "You mean like you have?"

His bright expression faded. "Well…I…"

"Never mind." Stretching, Edric arched his back with a crack and got to his feet. "I'm rested. Let's go on."

Azriel stood immobile for some time while Edric departed. Edric looked back and shrugged to himself. What did it matter? Perhaps it would not be so easy keeping the two of them fed after all. And what if the madman went into a rage again? Edric might be murdered in his sleep. He balanced the thought of death to his continued and unchanging existence, but thoughts of death, no matter how tormented by life he was, still frightened.

Flashes of his childhood intruded. It washed over him with the heat of humiliation. He recalled being cornered by the village youth when he was no more than ten. He even remembered the feel of the rough daub on his palms while he cringed against the wall, the stench of his own musky sweat fresh in his nostrils. They held stones in their hands—pebbles, really—and clods of dirt, and they laughed harder when he began to cry.

Just beyond them, he had spotted his father lumbering along the path between the houses, a wake of dust surrounding his straw gaiters. Edric's heart leapt. Hopeful, Edric looked toward him with a tear-streaked face. But his father had glanced at him only once with that coldness he always directed toward Edric. Only that time it was worse. Far worse.

Helplessly, Edric watched him continue on—never slowing—and left him to his fate. The pebbles and dirt stung, but not as much as that single glance of apathy.

Azriel was no different from anyone else…except that he did not seem to ridicule Edric. Perhaps that was part of Azriel's insanity.

"You never say or do anything for anyone else," said Azriel, startling Edric. He did not notice Azriel come up beside him. "Yet you bothered to save me when I lay in that ditch. Why?"

With curled fingers Edric plowed furrows through his hair before letting his hand drop. "I dunno. Sometimes I wish I hadn't. Some witless song made me do it." He shrugged, wondering. The Good Samaritan song lingered in his mind. "I dunno."

Azriel shook his head. Softly, almost too lightly for Edric to hear, he said, "Such a pity you cannot recognize your own compassion."

Edric rolled his shoulders, ignoring sentiments he could not comprehend. Why did Azriel have to say things like that? Was it a compliment? He did not like it. He did not like anything he could not understand.

A stubble of houses crested a rise and all the ill feelings were suddenly forgotten. Edric motioned Azriel to hurry and follow.

Mad he may be, but Azriel could do the one thing that enthralled Edric like no other. He could make music. Not just any music. Beautiful, coordinated, balanced music to Edric's own. His piping blended with Azriel's voice, as if they had sung together for years. The hurts of the world could be cast aside.

Once they reached the village, Edric lifted the reed to his lips and relaxed against a post, eagerly anticipating the sounds to come. Music flowed, a melody of sweet tones and mellow resonance. Closing his eyes, he fell into the song, breathing it…and then Azriel began to sing.

Edric's heart filled with something indefinable, warm and tingling. Was this joy? Surely it must be. For this one moment, it did not matter if they were successful, if any of these farmers threw bread or curses. Just for this moment, he was no longer Edric, no longer lame. He floated free of the earth, spiraling upward like a leaf on an updraft. The music upheld him, the weight of its gleeful timbre carried him along like some great river moving a heavy log on its current. They were one voice, that was it. His reed was a voice like Azriel's, and they melded to one round resonance.

Edric felt almost a physical pain when the song ended, and with a regretful sigh, he lowered the reed and opened his eyes, focusing gradually on the slack-jawed farmers encircling them. One moved forward, his grizzled beard dusted with crumbs from a recent meal. "That was a right good song of yours," he said appreciatively. Out of the satchel hanging from his waist, the farmer took out a slab of hard bread. "That's all I got, but it is worth it. Will you take it?"

Edric stared at the bread and breathed. Here was a man who possessed almost as little as he. Edric's mind wandered over the possibility of such gratitude. Would he be willing to give away his own bread for such little respite from life's harshness? He sensed Azriel beside him, but could not look at him.

Edric closed his fingers over the bread. "Thank you," he

mumbled. "Come along, Azriel," he said into his shirt, anxious to move on.

At day's end, a wine-stained sky stretched toward the horizon, and birds flitted across the bright expanse like ember smudges. He and Azriel made more music together beside their little fire while the sun set, and Edric felt that joy again.

Afterward, he yawned and stared into the fire, tasting the savory smoke in the back of his throat, and settled himself on his back to gaze into a sky darkening with night. The food the townsfolk gave them was already a memory and he patted his belly. He stretched his arms over his head and interlaced his fingers, resting his hair against them.

He watched the firelight scramble gold patterns on the dark trunks of the surrounding trees. Edric had imagined many things about Azriel, but never this.

It put him in a mellow mood, which always brought on thoughts of women, and that thought made him sigh. It caught the wind and sighed back to him, rustling his hair.

"What makes you sigh? Have I done something wrong again?"

"No," Edric answered softly. "I was just thinking of women. It's been a while since I've had one."

"'Had'?"

Edric frowned slightly, but Azriel's razor tongue could not stiffen his mellow humor. "Aye. Me. Is that so strange?"

"No. That is...what exactly do you mean by 'had'?"

Edric chuckled. "Lain with, you sarding lunatic."

Azriel snorted. "You mean sinned with."

Shrugging, Edric smiled. "As you will."

Silence sheltered them, disturbed only by a mournful birdcall, and the plop of a frog slipping into a pond. Shadows danced and dashed into the trees at the edge of the fireglow. Edric picked his teeth with a stick and dreamed wistfully of soft limbs and plump bodies. "Have you, Azriel?" he asked listlessly.

"Have I what?"

"Had a woman, you silly bastard."

From the corner of his eye, Edric saw Azriel stiffen, rolling his shoulders disdainfully against a tree. "No," he replied icily.

Half rising, Edric guffawed. "Go on! With a face like that? They'd fall at your feet, they would." He waved his hand in the air and lay back, chewing on the twig. "Do you even know what they're like? Ah Azriel. They're soft…tender…sweet." Aroused, Edric dropped a hand to his groin and squirmed. "God's teeth! All this talk makes me long for a bit of quim now."

Azriel blinked his indignity.

Edric shook his head, rolling it along the musty leaves. "If you've never had a woman, Azriel, then you've naught to say. A woman is like no sweetness the world has ever known. Richer than wine, sweeter than honey. Their bodies are like pillows, softer than down. And warm. The scent of them… I've not had many, mind. No one likes a cripple…" The smile washed from his lips. He spun the twig between his teeth a moment longer before spitting it out, watching it arc over his prone body before it rolled to the fire's edge.

"There must be something good in you."

"I'm not a whole man, Azriel, and that's the crux of it."

Azriel raised his knees and hugged them close to his grass-stained tunic. Slowly he shook his head. "I do not understand you creatures, and I never shall."

Edric huffed with irritation. The dry leaves at his head crunched in his ear. "I told you about that 'creature' talk. I should flatten your face."

"You have the gift of life, and yet you scorn it."

"The 'gift of life', is it? This is no gift, friend. Not my life."

"Every life."

"God's teeth! It's always the same argument with you. Just be still, Azriel, if you can't say naught else."

Solemnly, Azriel pressed his lips tightly and leaned his head back against the tree.

Edric mentally shook his head. Why did the man imagine himself an angel, and a fallen one at that? It came from too much study, of this he was certain. "I'll wager you read, don't you?" Eyes closed, Azriel nodded. Edric laughed. "And where's it gotten you, eh? Out in the freezing woods with a crippled beggar. That's book learning for you!"

"You put things so succinctly."

Edric did not like the sound of that but decided to ignore it. Heaving a sigh, he rolled onto his side, letting the fire warm his back. "There's no more food, Azriel. We'll have to bide nigh a town on the morrow. To sleep now. Maybe tonight I'll dream of women."

It was not long before Edric was snoring, but he did not dream of women the way he wanted. He awoke sour because of it, and said nothing to Azriel while he pissed into the bracken, scratching his backside when he was done.

They trudged in silence throughout the morning, staying just ahead of threatening clouds. When they reached the town walls they made it to the safety of an alehouse just before the sky opened, spilling a torrent into the dirt paths and alleyways.

The patrons glared at them when they stood by the large hearth fire and Edric wrestled uncomfortably with the unfamiliar setting before confidently withdrawing his reed. He knew now what to expect.

The stifled air was filled with the smell of sweat, wet wool, and smoke, but the patrons gathered when their music flowed, erasing the harshness of the room. When Edric and Azriel finished, the men cheered and bought the players a round of drinks in wooden cups.

Azriel drank the spirits tentatively, grimacing into his cup, but he smoothed his complexion when Edric gave him a warning glance.

"Thank you, good masters," said Edric, settling against the hearth again. Few seemed to notice his deformities. "Will you have another song?"

"What of the news?" asked a tall man in the back of the crowd.

"News?" Edric eyed the man, sliding his glance to the other

shining faces in the smoky room. *Christ! They think we're minstrels!* Why not? Better they should think that than that they were beggars. "Er…news. Well now…" Edric recounted all he heard in the last town and even embellished some half-heard imaginings he heard from the town before that. It did not seem to matter. When he talked, they brought more drink.

He and Azriel made a little more music before they were offered a platter of broken meats, cheese, and onions. Edric ate heartily while Azriel picked at it all like a stiff-nosed lord. When they were later given a place to sleep in a stable outside of town, Edric wore a smile from ear to ear. At last!

They settled in, each finding their own spot in the hay to sleep. Azriel tucked the cloak he was given up to his chin. It was soiled and torn but at least it offered warmth.

"They gave you a cloak, did they?"

Azriel smiled briefly, running his hand over the garment with a puzzled frown. "Yes. I was grateful. Gratitude is difficult to learn, but not impossible. I found I liked it."

"Tell me something, Azriel. Are all angels like you?"

"No. We are all different."

"That's a relief." Edric sat back, nestling half in the straw and half out of it. "I thought for a moment that Heaven might be full of smug knobs like you."

Azriel popped to his feet. "*What!* You…you witless Little Creature…"

"Here now. None of that." Edric's serious expression broke into a crooked smile. "Don't you know by now I like goading you? It's so easily done."

Azriel's stiff shoulders drooped and he slithered down to a prone position again. "Oh. I…I am unused to goading. I take it all very seriously."

"Believe me, friend." The laughter soured in Edric's throat. "I take it all seriously, too."

CHAPTER EIGHT

Hugh straightened painfully on the saddle, relieved Pershore Abbey was finally in view. He pretended not to notice Sebastian's look of concern, and sharply inhaled the morning instead, allowing the rim of the road and bounding starlings to capture his attention. He and his men rounded a curve and came at last to the abbey's gatehouse, where a nervous porter hurried them in. The two footmen, four archers, and servants plodded behind, never raising their eyes.

Sebastian moved quickly to help Hugh from his mount and the knight gratefully acknowledged him with a smile and a nod. They followed a long-legged monk over the mud of the courtyard and into the monastery grounds to the abbot's lodging.

Abbot Gervase rose to greet Hugh and offered him a chair, where he sat, wincing. "Is there something wrong, Sir Hugh? Are you unwell?"

Hugh acknowledged the abbot with a scowl. "No, Abbot. Quite well. Age and damp do me little good these days." He took the wine the chaplain offered and nodded for Sebastian to partake. The squire stood quietly behind his chair, the cup in his hand. Taking a sip, Hugh felt relieved that it calmed the wave of oncoming pain. He sighed, though the relief was short-lived. The reason for his being at the abbey tightened his gut. "What is all this about, Lord Abbot?"

Without sampling the wine, Gervase set his cup aside with a sigh. "I suppose it is time I tell you of Brother Peter."

Hugh hunched forward, balancing the wine bowl on his thigh. "You mean those rumors from all these years are true?"

"Well…rumors and truth, Sir Hugh—"

"Do not prevaricate with me. I am in no mood."

"Yes." The abbot stared into his untouched wine. "Brother Peter has been under our care for these last ten years."

"Blessed Virgin! And a secret all this time!"

"And under careful control," Gervase continued. "Except…for the incident with the church."

"You do not mean to say—"

"With sadness, yes. Brother Peter *was* responsible. In what way, we are uncertain. We tightened our control of him since, but apparently he only bided his time in order to outwit us."

Hugh felt weary. He had disappointed his family by delaying the hunt and Teffania by equally delaying the betrothal announcement, but secretly before he left he had chucked her chin while sliding his glance toward Sebastian, eliciting a smile from her. The more he listened to the monk's horrific explanation, the longer away the hunt seemed to be, and time was no longer a commodity he held in abundance. "Where is he now?" he asked thickly.

"God only knows."

Shifting his weight, he felt again a wave of oncoming pain. He downed several hefty gulps of wine. "No clue at all? Family? Acquaintances outside the monastery?"

"Brother Peter came to us the bastard son of a lord. Many such boys are given to the Church to…well…to keep them from sight. He has no acknowledged family."

Hugh's callused fingers tapped against the dented metal bowl.

"You have created quite a situation, Abbot. Taking a responsibility upon yourselves without alerting the proper authorities."

Gervase squared his shoulders. "What authorities do you mean, Sir Hugh? The bishop well knows—"

"Oh, the bishop. I see. But it is not the bishop riding out into the muck and the rain. No, my good Abbot. It is I, the bailiff. Should I not have been informed?"

"That ship has sailed, Sir Hugh," he said between stiffened lips. "We cannot spend our time arguing when Brother Peter is abroad."

"Is he dangerous?"

The abbot's glance darted momentarily toward the chaplain, but he dropped it quickly. "He…he might be considered so."

"'Might' be? A burner of churches?"

"Sir Hugh, this is a difficult problem. Each monk is like a son to me. Should I love any one of them less than the other?"

Hugh did not glance toward Sebastian, but he was aware of him standing behind him, the warmth of another human soul. If the squire were to go mad and pose a danger to Hugh's family… "You kept this one locked in a room. That speaks volumes."

"It is imperative he is quickly found."

Hugh slammed the bowl down, ejecting a crimson sunburst of wine upon the floor. "No more games! Is he a danger or isn't he?"

The abbot sobered. "Yes, Sir Hugh," he said softly. "Reluctantly, I must admit I believe he is."

"Then tell me why I am to go to such great pains to bring him home when my time might be better spent bringing him down like a stag."

Gervase lengthened in his seat. "Sir Hugh! One of God's creatures—insane though he may be—should not be killed like a mad dog! We want him back safe and sound!"

"Pardon me, Abbot, but I am under no such obligation. It is my duty to keep the peace under the direction of the Lord Sheriff. If a lunatic is free—monk or no—it is my duty to stop him. If death is the ready answer then death it must be."

The abbot shook his head worriedly. "Sir Hugh, if I knew you would take this course, I would never have alerted you!"

"And have on your head death and injuries caused by your own brother?" He glanced at last at Sebastian. He expected affirmation but found only a stony exterior. Hugh swiveled back toward Gervase, unsatisfied. "No, Abbot. I spare you that guilt at least."

Agitated, the abbot rose, turning his back to Hugh while he gazed out the window. "I have sent two brothers in search of him. They left yesterday. One is his oldest friend—a Brother Latimer—along with another monk—" He searched the air for the name, but looked to the chaplain to supply it.

"Brother Herbert," said the chaplain.

"Yes. Brother Herbert. They turned west from here."

"Then I shall go east. Were it up to me, I would fine your abbey for such negligence. I may yet suggest it to the Sheriff."

Gervase turned. "That is your right, Sir Hugh. But I always thought you a generous friend to this abbey. What so hardens your heart?"

Hugh rose, shaking off his discomfort. "My duty hardens it, Abbot. The plight of the innocents." He scanned the room, from its inviting hearth and tall arching windows, to its cozy corners and staid brothers watching from the guarded vantage of obscuring shadows. "You are all safe here. The world outside passes by your gates, and such sturdy gates they are. A soul within suffers and your solution is to conceal him in a cell. But the rest of us are out of our cells, Abbot, moving within the seething sin of the world. And now I am to clean up your muck the way you would have it. It is not that simple." He shook his furred cloak over his chest and whirled, stomping through the archway.

Sebastian stood dumbfounded and eventually turned toward the abbot. "It is not what you think," he said meekly. "He is not like this." But the abbot said nothing. He merely stared at the squire, who remained several more uncomfortable moments before reluctantly taking his leave.

"That was very rude, my lord," Sebastian grumbled to Hugh when he caught up to him.

"You are not my son-in-law yet. Best watch your tongue."

"He is a priest, my lord."

"A priest is still a man."

"Chosen by God," Sebastian insisted, stiffening.

"We are all chosen by God to do one thing or another…Ah, Sebastian. I apologize. I did not mean to vent my anger upon you."

"It is all well, my lord." Sebastian's waxen face hid nothing.

"No, it is not." At length, Sebastian's wounded expression faded away. Hugh huffed. "This is damnable! Letting a madman run loose!"

"They did not mean for him to have done."

Hugh dropped his hand on Sebastian's shoulder for support. "Yet he did."

The cloister walls drew up around them, shadows hunching inward. He raised his eyes and saw the monk's quarters, each dark window like a solemn eye watching him. Which one was Brother Peter's? The farthest from the others, no doubt, yet not far enough. A streak of sunlight bore suddenly through the clouds and rushed to the roughened wall, crawling upward until the whole face shown golden. "Angels and saints preserve us from holy men."

"What did you say, my lord?"

"Nothing. I only meant to say that these clerics were the only ones to truly know about Brother Peter, and that simply will not do, Sebastian. That will not do."

"What is to be done now, my lord?"

"We will find him."

"Will you…will you kill him, my lord?"

They reached the courtyard, and passed the dark forms of the monks in their disfiguring cassocks. White faces stared at him from beneath their cowls. "If it warrants it. I will risk none of my men in his capture." Sebastian quieted. Hugh listened to their footsteps crush the gravel, and raised his head to his men who stood at attention when he approached. "Tell me, Sebastian, if I were the madman, what would you do?"

Sebastian shrugged before helping Hugh mount, then reached for the saddle pommel of his own beast and hoisted himself aloft. "Dangerous, like this one?"

"Yes. And you were responsible for the safety of those in the shire."

Sebastian's gaze steadied while Hugh waited. "I would… examine the situation, my lord."

"Examine!" he snorted. "Sometimes—often—there is no time to examine it. Just imagine a lunatic bearing down on Teffania, eh? She is precious to you and to me—"

"I thought *you* were the lunatic."

"What? Oh. Quite right. So. Would you kill me?"

"If no one is in immediate danger—"

"Bollocks! You can never know that. Especially when the foe is someone you know well. They can be the most dangerous of enemies."

"You would prefer I kill you, my lord?"

A footman cocked his head in their direction before ducking under the shadow of his helmet.

"Yes, dammit! Of course you should kill me!" cried Hugh. The archers glanced toward Hugh and the squire. "You see. You are like these monks with their precious brother—and I mean that well. But imagine Teffania in danger. It is not such a matter to be ignored. I will not see the innocent in danger." He huffed a breath and straightened his tunic. "Shall we search the woods?"

Sebastian sobered. "Every trail is cold by now. Yet it may well be all we have, unless those monks find him."

"True enough. I saw a copse on a hill before we entered. That is a good view of the valley. Let us try there first."

The cancer suddenly made itself known again. Hugh pressed his hand into his side, pushing on the tumor to stamp out some of the pain. When it did no good, he threw back his shoulders with a bitter inhale of frigid air and trotted his horse across the yard under the gatehouse arch.

CHAPTER NINE

Brother Latimer splashed the icy water on his face and shook out his cheeks. He tucked his hands within his sleeves to warm them before casting a glance toward Herbert.

Latimer tried to forgive Herbert, tried to ignore him at the very least. But everything out of his mouth portrayed him as a weak creature, full of superstitions and sorrows.

"Where today, Brother?" Herbert asked. He asked the same thing every day.

Latimer said a silent prayer for patience and glanced at the gray light seeping through the shutters. They were fortunate to find charity at an inn, and were provided with an attic room and food. "There are no answers in this room, Brother," he said, blowing out the candle. He led the way down the dark stairway, and emerged into the hazy light of the great room below. A fire blazed in the hearth and many of the inn's travelers sat hunched over the tables, consuming bowls of viscous porridge. Seldom did they look up through the tangy hearth smoke, but when they did, it was to eye the monks with unveiled suspicion.

Latimer gauged the room uneasily. Taking the offered bowls and a chunk of brown bread, they sat at the end of a long bench.

Quietly, they ate until a merchant sitting across from them glanced up. His eyes traveled from one face to another and back again before he ventured, "Going on a pilgrimage?"

"Of a sort," said Latimer. He did not bother to refer to Herbert. He knew the young monk would concentrate on his food in order to avoid eye contact. "We search for…a lost brother."

Other heads rose, looking in their direction. Latimer cringed inwardly. Of course, no one cared about them until some prurient bit of business was revealed. Why where they looking for this brother, after all, they must be thinking? Did he run off with someone's daughter, perhaps? That was far more interesting than the truth of one man's solitary suffering. He did his best to hide his distaste. "He is ill," he said solemnly, "and lost his way. Have any one of you seen a man in this region who may seem out of place? He is not wearing a cassock and his tonsure has long since grown in and so he does not look to be a monk."

Blank faces regarded him, and his spirits drooped again. *You must have seen him!* he longed to scream. How could a man disappear so easily, yet he supposed it happened all the time; a body washes ashore after a frozen winter repose in an icy pond, or a robber leaves a man for dead under a log teeming with worms who do most of the work of eternal concealment, or a wounded man crawls into a rocky crevice, never to come out again until his bones are found by a rich man's greyhound. One heard of these things occasionally, but they never meant anything to Latimer before this.

Brother Peter, where are you? He scanned the room again, at all the blanched faces of indifference. How apathetic would they remain if they knew the truth, if they knew a dangerous madman were among them?

Latimer drew himself up. It was the first time he dared admit it. Peter *was* dangerous.

Latimer swiped a glance across the vague monk beside him and lowered his eyes. He never told the complete truth about that night of the fire. Peter did not attack him from behind. Instead, they argued for the hundredth time. Latimer foolishly thought he could confront Peter, make him see that his fantasy world was just that. But Peter did not want to listen. His new world was his own. Viciously, they struggled. Peter struck him, not once, but many times, each blow more and more violent. Latimer managed with ebbing strength to fend him off. The last thing he saw before losing consciousness was Peter's wild expression while he tore into the freedom of the dark corridor. Latimer had awakened fitfully to a haze of smoke and flickering light, to the noise of many feet running, and shouted prayers and entreaties, the sounds of cracking and falling timbers.

Peter was brought bodily back to his room, and that was when Latimer was discovered and ministered to. It took time to recover, not only from his wounds, but also from the horror and lasting scars of his friend's complete collapse into insanity. Latimer did not want to confront it, but now it stared him in the face with an incontrovertible scowl.

Slowly, an inescapable thought emerged amid the tangle of Latimer's mind. Did Latimer truly *want* to find him? He well knew what Peter's fate would be when he returned to the monastery. He would again be locked in his cell. And Peter would grow more insane while the years tolled on until he would need to be chained to restrain him. He shut his eyes to the painful indignities.

He breathed in the close air of the low-ceilinged room.

If Peter were already dead, then he rested in the arms of Christ and nothing further could harm him. Better to leave it alone. Better not to know.

His gaze fell on Herbert. It would be easy to misdirect their course. This one would never suspect and probably would not care. Herbert wanted to find Peter even less than Latimer did. Was it wrong to deceive them all so? He asked God this question but resisted listening to the reply. Instead, he said aloud, "The road is long, Brother. Shall we go and discover what we may in the nearby towns?"

"Yes, Brother," Herbert answered nervously, pushing his barely-touched bowl aside.

A wood mouse. That was the picture Latimer held in his mind of Herbert, bristling, quivering, eyes darting. All he need do, then, was throw the occasional piece of cheese. "Say your prayers often," he admonished the young monk. He rose and turned his back on the room. "It is what keeps us anchored to the ground and God in His Heaven."

CHAPTER TEN

Hugh's men were arrayed over their campfires in the misty velvet of night. A wind stirred the jagged flames upward where they petered to speckled flashes of embers.

Hugh inhaled the spicy aroma of wood fumes. He nestled within the warm musty furs bundled around him. Sitting at the pavilion tent's opened flap, he observed the night, listening detachedly to the buzz of the men's conversation. He always enjoyed the male camaraderie of a hunt or of battle. Ironically, even in the most ruthless foray, it was this camaraderie that made him feel alive. He clung to the notion, even though he could no longer conjure those same feelings.

Sebastian tried to occupy himself with other matters while Hugh sat. He sorted parchments and tended to the fire, even though the servants should have been doing that. *Good old Sebastian*, thought Hugh. How much longer would the two of them be able to conceal his illness?

"You are pensive, my lord?"

Hugh glanced at hazel eyes over a patrician nose. Sebastian's was a kindly face, fresh, untried, and pure without the scars of betrayal or disappointment. He little wondered why Teffania fell under its spell. "I only consider the future, Sebastian. I must speak frankly with you."

Used to their familiarity, Sebastian pulled up a stool and sat beside him. He pushed the furred collar of his own mantle up to his red-tipped ears. "I am always ready to listen, my lord."

"It is about my lands and chattels," said Hugh. "My sons are young yet, but I fear I will not be here to see them reach maturity." Sebastian offered no currying protest. The time for that was past. "There is no kinsman whom I trust to oversee the lands," Hugh went on. "What will become of them and my family without someone to protect them? I am glad you told me of you and Teffania. I plan to name you protector. I shall make a likewise document to send to the king. No one will dispute your right. And when my son Rauf comes of age, I also trust that you will release the reins to him. When we return, I shall announce your betrothal and further, Sebastian, I will also take that opportunity to knight you."

"My lord!" The fragile solemnity that composed Sebastian's features fell away.

Hugh raised his head. "Did you expect less than that? What knight would not repay loyal service in this manner? How many years have you been a part of my household, Sebastian? Do I not already see you as a son? Should a man not knight his son?" Sebastian's face grew taut. He struggled before lowering his head. He nodded, but said nothing. "I understand the difficulty," said Hugh. "Such happiness bound up with my death. It puts any loyal man out of sorts."

Looking up, Sebastian's cheek was wet with streaks of tears. "How well you know me, my lord."

"Well, then. It is settled. As soon as this monk business is finished, we will draw up the documents. How relieved I shall be. You have lifted a great weight from my shoulders, lad."

"My lord—"

"Do you think you will ever be able to call me Hugh?"

The sparkle in Hugh's eye was reflected in Sebastian's. The

squire smiled, sniffed, and wiped his face with his palm. "I do not think so, my lord."

Hugh chuckled. "I do not suppose it matters." He fell silent, lolling in the encompassing sensations of night and men and his own vivacity. Hugh recognized the fleeting wisp of happiness in just being alive, but even that notion flitted away again, leaving only a bitter slash of a smile on his face. "Sebastian, do you ever think about Heaven?"

"As much as any man, my lord. I hope to get there someday."

"We all hope to get there. But how many of us do, I wonder?"

"*You* will, my lord."

Hugh waved his hand in the air dismissively. "That is not what I meant." The brazier's light from within the tent gilded Sebastian's cheek. Absently, Hugh watched the meandering shapes of light play on the smooth planes of the boy's face. "I mean to say, that…well…where *is* Heaven exactly?"

"I am not certain I understand you."

"If I were to reach through the ether now, do you think I could touch it? Grasp the hem of an angel's gown?" Gently Hugh lifted his hand. It appeared small against the background of a star-peppered sky.

"I…do not know, my lord."

Dropping his hand, Hugh's fingers curled around the chair arm. "Because you see, when a man comes to the end of his life, he is no longer certain that his good deeds were all that good, or his prayers fervent and often enough. What if no man was good enough to get into Heaven? I am a warrior, Sebastian. Maybe I can fight my way there mid the ghastly demons and the dark. If I struggled upward with sword in hand, could I hack my way through strangling serpents into the presence of the Almighty?"

Thoughtful, Sebastian folded his hands in his lap. "I never thought of it like that. Does not the Church teach that once we die it is no longer for us to decide, that only the prayers of the living intercede for us?"

"Just the same…I should like to be buried with my sword. Will you do that, Sebastian? Just like the Vikings of old, eh? A true warrior's funeral."

"With a pyre, my lord?"

Hugh caught the edge of a smile on the squire's face. "No. A pyre would be too much, I think. And the bishop would never allow it. Only the sword, for I feel, somehow, that there is more to dying than giving up one's life."

"Are you afraid, my lord?" Sebastian's eyes were bright.

Perhaps he is more afraid than I. "Sometimes I am. Other times I am angry. And other times…awed."

"I am angry. And afraid."

"Maybe the thought of death is only difficult now," said Hugh. "When it is finally your time, the notion may be welcomed. I am counting on that."

"And amid all this, we have this wretched monk business."

"I am almost grateful for it. It takes my mind from myself." The crackle of flames grew loud while the men quieted under their blankets and furs. The spears lay beside them while the unstrung bows stood propped against a tree, gleaming silver in the firelight. Hugh frowned. "I do not like this whole affair. I do not mind admitting it makes me angry. Perhaps this Brother Peter will grant us the favor of his already being dead."

"I have never dealt with a madman before. Do madmen…look mad?"

Hugh rested his chin on his fist. "Not all madmen. But they are unpredictable. That is the one thing I cannot stomach."

Sebastian leaned forward out of the wind. "No one in these parts seems to have seen a madman. At least no one has said."

Hugh nodded "I believe them. They would not have cause to hide such a man. Did you see how they trembled when we told them he was mad?"

Nodding, Sebastian shivered. "Yes. How long will we search, my lord?"

"Until we find him…or at least until we are certain he is dead. I hope the latter. No. Perhaps it is not good for a man to wish for the death of another. I do not know anymore, Sebastian. My life is suddenly a puzzle to me. All that I have done—was it wrong, I wonder?"

"My lord, it is best not to travel that route. You cannot walk backwards into your own footsteps, after all." Hugh nodded. The squire rose and stretched. "Will you retire now, my lord?"

"No. I want to think for a while longer. You go on to bed, though. No reason for you to keep me company."

"Are you certain?" he asked, restraining a yawn.

Hugh chuckled. "I am certain. To bed with you!" The squire moved into the tent, but turned back when Hugh called out to him, "Just once. I would hear you say it."

The squire's face blanked until it slowly crimsoned, and a smile crept to the edges of his mouth. "Very well…*Hugh*."

"That was not so bad, was it?"

"No, my lord," he answered curtly, ducking into the far corner where his pallet lay.

Grinning, Hugh settled into his seat, scanning the sky and its stars. He sighed. If Heaven were hidden there, it was like no other concealed place. And why should it not be? He wished there was a priest with him to ask all these questions, but he knew most clerics possessed very little imagination where God was concerned. They only knew what they read, and this pragmatic musing did not seem to be something one could read in Scripture. He was aware he would know soon enough, but that was unsatisfying. He wanted to know now, before he must. Was that too much to ask?

Craning his neck, he looked upward. How they glittered! The stars stretched across the uneven velvet darkness in a milky river. There were so many. He once heard that these were the souls of all who ever lived. Was it true? Is this how they lived in eternity then, this endless assembly in the sky? Was he looking at Heaven now without realizing it?

"O God Eternal, bring me peace. Give me some portion of Your grace now so that I may not fear what lies ahead. Can You not give me a sign, some notion? For I would know where I will tread before I set my foot on that distant shore. It need not be a big sign, only so that I can know. So I can die a man."

The sky did not change. Not even a cloud marred its clarity. No shooting star streaked a heavenly message. There was only dark, and the quiet of the night. As quiet as the grave.

CHAPTER ELEVEN

Edric decided they should spend several days in the town. He liked sleeping indoors and was loath to give it up. For once, they ate well, slept well, and with plenty of kind company. After all, they were thought to be minstrels, not beggars.

He looked over at Azriel in the bonfire's light. Azriel did not lose control like he did before, managing to temper himself, saying nothing to anyone about being an angel. Edric found much relief in that.

Edric settled his rump on the ground, clenching his arms around his knees. The farmers had built a bonfire to celebrate the first greening of the fields and all the townsfolk were there. Edric played his pipe for a while, until the others began with their own drums, bagpipes, and noisemakers. They told him to take his ease, and he yielded gratefully, yet he watched them all with a cautious eye. It did not do to let one's guard down.

He glanced at the edge of the blaze and scowled. She was looking at him again, the comely lass with the ginger hair and greenish eyes. He did not like it. Hunkering down before the fire, he pointedly turned away.

The first time he noticed her was early in the evening. Azriel sat before him singing his melodies, and the two blended naturally. The dancing light from the fire illumined the faces of the crowd, revealing some and hiding others. He noticed her among the dirty faces of farmers and farmwives, not for any particular reason except that she showed such fascinated interest in them. After a time he realized it must be due to Azriel's handsome features. Women harassed them wherever they wandered, but Azriel's cool indifference soon dampened their ardor.

Edric sniffed at this one. She would find out soon enough that Azriel was a man unlike most. No pretty face or heaving bosom could crack his icy exterior. It was as if he were not a man at all…but that idea made Edric scowl.

The sudden touch on his shoulder startled him. Coloring with embarrassment, Edric looked up at the woman. "I like the way you play that reed," she said. Arrested momentarily by her words, Edric only stared. She dropped down beside him, skirts pooling under her. "I've never heard the like. Are they your own songs?"

Surreptitiously, his eyes scanned over the heads of the others crouched around the fire. Where was Azriel? His glance caught the woman's again, and he finally nodded in answer to her question.

She smiled, bobbing her head. "That's a fair talent, that. I couldn't do that if I had from now till doomsday."

"He isn't here."

Her eyes caught the firelight. Round, bright and green like sage, they were framed with a spray of dark lashes. Her expectant mouth stood open, poised between a smile and caution. "Who do you mean?"

"Azriel. The singer. He isn't here. He's about, though. You'd best look for him."

Laughing, her eyes squinted at him. "But I'm not looking for *him*."

"Oh." Edric sniffed and turned from her, drawing himself in tightly to keep warm. The fire was a pleasant thing and his belly was full. His mouth still tasted of savory roast fowl and nutty cheese. It was almost unbelievable the good fortune he found. Was it Azriel's doing? Did it only take a handsome face to counter his own? Not that his was that bad a face. He even shaved that morning.

There was still so much Edric did not know about his mysterious companion. He harbored his suspicions: that Azriel was a lord that no one wanted to find, or an heir who was too much trouble to murder. Edric's current good fortune proved how valuable he was, and he did not desire to change the circumstances. *Besides*, Edric thought grudgingly, *I like making music with the fool.*

Edric jumped again when the woman lightly touched his shoulder. "Will you dance?"

Looking into those glittering eyes, Edric paused. Was she daft? Vigorously, he shook his head. "No."

"Oh, come." She pulled on his arm, but he shook it off.

"No!" Again, she took his arm, laughing, and even though she was small she managed to pull him to his feet. He stumbled forward, straightening with sparse dignity. "I don't dance!"

She looked down when he said it, her eyes following his own quick glance to his foot. A frown creased her forehead. "Does it hurt, then?"

"It don't do naught. Now off with you, woman!"

Her face collapsed into mortification and her fingers rose to her flaming cheeks before she turned and ran off between the dancers into the flickering shadows.

Satisfied, Edric pulled on the hem of his tunic before dropping heavily to his place. He found himself facing Azriel again, but before Edric could ask where Azriel had disappeared to, the madman's eyes narrowed to dangerous slits. "Go apologize to her at once!"

"Apologize?" He grunted. "Where the hell have you been?"

"She was only trying to be kind to you, though little you deserve it."

"She was mocking me."

"Mocking you?" Azriel laughed. "What supreme vanity! To think that all the world cares for only the one thing: to mock *you*!"

"I said off with you, Azriel. I'm not in the mood for you tonight." His pleasant mood was ruined. Perhaps they had overstayed their welcome.

"Why she wanted to be kind to you is a wonder. I see now why women are so much of a mystery to you men. Men little understand themselves let alone the female of the breed."

Without answering, Edric flipped his hood up and turned his face deliberately away.

With a huff of irritation, Azriel rose and picked his way through the crowd until he found the woman.

From the edge of his hood Edric watched with a frown while she assessed Azriel. He spoke gently to her, angling his head toward Edric. Edric drooped, hiding within his own shadow. She shrugged to whatever comment Azriel made and bobbed her chin. Her curved neck allowed her head a graceful drape when she looked back at Edric, who slid further down. She brightened the longer they conversed, and Edric could easily imagine their exchange. She laughed, but Azriel shook his head, looking dour. *Sarding fool! She looks interested, Azriel. Don't muck it up!* Azriel shook his head again, but she took his hands, and without warning, whirled him, throwing her weight to fling Azriel outward with the momentum of the music.

Edric watched them ramble by and he lifted his hooded head only slightly. Perhaps it was her attractiveness that startled him. Pretty women like that seldom paid him any attention. Of course, it was dark and his features were hard to discern. Especially the foot.

Azriel wore a concentrated expression while he stiffly followed her movements. She glowed with the heat of the dance. Whenever she turned to the firelight, her round countenance gleamed, springtime to Azriel's winter.

Rolling his shoulders, Edric nodded to himself. He wondered how long it would take for her to see that Azriel held no interest in her.

Turning away, he saw the woman in his mind's eye. He did not remember seeing her before in the town. Her face and curvaceous body caused a familiar ache in his groin. He spat dispiritedly into the fire. She was not the only woman. Now that he held coins in his purse, he wondered if he could not buy a little relief.

Drawn again to the dancers, Edric slipped his glance over his shoulder and watched Azriel try to follow her steps.

Azriel's brow was thoroughly furrowed and he gripped her fingertips trying to keep from stumbling. He lifted his feet heavily and dropped them the same way, kicking up a cloud of dust. Edric made a scoffing noise. "That's the most pathetic thing I've ever seen." She tried to spin Azriel outward by extending her arms and whirling, but Azriel misinterpreted and stumbled after her, attempting to catch up. Finally Edric could watch no more and huddled over his knees, chuckling softly.

A flourish of skirts fanned the air and the musky scent of woman clouded about Edric's head when she flopped down beside him. Azriel had disappeared again and Edric was left alone with the ginger-haired woman with the broad smile. What was she up to, he wondered, sitting beside him like nothing happened? He scowled pointedly at her before turning away.

"Such a clear night," she purred, her voice soothing like the cool breeze just sweeping up Edric's back. "You can see all the stars."

If he did not answer, he decided, perhaps she would go away, though a spark of arousal warmed him from her being so close.

She was silent for a time and Edric thought she might have given up at last when he felt her breath unexpectedly at his ear. "I'm Margery."

He ignored her.

She touched his shoulder. "I'm Margery," she persisted.

Slowly he glanced her way. "You talking to me?"

Her throaty laugh thickened the night. "You're Edric, aren't you?"

The edge of his lips levered open just enough to mouth, "aye."

"What village you from, Edric?"

"The village of none of your sarding business."

"Why are you so sour on a night like this? I'm only trying to be friendly."

"Who asked you to?" A gray coal tumbled from the fire and he kicked it back with his good foot.

He felt her warmth as she leaned closer and said, "I dunno. I just took a fancy to your face."

"Well it goes with the rest of me, don't it? You satisfied now?"

"I see," she said with a low laugh. If it were not so seductive a sound it might have irritated. "You've an air about you, haven't you? Your friend told me to give you another chance."

"Another chance for what?

"Told me you weren't used to talking with women. That's why you were so rude and all."

"I know enough to ask how much coin they want for a tumble. How much do *you* want?" He leered, looking her up and down. "You're a fair lass. I wouldn't mind laying with you." Expecting it, the slap she delivered to his face somehow pleased. It was at least sincere. "The way you carried on, I just reckoned you were a whore—" She slapped him again, but this time he was not so amused. His cheek stung, and his hand cupped its swelling warmth. "As you will. Off with you, then. If you're no whore then I've no use for you."

With an unintelligible sound, she shot to her feet and escaped, shoving Azriel aside just as he returned again. Azriel stared after Margery, and then glowered down at Edric. "*Now* what have you done?"

"Naught. I just asked her how much money she wanted to lay with me."

"I have never heard of such a thing! You…you are the most appalling creature I have ever met!"

"I'm just practical. Woman are for swiving and making babies. That's all they're good for. Don't you know naught?"

Azriel made a choking sound before he finally sat. "Edric, why do you turn love and kindness away from you? Don't you think you deserve it?"

Edric held his hands toward the flames, warming one side and then the other. "What sort of fool talk is that? Shows what you know. I don't turn it away. It turns from me!"

"And you believe that. You did not see that Margery was being kind to you because—God help her—she seemed to be actually attracted to you?"

"You're truly addled, aren't you? It was you she wanted."

"She has paid me nothing but a passing interest, and only to ask about you."

"You're mad!" He pulled the mantle taut over his shoulders, rubbing his stubbly chin against the hood. "What are you now, Azriel? Some matchmaking pixie?"

Posturing, Azriel raised his chin. "You know perfectly well what I am."

Edric surveyed the dancers, musicians, and other merry-makers—all too far away to hear. None took notice of them. "Just keep it down, you," he said huskily.

"Perhaps I *am* your Guardian Angel. Little wonder I am being punished!"

Edric laughed, each raucous guffaw ruffling Azriel all the more. "*My* guardian angel. That's perfect. You're just the sort of angel I'd have."

"You are most difficult to like."

That particular frown Azriel wore rubbed Edric raw like a new scab on an old wound. He turned away again. "Who asked you to?"

Azriel contemplated the flames. His voice took on his singing voice's tone, fluid and airy. Its intimacy gave Edric the sensation they were the only two there. "Edric, love and friendship are not curses. You should learn to enjoy them. I am only beginning to myself."

Edric took a long moment to think. He could not remember the last time someone took so much effort to talk with him. Though mad, Azriel sometimes seemed like the sanest man he knew. Why did it have to be that way? Why couldn't someone from his own village have treated him with this much kindness? He might have stayed, might have felt at home, and might have become something. But even his own father…

Edric shook his head at it.

Azriel's eyes glistened. They followed Edric's hands when they rubbed each other, and then Edric's feet when they stretched forward seeking warmth.

Edric squinted back at the man who thought himself an angel. "Are you…are you saying…you are my friend?"

Azriel's gaze drifted into the fathomless flames. The fire wavered in his eyes, glazing the blue to silver. "That might characterize our relationship."

Edric heaved a frustrated sigh. "Does that mean 'yes'?"

Azriel smiled. "Yes."

The answer, though half-expected, still caught Edric off guard. "Why?"

Shrugging, Azriel tucked his worn cloak around him. "I think we need each other."

"I don't need no one!"

"Do you not? Men are not meant to be alone. The Divine Father made you Man and Woman, the one cleaving to the other. He made other creatures like yourself with which to live in community. You are not meant to be alone. Solitude is cruel…as devastating as my own abandonment."

"It isn't my choice, Azriel."

"Margery openly invited you and you scorned her. I offer my sage advice and you spit upon it." Azriel spoke in mellow tones. They were like the tawny fire, warm and enthralling. "I am not afraid to admit that I need you, Edric. I need you as I have never needed anything before. You must realize how great an admission that is for me. I, who was one of the greatest Angels… But what does that matter now? Now I am here. You plucked me from the mud. You succored me. You were my reluctant Good Samaritan. And yet, what is my purpose here? What is *my* goal? Maybe you were right in that as well, that I am to seek out humility." He shook his head. The curled points of his golden hair gleamed from the fire glow. "I am completely lost," he said mournfully. "If it were not for you, I should be the most forlorn creature on this earth."

An uncomfortable tingle rippled down Edric's flesh. He stared at his feet. The one on the left appeared perfectly normal within its leather shoe. But the other beside it was its bastard brother. Twisted by confused bone and gnarled muscles, it curled unnaturally toward the instep and downward. Toenails grew where they should not, and extra creases in the flesh often became red and full of pus. Forced to walk on the callused toes and side of the foot, it was often painful on stony roads, and so he padded it with bundles of cloth, encasing the whole in a sturdy binding of leather he seldom removed and that more resembled a sack. Men who might have been his friend shunned him because of it. Women never approached. What woman could? He hated it with every fiber of his being. It might have been better to cut it off than to have this miserable mass of flesh instead.

Yet here was Azriel, more lonely and dejected than he. Or was he? *Did* he need Edric? If Azriel with that face and voice felt alone, then what chance did Edric have?

"I didn't know you felt that way," Edric answered softly, staring into the fire. His throat warmed with unnatural emotion. "I've never been needed before. You sure?"

"Yes. Did you not realize it?"

"I dunno. I've been alone so long I got used to the sound of me own voice."

"Am I so bad?"

"No." He eyed him critically. "I reckon not." The startling thought that Azriel just might be a friend became overshadowed by visions of the curvaceous woman.

Edric ran a hand over his clammy neck. "Do you…do you think I should go over and talk to her, then? You know. Margery."

A brilliant smile brightened Azriel's face. "What do *you* want to do?"

Shrugging, Edric rocked back on his haunches. "I reckon…it couldn't hurt." Slowly, reluctantly, he got to his feet, rested his hands on his hips, and swiveled, looking for her.

Alone, she sat away from the fire. Her curling hair fell over her eyes and gathered over her shoulders. When he turned back, Azriel gave him a smile of reassurance, though Edric felt it was going to take far more than that.

Exhaling a long breath, Edric ambled toward her and stopped a few paces away. Shuffling, he tried to smile, and finally leaned against a tree. "Erm…Look here. I didn't reckon you meant what you said before. I thought you were looking for *him.* And then I reckoned you meant to mock me, see. Everyone does. But…well. That's it."

She lifted her face to him, but said nothing.

Heat flushed his cheeks. "Well…I've said me piece." If he were to turn away immediately the embarrassment would lessen and then he and Azriel could slip out of town at first light.

"Wait." With a delicate hand, she brushed the heavy tendrils of hair out of her eyes. "If you won't dance with me, will you at least bide a while?"

His first instinct was to run, but her manner gave him pause. He liked the shape of her arm and the curve of her jaw, the way her cheeks plumped when she said his name, and the way she never stared at his foot or crooked back. He tried to spy Azriel over his shoulder, but could not see him.

Shrugging, he sat, easing the pressure on his foot. "I've got naught better to do."

"Now why do you say things like that?"

Picking at a small root until he yanked it free, Edric drew mindless scribbles in the dust with it. "Like what?"

"'I've got naught better to do.' Sounds like you don't care at all."

He smiled and tossed the root away. It disappeared into the dark. Slumping forward, he wrapped his arms protectively across his chest. "I didn't mean it like that. I'm not used to talking to women."

"You're learning." She peered at him in the scant light. It only made him cringe further into the darkness. "You play that reed right well. How long you been here?"

"Two nights. We'll be going in the morning." Did her shoulders droop in disappointment? Surely that was his imagination.

"So few things happen here. A new face is always welcomed."

"What do you want the likes of me for?"

She cocked her head back and a brassy curl fell forward, nuzzling a shoulder. "You've got a nice face…if you didn't grimace so much."

"Grimace?"

"Like you're doing now."

It was useless. He slumped with a sigh. "I'm not one for pretty words, lass, and I've been on the road a long time. I've got a coin. So will you or won't you?"

"Won't I what?"

"Lie with me."

The round eyes narrowed. "Blessed Virgin! Is that all you think of me? Of every woman?"

"What *should* I think? I know what I am. I know what I can expect."

"Have you never learned to say a kind word to nobody?"

"And what would I say? 'Come, pretty lass. Come lie with the cripple. He's got a nice face…If he don't grimace.'"

Anger welled up in her eyes but just as suddenly wisped away. She softened and leaned closer. "I'm no whore, Edric," she said gently. "I…I'm a maiden, that's the truth of it."

He could not believe it, but vaguely wondered why her cheek darkened with a blush. It was a charming sight even in the near-darkness.

"Now I've said you've got a nice face," she went on, eyes still lowered, "and nice it is. It might be even nicer in the daylight, but mayhap I'll never know because you'll be gone. I've got no man, Edric, and I've got no family, so I'm on me own. A body gets lonely." She blushed again, lashes feathering her cheek. "I thought you were lonely, too, is all."

Eyes wide, Edric regarded her. He could be drunk, but he did not take that much beer. Warmth emanated from her skin like the bonfire's warmth. Was her hair afire? Is that what made it so red? Who was this woman who liked his face and wanted only his company? *His!* He leaned forward and stared at her. A shiver ran down his uneven spine. What had Azriel said to her?

Edric's voice was softer than usual, its coarse, jagged surface brushed smooth by unfamiliar emotions. "Ever met an angel before?"

"An angel?" Her small teeth glimmered in the dying bonfire. "No. Have you?"

He smiled, headiness making him dizzy. "Aye. I might have."

CHAPTER TWELVE

Her skin was smooth under her clothing. Edric tried to nuzzle her, savoring the saltiness of her neck, but she squirmed and squealed. Frustrated, he shoved her against a tree. "I can't wait no more, woman," Edric said huskily. Fumbling at his own braies before yanking up her skirts, he strove to couple, but her struggling confounded the effort. His fingers pressed harshly into her flesh in an attempt to hold her steady, but Margery gave a grunting cry before shoving him back, swatting at her skirts to swish them back into place.

She drew back her foot and kicked him hard in his good shin.

"Oi! What's that for?" Angrily he dragged his breeches back into place before rubbing the shin. "What the hell's wrong with you, woman?"

"That's for being a pig!"

Startled, all Edric saw was a whirl of disappearing skirts and shadows. He hobbled after her. "What you mean? You wanted it, didn't you? Or are you just a trifler?"

"It isn't because you're a cripple you haven't got a woman!"

Ears warming, Edric drew himself up. "I'm no gelding! You can't complain about that!"

"You weren't lacking, you idiot. You just don't care about me or what I want. I could be a sheep for all the care you gave it"

"A sheep? More like a bitch!"

Her lips hung open, glistening in the moonlight. Edric cringed when she raised a hand to slap him, but she changed her mind, whirling away instead. "You're not worth it," she cast over her shoulder.

"So what was all this, then? Pity for a cripple? I don't need your pity!"

Stopping, she spun, posturing against the firelight. "Pity? Is that what you make of it? You're as dense as cheese, Edric. You're a witless man and you don't know naught!" She cast her hands in the air, exasperated. "It isn't like you think. It's just…I thought you had a nice face. I thought the rest of you was just hard crust, but I see now how it's gone all the way through you."

Speechless, he watched her shadow retreat toward the fire. How was he ever to understand women? Was she mad like Azriel?

Limping, he followed and reached for her. She swung her other hand outward and connected with the side of his jaw. Edric drew his own arm back to deliver a blow when something gripped it.

"What are you *doing*?" cried Azriel.

"She's a bitch what needs a good smack." He wrestled his wrist away. "And you! 'Be nice to her,' he says. 'She likes you,' he says. More pig shit!"

Azriel's eyes drew down to slits. "The whole world is wrong and you are right, I suppose."

"Aye. That's it. That's just it! You in your little world of saints and angels. You're a piece of work, Azriel. A piece of work! Everything's newborn just cause you say a kind word to someone. Where's it ever gotten me, eh?"

"Have you ever *said* a kind word?"

"That's beside the point!" Glaring, Edric's glance swept both Azriel and Margery. Azriel stood taller than the both of them, broader and with more authority. Margery's face flickered a chaos of anger and confusion, before Azriel stepped in front of her, blocking her from Edric's view.

"Where were you?" Azriel asked Edric. "I looked for you."

"We were having a bit of sport back there."

Azriel's imperious expression elongated to horror. "Gracious God! Were you sinning?"

Edric dropped his chin though he tried to catch a glimpse of Margery. "I was *trying* to!"

Azriel looked back at Margery. "I expected better of you. If I had known, I would not have suggested you try to speak with him again. I see a lot of good it has done the both of you. Well! There is little to be done here. I cannot help you if you will not help yourselves."

Azriel dismissed them both, but Edric's flaring anger propelled him forward, and he gripped Azriel's arm. "What's the matter, Angel? Didn't do the job of guarding me from sin? What's to do now? A little flying maybe?" Edric waited, amused and frightened by what might come.

Azriel only glared down at Edric's dirty fingers, his face taking on an unexpectedly mild cast of surrender. He raised his chin and looked from Edric to Margery. "I opened my being to you, Edric, because you are the only creature on this earth who might understand. Do you think I play at a game? Oh I know…you think me a lunatic. Perhaps on this world that is all that I am. But to you I thought I was more. You are my friend. I thought *you* also needed one."

He turned to Margery, who shuffled under his reproachful and perplexing scrutiny. "I thought *she* might…well…I was wrong about that, too. You cannot recognize God's greatest gift, Edric. It is like a fog to you. How can you possibly limp through life without love?"

"I manage."

"You 'manage.' What sort of life is that?"

"What would you know of it?"

Stopped short, Azriel stiffened. "Well…I suppose that is true. Perhaps you are opening my eyes to my own ignorance. Perhaps—though you do not know it—you are helping me."

Edric scowled, eyeing Azriel first, then Margery, who stared critically at their glowering exchange. "Well isn't that pretty," he said to Azriel. "I'm happy for you."

"And therein lies the problem," Azriel said, broad shoulders rising in renewed outrage. "You are *not* happy for me. You are so sour about life that you shun every emotion but hate."

"Leave off, Azriel," he sneered, pushing up his right sleeve, "or you'll get another lesson in humility."

"If it pleases you that much to strike me, then go ahead." Scowling, Edric drew back his fist and delivered a blow to Azriel's unprotected chin.

Azriel staggered backwards and Margery screamed. Azriel grabbed his bruised jaw in horrified amazement. "You *did* it!" Azriel cried. "You actually did it. And you enjoyed it!"

Rubbing his knuckles, Edric nodded. "I must admit."

Azriel's scowl drew deep lines in his cheeks. Methodically he straightened his tunic and pulled taut his ragged cloak over his shoulders. "No, Edric," he said in a strangely calmed voice. "I truly cannot imagine why a woman would want you. Why anyone would attach themselves to you. You cannot *be* helped. Do you know why? It is not part of your vocabulary." He shook his head, sadness cloaking his eyes. "I cannot help you anymore, Edric. Perhaps I was not meant to help you. I only feel pity for you, for all Mankind. The greatest gift has been given you all, and all of you do not have the least idea what to do with it. It is Love, Edric. Love. You do not know Love. You do not know what it is, and worse—you do not want to know. Well!" he huffed. "Good luck to you. I pray your life is all that you hope it is." With one last glare at Edric, he tugged at his tunic and slowly pivoted. "You may find me back at the stable should you care to join me again. If I do not see you by morning, then I suppose I shall move on without you. And only the Divine Father knows where I shall be after that."

Brusquely, Azriel brushed past Edric and disappeared into the dark. Edric and Margery silently watched him depart for a moment before Margery drew up and clubbed Edric's shoulder. "That's for making him unhappy!"

Edric cringed. "I didn't mean to!"

"You don't mean a lot of things but you make lots of people unhappy."

"And just what did I do, eh? You wanted it."

"He's right. You're selfish. You take without giving."

"You'd've gotten plenty."

Margery blocked the bonfire's light with her silhouette. A nimbus of fire glowed about her hair. Her face fell into shadow except for the gloss in her eyes. "Haven't you ever been tender? Haven't you ever kissed a woman, Edric? You didn't even try to kiss me. Not once."

He clenched his fists. Anger at Azriel's words—some he did not even understand—was eclipsed by the heavy embarrassment that suddenly settled upon him. "You want kisses? Aren't I just another man in the dark?"

"Are you?" She drew closer and Edric felt her warmth again. It galled him that Azriel might be right, or he himself might be wrong.

With effort, he concentrated on Margery staring so earnestly at him in the dark. Why was she not running from him, slapping him again?

A bagpipe began playing and a cheer went up. Dancing figures wavered before the yellow blaze, all of it receding distantly.

Margery's breath puffed against his cheek and a heat hotter than the farmer's bonfire flared in his chest.

"Haven't you ever kissed a woman?" she breathed. "Truly kissed her?"

He only raised his face slightly when he felt her mouth timidly touching his. Soft and moist, her lips caressed in a slow seduction. He did nothing, allowing her mouth to stroke across his and then back again. It was a strange sensation, for he realized he never had kissed any women, not truly. Not like this.

His heart pounded, constricting the breath in his aching chest. Edric fought his own emotions. The false boasting he made to

Azriel did not compare to this sudden reality. He never knew anything could be this sweet. He wanted to surrender, but always there was something tingling in the back of his mind to be wary, to be on guard.

She moved her body closer. He tasted her mouth, releasing an unexpected sigh. Her fingers clutched his head, slipping into his hair. Weakening, Edric embraced her, arms enfolding her. He kissed her back with gusto, gently exploring, tasting.

After a time, her lips pulled away from his. Breathlessly he stared at her, her face barely inches from his own. So warm. Everything about her was warm like a thick fleece. How he wanted to remain in the haze of her, that radiance of intoxicating sweetness. But though he tried to fend it off, a cold reality slipped in, twisting his gut and forming a lump in his throat.

Reluctantly, he drew back. His head hung low on his chest. "I…don't want to play this game," he rasped.

"What game?"

"Whatever you're playing at. I don't want it."

"There's no game," she said, shaking her head gently. The curled tendrils of her long hair still clung to his shoulders. "It's as far from a game as can be, Edric. It's true."

Why was his heart trying to force its way out? At least that is what the pain felt like. "Why do you do this?"

"Can't a woman like you, Edric, even as mean and as rude as you are? Can't a woman like your face despite your manner?"

He could not lift his eyes to her. His head felt too heavy for that, too heavy to see the honesty in her eyes if she were lying. He clenched his teeth till his jaw hurt. "Do *you*?"

"Aye." A simple word. She did not even hesitate saying it. But he knew she could not mean it. They never meant it. Suddenly he could not move. Feeling too horrible to even leave her presence, he stood there dumbly. Her kiss lingered too much in his mind and on his lips, tingling even now.

He jumped, startled, when her hands grasped his cheeks and forcefully lifted his face. Again her mouth descended again, opening over his. The kiss deepened, more so than the last time. His arms wrapped around her tightly. She was soft and pliant, every part of her touching him. He returned the kiss, lapping his lips over hers while heat rippled throughout his body and made him completely forget—for once—that he was not a whole man.

After a long interval, he broke away and drew back, gazing at her, amazement in his heart.

There was no mockery on her round cheek, no unkind laughter in her eyes.

"I wonder what you look like in the sunshine," he whispered, unnaturally tender. Lightly, he touched the curled ends of her hair. "Your hair must be like flames. And your eyes—" He leaned forward and kissed the lids, feeling the ticklish softness of her lashes. His lips caressed her skin. "They must be like wet stones sparkling deep in a brook. Are they?"

She giggled. "I don't know."

"They must be…Margery… Why—"

"No." She laid her fingers over his mouth. "If we see each other come morning, we'll see what the sunshine does."

The floating sensation deflated and he felt heavy within himself again. He pushed her away. His voice cracked when he said, "It will make you hate me."

She smiled. There was just enough reflected firelight to glisten the moisture of their kiss on her mouth. "I doubt that."

"What if it does?" he asked fearfully.

"You think so little of me?"

"I don't even know you!"

"Poor Edric. Why don't you beseech your angel? He'd help you lose your fear."

The words yanked him back to the chill of reality. It washed through him, erasing the warmth inflating his chest. "Angel? What are you talking about, woman?" Did she overhear them? What did she know about him and Azriel? Had the fool gone and said?

"You asked me before if I'd ever met one."

"Oh. Aye. Margery…" His relief was short-lived. "Hell! You

just met me. You don't know. Everything Azriel said about me…it's probably true."

"I know more about you than you think. There's loneliness in your eyes."

He should have been angry. If Azriel had said it…but from her it was different, sincere. Arousal flushed him with renewed heat and he embraced her, roughly handling her breasts and sinking his face beneath the waves of her hair. With an exasperated grunt, she shoved him again. "Edric…no!"

"What now?" he bellowed, drawing back. "I kissed you, didn't I? Isn't that what you wanted?"

Arms clasped protectively across her bosom, Margery glowered. "If you want more, you can go and buy it in town. There's women there who will whore for you."

What was she saying? Everything about her seemed to call him, and yet every time he drew closer she shied away. Could she really be a virgin? If she were, he wondered what she wanted with him. He liked the way she kissed. It was warm and soft, her lips nibbling on his in a way that aroused not only his flesh, but also his soul. It might be just a trifle, mocking him like so many others had, but there was no malice to be found in her voice or her eyes. "Well…a man isn't used to…"

"Isn't used to tenderness and being gentle?"

"I…well it's…" He took a deep breath and scowled. "Are you mocking me? I'll knock your head in if you are!"

She wore no fear and even smiled. "I'm not mocking you. You're a comely man and I like kissing you. Sometimes I'm lonely, too, Edric, and just want a man's arms about me. That's all. If you don't want it, then say so."

What were her eyes telling him? He could not guess. He never saw that expression before, not directed at him. Azriel told Edric he could not love, and maybe that was true, but there was something about this woman that made him weak. It was not a bad feeling but neither did he know if it was a good one.

"I want you, Margery," he whispered harshly to her ear. She

shivered. "But…" He cowered back, indecisive. His instinct was to move toward her, but his instincts had been wrong before. He could not seem to trust anything. *Damn Azriel!* "What must I do?" he rasped. "Tell me, lass. Tell me what to do and I'll do it."

She smiled and then slowly kneeled. Still grasping his hand, she pulled him down with her into the damp bracken, not more than ten paces from the merry-makers and the bonfire. Slowly, softly, she touched her lips to the side of his mouth.

Closing his eyes and deeply inhaling, Edric trembled at the unexpected sensation.

"Just kiss me, Edric. That's all. Just kiss me, and that'll be enough."

CHAPTER THIRTEEN

Turning his head, Edric spied the curve of her jaw gilded by a climbing sun. He sat up, and leaned his stubbled cheek on a fist. With his other hand, he brushed the hair away from Margery's face, awakening her. "Well?" he said cautiously. "Here's that face in the sunlight. What say you?"

She stretched, shivering with cold. Without thinking, he threw the ends of his cloak over her and she grasped it, bringing it up under her chin. "It's still a nice face. That *is you* Edric, isn't it?"

He nervously chuckled. "You're a stoat, aren't you? But I knew I'd like yours in the sunshine. It's pretty, even in the dark."

She leaned upward to deliver a quick kiss, but Edric held her face, her hair weaving between his fingers. The kiss lingered until he pulled gradually away. Sadness, sticky like syrup, hindered him, and he sat back, rolling an arm around his upraised leg. "But now it is the morn," he said without emotion. "What do we do now?"

"I don't know." She sat up, sitting on her haunches. Her own cloak twisted around her. "That depends on you."

"On me? Why?"

"If you'll be staying…or going."

"Stay? What would I do? I can't make no living hereabouts. I'm no farmer. I don't know a trade. I'm just…hell. I'm not even a minstrel. I'm just a crippled beggar what plays a pipe."

She ran her red-chapped fingers over one another. "You're a beggar?"

"Aye. Didn't you know?"

"No."

Emptiness, deep and appalling, opened wide his chest. He had been a beggar for many years, eking out a life from almoners, knights, and townsfolk. He hated it, cursed it, but accepted it as his lot. Yet never before did he feel ashamed of it.

Last night had been unreal, ethereal. He felt alive and unencumbered. But like all dreams, the waking sky chases them away and they never return.

Clumsily, he got to his feet and shook the morning damp from his cloak. There was no need to look at the woman. He could conjure that expression in his mind from any number of females.

Margery rose and shook out her skirt.

It suddenly stabbed his heart to leave her. This was not love, was it? If it was, he had no more use for it than an empty belly. It was just as painful.

Lobbing the hood over her wild tresses, she stared at the ground. "I've got to get to the baker's. He's probably bellowing, wondering where I am." She said nothing else and stood for a long moment, yet Edric felt somehow she wanted to say more. The air hung still with anticipation, and then a breeze blew up, just enough to move his hair, but also enough to chase away any last vestiges of hope. "Farewell, Edric," she said at last. "God's grace to you."

For a long time he remained frozen except to heave a deep sigh. The crunch of thickets and the thud of her footsteps eventually petered out, and by that he knew she was gone.

Gradually, he lifted his face to the sky. He could not shake the feeling that something huge had passed him by. Last night with her, he did not feel like a cripple. But this morning he wore that mantle once again, like strapping on a piece of heavy armor. The burden of it pulled him into the ground. He lifted a foot—the good one—but it felt almost as oppressive as the other. *She likes your face well enough—but you're a beggar…and she didn't yet see the foot.* That was a crevasse he was not willing to cross. To see her wince in disgust—even to picture it in his mind—stabbed an ache in his heart. No. She was better off without him. That took no reflection at all.

He stood for a long time, gazing into the foggy patches milling like sheep along the rutted road.

"Bah! You're a fool, Edric," he grumbled aloud. A lone crow chuckled back at him. He raised his head to stare at the bird, its feathers slick and highlighted in blue. It called again before it opened its wings, pumped the air, and dove behind the copse. He thought he heard its lonely voice farther on but it might be the wind in the brake thrashing dead twigs. Finally, he turned toward the stable where he and Azriel made their beds. He hobbled over the rise, the narrow dirt holloway almost too cramped for his loping gait.

The farmer and his family were already out with their animals when they raised their heads at Edric's passing. Edric almost reached the stable when the man stopped him and said, "He's gone already."

Edric cupped his hand to his ear. "What's that you said?"

"I said your friend. He's already gone. Left at first light."

Limping quickly forward, Edric closed on the man. "What you mean 'left'?"

"He's gone. Gave us his thanks and a blessing and went off."

Panicked, Edric quickly limped to the stable and searched the empty space with his eyes. Gray light angled through the slats, illuminating patches of floor, piles of straw, and dark enclosures. Vaguely, he remembered Azriel promising to leave if Edric did not return, but Edric hadn't believed Azriel would actually do it.

There was no sign of Azriel, no indication he even spent the night.

Breathless, Edric ambled back outside and hailed the farmer. "Which way did he go?"

"Toward Evesham."

His heart sank. Azriel would be quite far along if he left at first light. Azriel's gait was good and steady. "The sarding fool!" he rasped. What was he to do? He had not said very kind words to Azriel, even after the man had opened his soul to Edric. No one had ever done that before. No one thought him worth the trouble. Was it Azriel's madness that made the would-be angel think such a thing? Edric did not think so. There was something to that lunatic, something deeply imbedded in his eyes…

An unaccustomed heaviness planted itself in Edric's belly and drew out a deep-seated moan. The only friend he ever had, the only woman who ever showed an interest…

He glared heavenward. "This is Your idea of a jest, is it?"

The farmer eyed him warily and trudged away, tossing more scraps to the hens and swine.

Edric knew he would have to go after Azriel. Alone, Azriel was a danger to himself. He was bound to tell the wrong person his fool tale and get himself killed.

Edric jerked forward but stopped abruptly. After he found Azriel, then what? The man was foully angry with him. Would Azriel even want to see Edric again?

Tottering against the rough stone of the stable, Edric slid down until he sat in the muck, gathering his thoughts. Life was no better before all this, but it was a damn sight simpler. He could go on like before. It would mean no shelter and few coins. Bitterly, he felt the disks in his pouch. *Azriel, you fool! You left without money.*

After all the preaching by well-meaning and self-serving clerics, none managed to ravage his soul as much as Azriel's lunatic railings. Nothing would ever be the same again. His life was surely miserable enough without all this. Why had Edric even stopped to rescue him in the first place?

Without warning, the monastery song welled up irresistibly inside of him, clattering against the unprotected crevices of his soul. He slowly pulled forth the pipe and played it again. The lonely notes spun into the air and swirled about his head, balancing precariously on the filtered light of the morning. The music traveled outward and seemed to disappear over the treetops, blanketing the countryside in mournful song. When the echoes completely died away, he pulled the pipe sluggishly from his lips and rested it in his lap. The Good Samaritan. Azriel had also called Edric that. What did that mean exactly? Only Azriel would know. He would have to ask him.

It was strange how it seemed decided for him. Was he mad like Azriel? He stuffed the pipe away and hoisted himself to his feet. The day was already drawing on. He had spent too long with Margery this morning…

Edric winced. Thoughts of her ached his chest with added discomfort. The two thoughts mingled. Azriel was far ahead. Margery. Margery had two good feet. She could move faster, if need be.

He did not know anyone else to help him…and he wanted an excuse to see her again. Of course there was no reason to expect she would go with him. He remembered her face when he admitted to being a beggar. "What of it?" he spat. "If she don't go, she's just a silly cow like all the other women." He would just ask. No loss if she declined.

Raggedly, he limped toward town, passing the hedgerows and budding lupines without pause. He ambled along the main thoroughfare, avoiding a mucky ditch trickling with refuse. Steamy smoke rippled along the thatched rooftops, and he followed that to the shopfront and clung to the doorway, panting. The yeasty aroma of bread rose about him.

"Margery? Where is she?" he gasped to the baker's wife. She looked at him oddly, but jabbed behind her with a thumb, indicating the back room. Edric rumbled by her, ignoring her disquieting scrutiny, and cast the curtain aside.

Margery's hands were deep within a wad of dough when she looked up, surprised. "Edric! What you doing here? Begging for bread, are you?"

It hurt. It was too quick for him to shield himself. He swallowed the curse he planned to hurl at her, and said instead, "Azriel's gone and I've got to find him. But I need help."

She pulled her hands free and wiped them long down her apron. "So?"

His eyes could not help but dart around the warm surroundings. A heavy wooden table dominated a room crowded with barrels. The floor and every other surface were dusted white with flour. Three kneading troughs lined the table with a piglet-sized mound of rising dough in each one. A small hearth with blackened stones smoked from one wall, while in a far corner lay a straw pallet, and beside it a chipped clay jug. He guessed it was Margery's bed.

Inhaling the warmth and the sweet aromas of bread along with the wood smoke, he pushed aside a shard of envy. It was just the kind of place he imagined living in when he dared dream.

"Well…I need help."

"What kind of help?"

"Dammit, woman," he grumbled. "I need yours. Two strong legs to scout ahead. I haven't got them."

"Why me?"

"Why not you? I don't know another soul here."

"What will you pay?"

"Pay? You think I'm a lord? I got naught."

She jerked her head toward the pouch at his belt. "I see coins there. If I go with you, I'm liable to lose me situation here."

Leaning on his good leg, he smoldered. "A man's got to eat, hasn't he?"

"So's a woman."

The flour-dusted floor held his interest for a long time. To be without money… He'd been there often, but the thought of giving it up for the likes of Azriel galled.

"I've…I've got a few coin," he admitted. She squinted at him a long time, just enough to unnerve. He grimaced. "Will you or won't you?"

Without a word, Margery moved to the peg at the wall and took down her cloak. Draping it over her shoulders she brushed passed him, but stopped long enough to turn back. "You coming?" she asked, rolling her sleeves down.

The ache he stored in his chest filled with warmth.

She moved forward into the shop and scooped a day-old loaf from a table. "I'll be needing this," she said to the baker. "I've a long way to go."

"Here woman! What do you think you're doing?" The baker lunged forward. His broad face reddened, and the dark eyes widened. "Running off to do your mischief in the middle of the morn? Weren't you late enough?"

"That's enough of that!" said Edric, pushing him aside. "You heard her."

"I'll not have this."

"You want payment for her?" Edric snarled. "Here's payment." Swiftly, he drew his knife and held it up. The baker staggered back. His wife shrieked and ran into the back room.

"Edric!"

"I won't hurt him," he said over his shoulder to Margery. "I just want him to know that you're going with me without trouble. Isn't she?"

"I'll get the law on you."

"I've had worse, friend." He took her arm and moved quickly out the door and sheathed his knife.

Once they reached the surrounding hills he looked at her with some surprise. Her grin spilled outward into a laugh. "What's so damned funny?"

"You took a knife to the baker for me. That's something, isn't it?"

He chuckled half-heartedly. "I never done the like before, that's the truth."

"You didn't have to, you know. He'd have let me go. We're almost family, him and me."

He stopped, leaned against a tree, and looked back. Nothing changed in the little town from his actions. Smoke still curled from chimneys, dogs scampered along the lanes, men lingered in their fields with wooden hoes poised over their shoulders. The main road wriggled outward in its usual fashion, braving the headlands and avoiding the river. Yet all was different.

"Margery, I need to tell you why I'm going in search of Azriel."

"I reckon you're his friend. There's naught *to* say."

"No. There's more. You'd best sit."

Easing down beside him, she looked up expectantly. She was close enough for him to see the sprinkling of freckles across her cheeks and forehead. Even her blunt nose sported several. Her verdant eyes were greener in the sunshine, reminiscent of the greening hills behind her. He could not stare into those eyes for very long without a feeling of craving dragging at him, so he moved away and turned his back to her. His shoulder nuzzled an oak's rough bark.

"Azriel…well…he isn't right in the head, see? When I found him a sennight ago he'd been coshed. I don't know if he'd been coshed because of his madness or became mad after. All I know is he thinks he's…he thinks he's an angel."

"Are you saying he's a madman?"

"Well…aye. That he is. A ripe one."

Edric cringed when she rocked with a laugh. "He thinks he's an angel?"

"It isn't all that funny, Margery. And aye, he truly does think it. He's got a whole dream world attached to it. Oh, I don't know what he was before or who he really is. Does it matter? He's been right kind to me when no one was, and he tries to please, even though he can be an arrogant bastard."

"You like him, don't you?"

Edric rolled along the tree trunk until he faced her. Biting his lower lip he reluctantly nodded. "Aye. I do. Don't ask me why. But he can't be on his own. He'll say something or do something and he'll get hurt. I never asked to be no nursemaid to no fool but…there it is."

Her arms crossed over her chest and a small smile curved her lips. "You're a one, Edric. You *are* all crust. You don't want no one to know there's melted butter inside."

He frowned. "So how much coin do you want? I haven't

much."

"Why'd you need my help, then?"

He wiped his sweaty palm down his tunic front. Her unnerving scrutiny made it difficult to think. "What you staring at, you silly cow? I just need your help, is all. You need a sarding song for it?"

Her smile faded, and she rose with a sigh. "No. I just thought you might say."

"There's naught *to* say. If you don't want to go, then back lies the town. It's no secret I can't move as fast as he can. Why'd *you* come along so quick if you hate beggars so much?"

Picking at her cloak, she sniffed the morning air, watching the white puffs rise above her. "We're wasting time."

"Well then."

They walked for an hour, Edric all the while watching her skirt drag at the dusty road. From his rearguard position he was able to watch her slim form. Her hips rocked and swung. He found it hypnotic and arousing. It was maddening watching her without being able to touch!

Margery suddenly turned, startling him. "I can't let you walk behind me like that anymore," she called back.

"Why not? I'm used to it."

"Well I'm not!" She stopped, awaiting him, but he refused to move.

"What's the point of this? You're supposed to go on ahead."

Her hair quivered out from under her hood. The wind took it up and suspended it sideways across one shoulder. It rippled, glimmering copper and gold. "I can't," she said, her hand punching her hip, "not with you skittering behind."

"Skittering?" Limping forward, he stood with his eyes just up to her chin.

"It just don't seem right," she said softly.

Taken aback, Edric lowered his face. "Well…what good are you then as a scout?"

"We'll do it together, Edric. We'll find him."

He began to wonder if she wasn't right in the head either. Why would a woman want to be in his company? Surely she did not mean to rob him? The thought amused; someone having the gall to steal from *him*? They would have to be desperate, though it *was* the first time he actually had coin in his purse.

Reluctantly, he nodded. They set off again side by side. It was a peculiar sensation.

Margery sighed, tucking her hair within her hood again. "Have you ever traveled this way before, Edric?"

"Aye. I reckon I've been all over this part of England."

"Ever go to sea?"

"What? Beg at sea? From mermaids?"

She laughed, the first relaxed sound all morning. "I reckon not." After a few paces of pensive silence, she asked, "Is it hard? Begging, I mean."

"What you mean 'hard'? You mean asking folk for charity? No. It isn't hard. Well…maybe at first, but that was a long time ago."

"Did you have no parents to care for you, Edric?"

"My sire. He didn't want me about, so I left. But I've learned no trade and being a cripple and all, well…" He saw her shake her head. Her pity left a sour taste in his mouth. "Don't feel sorry for me! I can't stomach it."

She tilted up her head. "It seems to me that that's exactly what you want of people. Isn't that why they throw coins to you? Out of pity? Or is that why you play that reed…so it'll feel like you're earning it?"

"You're a sly bitch, aren't you? Think you've got me all figured out. Women!" By her expression, he knew he bested her to silence but it did not sit as well as when he did the same to Azriel.

The icy reticence took them to nightfall, where he built a fire and they settled on opposite sides of it. Edric folded into himself, hanging his head low over his chest inside his hood. Margery shivered and again raised her eyes to Edric. They already ate a small portion of the bread and planned to save the rest for tomorrow.

Edric listened to the quiet and the crackling flames for a time before pulling out the reed and softly playing a tune. The music began intimately enough, but slowly the tune billowed, surrounding them, and filled the night. Edric closed his eyes and flew away with it, free of cumbersome limbs and painful memories. He wasn't only a beggar, he thought. He played his reed. He was nearly as good as a minstrel was. He *did* earn coin when he played. A man gives coins when he feels the need to give to the lowly. Or he pays for a service rendered, and wasn't playing a reed for the pleasure of others a service? By the saints, of course it was! Whether Margery thought so or not!

He played on, opening his eyes once to glance at Margery. But at the sight of her he drew the pipe away from his lips.

She leaned forward. Silver tears coursed down her cheeks. "Why'd you stop?" she asked.

Horrified, he stared at her luminous face, shining with tears. "Why are you crying?" he softly asked.

"Why? Your playing. It's beautiful."

Edric lowered the reed to his lap. Coins, bread, curses. All of these he received from his playing, but never tears. He lowered his head. It was impossible to look at her. He tucked the pipe away and commenced making himself a bed of rusty bracken.

Edric tried to settle in until Margery's timid voice rose above the weak crackling of fire. "It's cold. Aren't we going to get closer?"

He tried to ignore it all evening. The twilight darkened, and the little fire reminded so much of the night before. Both had remained silent without referring to those events. But now her unexpected words fiercely aroused him, and he was reluctant to move.

"Did you hear me, Edric?"

"I heard you."

Sighing, she huddled in her mantle. "It's a cold night."

He lifted his head and stared at her from under the hood rim. "But—"

"But what? I'm freezing over here, Edric!"

Without hesitation, he jumped up, scooted around the fire, and huddled beside her. She closed her arms swiftly around him under his cloak and she nuzzled her face against his chest, making a sound like a purr. Her curled hair was at his nose and he inhaled its fragrance of baking bread, spice, and sweat. Slowly, he brought his own arms around her, eliciting from her another sound of pleasure. She wriggled closer. "Margery," he moaned.

She raised her face and he gazed at it, running his eyes over the shadowed lids and round cheeks. He could not see the freckles in the dark but knew them like a friendly landscape.

Gingerly, he lowered his head and touched her mouth gently with his lips. For a fearful moment, he thought she might pull away. But instead she returned the kiss and added her own passion to it. He wanted her. His hand on her face, thumb caressing her cheek seemed to ask.

Her bright eyes gazed at him and her smile told him what he wanted. He leaned in again, mouth finding the salty warmth of her neck.

Sleeping on and off, he awoke near midnight, amazed to the feel of a warm body against his. She opened her eyes and looked at him a long time through their foggy breaths. "I've never been with a woman all night before," he whispered.

She smiled. "What of the last time with me?" Her giggle quivered her hair, tickling him.

He ran his lips over her forehead, deeply inhaling. "I like the way you smell."

"The way I smell?" Her laughter did not hurt his feelings. Besides, the trembling of her body against his was quite agreeable.

"Aye. I like it." Her smile gleamed. He could almost count every tooth even in the scant glow of dying embers.

"What else?" she urged.

He leaned over and nuzzled her neck, sighing. "I like the way you taste, salty and all."

She giggled again. "What else?"

His hand reached and closed over her haunch. He squeezed gently. "I like the way you feel," he said huskily.

Her giggles grew softer. "What else?"

This time, her eyes captured him. He could find no malice there. It was easy to slip peacefully into her toasty warm gaze. "I…I like the way you look at me…like I was a man."

Tenderness furrowed her brow, and she raised her hand to stroke his stubble-roughened cheek. The fingers rose higher to push the dark strands of his hair aside.

"What do you want with the likes of me, Margery? You could have your pick. I'd have thought you'd be wanting Azriel."

"No. His manner…it frightened me a bit."

He chuckled, breaking the tension. "And I don't?"

"No. You seem…lost."

He rolled away to lay on his back with an exasperated huff. "Christ! Do all women want to mother men?"

Edging closer, she rumpled her hands under his cloak. "Aye. Because they all need it so much. You can't tell me you don't like to be mothered."

"I don't. Quit fussing!"

"Ah, Edric. Won't you let me? Just a little?"

"Curse it, woman!" He felt her fingers creep up inside his shirt, and he thawed. "Well… If you must…"

Her lips touched his ear. "Isn't that better than curses?" she whispered.

"I suppose," he said dazedly.

Turning his face toward her, she kissed him and then smiled. "You've a generous sweet mouth, Edric, when you want it to be."

"What's that supposed to mean?" he mumbled into her lips.

"If you try, you can be sweet." She ran her hands over him, and he turned with a capitulating sigh, throwing his leg over her. She looked down with a growing frown. "Don't you ever take off your shoes?"

His ardor drained. He rolled away again. "Why should I?"

"It's more comfortable."

"I'm used to it."

He felt her stare at the back of his shoulder for a long time, each eye boring a hole. He was about to tell her to be still and go to sleep when she softly offered, "You needn't mind me, Edric."

With anger too far along and building, Edric crumpled even tighter to a protective ball. "Is that what you want to see? Are you *that* kind?" The force of his voice slashed the night, startling a mouse in the undergrowth.

"Why are you so angry? I didn't say naught—"

"Just leave it, Margery!"

"It might need caring for."

He whipped about. "I don't need your mothering me! I been this way a long time, but God willing I won't be on this earth much longer. So leave it!"

He settled down, his back to her. He could hear her angry breathing, but he tried to shut his mind to it. Nothing was different. Why did he keep torturing himself that it was?

His eyes warmed and threatened a tear, but he pushed into the socket with a knuckle. Tears were futile. He had not wept about his state since he was a child. *That's what comes from all this mothering!*

"You can't mean you'd rather die, Edric." He would have sharply replied, but his throat was so swollen with an ache that he dared not say anything lest he unman himself. "Edric, you've got to learn to trust someone. I reckon you trust Azriel or you wouldn't be taking so much effort to find him. And I reckon—in a way—you trust me, or you wouldn't have asked me to come with you."

"You still haven't told me how much coin you want," he croaked.

"I don't want no money. I just said that to make you cross."

Edric released an irritated puff. "Well it worked, didn't it!"

Sighing, she edged closer. "I'm not afraid of your foot... because my own father was a cripple and his back was bent far more than yours."

His breath caught. What trick was this? In his soul, he did not think Margery was capable of such blatant lies. He found himself rolling back toward her.

"He was a kind and gentle man," she went on with a smile,

remembering. "Everyone liked him. Nobody feared him. And I don't fear you. Is that what you're afraid of? That I fear you?"

"It's what I'm used to," he replied hoarsely.

"Poor Edric. It isn't that way with me."

"Curse it, woman. Why didn't you say so before?"

"Would it have made a difference?"

He scowled, thinking of all Azriel said to him. Thoughtfully, he shook his head. "I…I don't rightly know." He blinked hard. "Let's to sleep," he grumbled. "We've got a long day tomorrow."

He heard her settle back, the bracken crunching beneath her. The night seemed to settle over them like a mantle, pensive, waiting. He did not get much sleep after that. His mind was too full of anxious thoughts. When he rose in the morning and disappeared briefly to attend to his bowels, he still thought of Margery's confession, but not with relief. It created a new set of anxieties to contend with.

When he returned she was toasting slices of bread over the renewed campfire. She said nothing when she looked up at him, and he said nothing to her. After a time, they gathered their meager belongings and began again along the winding road.

CHAPTER FOURTEEN

"Have you seen a man who may seem out of place?"

Latimer repeated it by rote, just as he repeated it during the week they searched. But always the answer was in the negative. Even the few times a traveler seemed to fit that description, it always proved false.

The monk glanced disdainfully at the many unclean faces in the square. Traveling among the laity was tiring. He longed to return to the monastery, but they received no reports of any strangers or of mysterious bodies found in the woods. Soon he would give up and return to Pershore. The abbot would be displeased, but what was he to do? He wondered if Hugh Varney was searching and what his investigations revealed.

Herbert's face was dusty and appeared haggard from weariness. Latimer had accustomed himself over the long years in cloistered life to falling asleep quickly and awakening automatically before the midnight bell. He could sleep in almost any position and under any circumstance, but it did not seem that Herbert had yet mastered this practice.

"When we return our brother to the monastery, Brother

Latimer," said Herbert, "what shall be done with him?"

Latimer scowled. "I expect he would be locked in his room again."

"I should suggest shackles to the abbot," muttered Herbert, rubbing chapped fingers. "And bars upon the windows. I am surprised at Abbot Gervase for being so lenient."

Coldness throbbed in Latimer's chest. Barely controllable rage trembled his limbs, but his features, as always, were composed like a saint's carved, wooden face. "Such uncharitable words, Brother, for a man you have never met."

"In all honesty, I do not wish to meet him…but I know we must."

Latimer's mind worked, one cogwheel moving another and another. "Are you weary, Brother?" he asked suddenly, with a gentle tone. "Would you rest yourself a while?"

"No, Brother," Herbert said with a sigh. "I would not leave you to this alone."

"Oh, but as you see I am not weary at all. Perhaps it would be wiser if we split up. More ground could be covered."

Herbert's eyes, though bloodshot, wore a tentative luster. "You want me to go on alone?"

"It might be more expedient. You can ask your questions in those parts of town I have not yet been. There. You can take the northern sector and I can scour the southern. We can meet in the middle."

"Do you truly think that wise?"

"Of course if you are uncertain. A proper monk is capable of being on his own. Especially if he possesses a full trust in God. If you feel inadequate to the task, Brother, perhaps you best pray on it back at the inn."

Herbert dropped his eyes and jutted out his lower lip in thought. A twinge of guilt tugged at Latimer, but he narrowed his eyes and stood steadfast. He would confess it. Later.

At length, the young monk nodded his head. "I…I think you must know best, Brother. I should take the south?"

"The north. We will meet back at the inn. The blessings of God and Saint Eadburga on you, Brother."

"And also to you…Brother."

Latimer shook his head and watched the monk recede with distance. Herbert walked carefully over the rutted lane, turning uncertainly toward all he passed and timidly gesturing when he spoke. "Well, it will do him good," Latimer muttered. He turned the corner out of Herbert's sight and sat on a stone in front of a basketweaver's shop.

Sitting for a time with nothing on his mind, he watched the people pass. Laborers and bondsmen marched before him, while wives and maidens clucked along together, pushing carts, carrying burdens, or dragging on the hands of uncooperative children.

Lying his head back against the rough wall, Latimer filled his nose with the smells of the town, from its savory cooking odors and sweaty horses, to wood smoke and the grassy tang of a thatched roof newly repaired and sheared. Latimer would commit another sin and lie, saying he discovered nothing. Chuckling, he rubbed his shoulders against the wall to chase an itch. Perhaps it would not be so much of a lie, he thought. After all, if he sat there all day, he was, indeed, bound to discover nothing!

Reaching back, he drew his cowl over his head and settled comfortably, ignoring the odd stares of the passersby. The best thing was to let Brother Peter go to whatever fate awaited. At least it was better than his being shut in a cell and shackled, like Herbert and all the other dull monks would have it.

Rearranging this casual reflection in his mind, he sunk into a deep reverie, eyes barely open and mind scarcely aware of his surroundings.

His faith sustained him. How could he have endured the last ten years if God did not rush through his sinews and veins, if God had not upheld him in his fiercest hour of loneliness, giving him understanding at last that Peter would not recover? God was all, yet Peter enthralled, too. Still, when Peter attacked him, the pain of those blows could not match that of a dread realization: it signaled the end of their dear friendship. He remembered raising his arms to guard his face and how useless it was under the power of Peter's fists. Even Peter's eyes were different, seeing not Latimer, surely, but some demon. It was easy to forgive Peter. There was nothing he could refuse him…except his freedom. Now he saw what a mistake that was. *Forgive me for all those useless years of captivity, Peter. I will make amends. I will give it to you now.*

Peter could be an amiable man when he wanted to be, and had attracted followers at the abbey. It happened often at the monastery when they were younger. Perhaps Latimer was one of them, too…at first. But Peter latched onto Latimer just as quickly. It was interesting how the right mix of two separate personalities could enmesh and become almost one soul, he thought. Yes. That was him and Peter, and it was because of this he would keep Peter alive and out of harm's way for as long as it was possible. Knights and monks be damned.

His meditation went on until he felt the disturbance. Latimer tried to ignore it. He felt the shadow first before opening his eyes and stared at the man who blocked the meager sunlight. Latimer blinked at him for a moment before taking a wearied breath. "Peace be to you," said Latimer sluggishly.

The man's face reddened and he bowed, not knowing how else to respond. "Are you the monk what's looking for someone?"

Jerking forward he rose. "Yes?"

"Well *I* seen a man. He was a strange one. Treated the world like no one else was there, you ken?"

Latimer measured the man from his straw gaiters to his patched tunic. "Yes. I think I do."

The man's fingers clutched a sack over his shoulder. The fingernails were rimmed with black dirt.

Latimer's heart thumped in his chest. Did God answer his prayers at last? "He was a strange one," the man went on. "Didn't much like to get near him. But he sang like naught I ever heard. It was not of this world, I can tell you. That voice—it came from someplace else."

Eyes hot, Latimer blinked away the moisture. "He sang?" Oh those blessed days beside Brother Peter when they chanted in the quire! Peter's mellow voice could melt even the stone statues. It was an extraordinary talent among so many. Peter could hear a tune once and repeat it, adding an insight and a timbre all his own, remaking it his.

Latimer looked anew at the stranger before him. There was no doubt. Anxiously, he asked, "When did you see him last?"

"Oh…let me see. That was days ago. Just outside of Pershore. He was with another man what played a reed. They were beggars, I thought."

Pershore? Then he did not get far at all. How did they miss that? Were not he and Herbert thorough enough?

But then the other words of the man awakened Latimer. "Another man?"

"Aye. He seemed to lead the singer about, and a crusty fellow he was. The singer possessed an air about him like he was too good for the other, yet he still let the little fellow lead him by the nose. They were a pair! One handsome and the other a cripple."

"The man with him—the reed player—was a cripple?"

"Aye. There's too many about, the poor souls. I threw them a few coins. Out of charity and on account of their skill with song."

Excited, Latimer closed on the man. He held himself back from grasping him by the tunic, controlling his voice with care. "Are they still near Pershore?"

"Oh no! Left before me. Don't know where they went. But anyone is likely to recall them two."

Latimer breathed his relief. Peter was not dead. It made his heart glad yet stabbed it with renewed fear. "I thank you, Master," he offered sincerely. "God's blessing upon you."

"Thank *you*, Brother. Always in need of a blessing. God keep you." He shuffled and walked away, looking back only once in case Latimer might offer more than prayers.

The monk sat again, trying to decide what next to do. Peter was alive! That was a miracle, but on the tail of this happy news was the misery of knowing his freedom was limited. If Hugh Varney searched, he might find him before Latimer. It was imperative to let Peter know to hide himself, but in his state would Peter take Latimer's advice? Who knew how far he had fallen into insanity. The man was singing with beggars, after all. Was it wiser to lead Herbert *away* from Peter or *to* him? He could not just order the fool to go home. Latimer scowled, thinking uncharitable thoughts of Herbert.

Dismissing the monk from his mind, he mulled over what the stranger had said. There were many villages and hamlets between here and Pershore. Peter might still be heading away from them, yet at least now there was more significant information. Peter had allied himself. But who was this beggar? And why was Peter allowing himself to be led by him?

With a cold quiver to his heart, Latimer realized this beggar was probably in danger. No one ever knew when Peter would suddenly explode in a frenzy of emotion.

He hoped Peter would not hurt the man, but suspected it was already too late.

CHAPTER FIFTEEN

Pungent odors of rotting peels, musty greens, and roasted bones sitting too long in the sun lingered in the thickened air. These along with dunghills lay in heaps in the ravine at the other end of town where the walls were left unprotected.

Edric led Margery through the stench and passed the gate hanging on its rotted hinge. Reluctant at first, she held her apron to her face, wizened up her eyes and nose, and followed him.

"It's one way into town without notice," he said. "I don't always like to attract notice to m'self."

They reached the fresher air above the stink and Margery squinted back. "Don't it bother you at all?"

"The smell?" He almost said he ate things that smelled worse, but decided against it.

He would ordinarily have rummaged for scraps to eat or possibly something to wear, not particularly caring if it was clean or not. Edric did not care if such actions disgusted Azriel, but he somehow cared what Margery thought.

What was he to do? They ate all the bread.

Remembering, he grasped the coins clinking in his purse. It was a startling notion, but he could *buy* them food. But waste the coin on food when he could surely beg it? It seemed immoral!

"How should we find him now we're here, Edric?"

Sunlight caught the feathery contours of her lashes, generously spraying them with gold. Swallowing, he inhaled and bobbed his head to hide a blush. "I suppose we ask around for a man what sings."

"What if he did no singing?"

"If you've got any better ideas, woman, I'd be obliged to hear them."

She fell silent, dropping into step slightly behind him. He led the way into the main thoroughfare and gauged his surroundings. "There looks to be an inn there up the road. We could ask."

More self-conscious than usual, Edric endured the stares of the passersby, ducking his head to hide his eyes. All at once, little fingers clutched his sleeve and her body closed behind him. Entering the smoky room, a unique sensation tickled a smile from his lips. She sought protection from *him*! He dared a sidelong glance, measuring the uncertainty in her eyes. Strutting forward, he pushed his way close to the fire.

"You're not going to beg in here, are you?" she whispered close to his ear.

"Don't be a dunderpate. I got coin, haven't I?"

She relaxed. The warmth that began like an ember remained in him, glowing. Glancing down the long row of disreputable tables and benches, and the curious faces peering at him, he lowered to a seat and tugged Margery down next to him. Slyly, he moved his hand over the knife. It was a distinctly uncomfortable feeling to sense the many eyes of the men travel over her. She did not seem to notice, but it grew to unseemly proportion in his mind.

"You going to ask, Edric?" she asked.

The tall innkeeper suddenly towered over him. "What do the likes of you want?"

Edric squinted up at him. With a jerk, he tore the pouch from his belt and slammed it on the table. "We want your miserable food. What's two pence buy?"

"Soup, bread, cheese, and beer."

"That soup better not be water!" Edric said before turning his back on him. Amazingly, the man went away to fetch a wooden tray. Quickly, Edric wrestled two slim coins from the pouch and slid it across the table. By then the man returned, scooping the coins before he laid down the tray. Eyeing Edric one last time, he departed.

There, set before Edric, was a half-round loaf of dark, coarse bread, a generous slab of hard cheese, and two wooden bowls of steaming soup with large oxtail bones forcing their way through the greasy surface. A feeling of accomplishment surged up in him and he shifted his glance toward Margery to take his due, but she did not seem aware that anything amazing had transpired. She simply took one of the bowls in her hands and blew on the soup before taking a sip.

He looked at the bowl between his fingers and raised it. The bone swayed in the hearty broth. Sniffing the salty aromas of the meat and tangy vegetables, he watched the steam rise. Here in his hands was hot food for once, not some cold leavings from someone else's table, and bought with coin he himself earned. It was almost overwhelming, but not more than his hunger. He tipped the bowl and sipped, throat warming when the savory broth trickled down. He tore a hunk of bread and almost took a bite before he thought to offer it instead to Margery. She took it with a charming smile before he tore himself another. Chewing, he could not wipe the astonished smile from his face. Sending a curse to his father—not knowing whether he was alive or dead—he mentally snapped his fingers at him. *That's for you, old man! Didn't think I'd amount to anything, eh? Didn't think I could provide for anyone, eh? Didn't think I'd get a woman, eh?* Downing a healthy gulp of beer, he wiped his mouth with his sleeve and set the wooden cup aside.

"How long have you served the baker?" he asked her, grabbing a piece of cheese and stuffing it into a mouth already bulging with a hunk of bread.

She dabbed at the crumbs at the corner of her mouth with a soup-smeared finger. "Many years. My father was killed accidental. After my mother died, the baker took me in."

He chewed for a moment, trying not to blush. "How come you never married?"

Brightly, she stared at him, her cheek delightfully dimpling. "How old do you think I am?"

He shrugged and positioned himself over his bowl, arms lying on the table and encircling the soup protectively. "I dunno. Five and twenty? Six and twenty?"

She touched her face. "*That* old? I'm only nineteen, Edric."

"Christ, woman." Milling the wad of bread in his mouth he finally swallowed. He rubbed the uneven stubble of his chin. "Well…*I* probably look eighty. How old do you reckon *I* am?"

"Forty?"

"See," he said with a shrug. "I'm only five-and-twenty m'self…or so."

Horrified, she chewed more slowly. "Maybe we *are* old, Edric. Too old for ourselves."

"Aye." Fisting a dagger-length of bread he stirred it around in the bowl, soaking the end of it before lifting it to his mouth. "Do you ever think about getting old, Margery?"

"No. But I do think about children and such. Do you have any children, Edric?"

Aghast, he drew back. "Me? No." The notion was impossible, and yet Margery claimed to be a union of a woman and a cripple like himself. How could a woman stand it? Huskily, he asked, "Your father…was he truly…you know?"

"Same foot, too," she said, jerking her head matter-of-factly toward the floor. Edric slid his foot under the table's shadow. "My mother would fuss over him. He used a stick to get around. He spent a lot of time just talking to folks."

"He wasn't a beggar?"

"My father? No. He drove the cart from the mill to the baker. And then my mother did it after him, but it wasn't no work for a woman. They say it was her heart." Wistfully, she gazed into the hearth's flicker, the warm glow lighting her cheek. "I think that her heart was broken when my father died. They loved each other, you see."

He slurped the soup, holding the bowl before his face. His voice echoed into it. "What she go and see in a cripple?"

"I don't think she saw him that way. Funny thing, he never saw himself that way."

He reached the bottom of the bowl, slurping the last of the dregs before picking up the bone. Turning it in his greasy fingers, he examined it before sucking the last of the gray meat from it and licking out the marrow. That was fool talk. There was not a crippled man in the world that never thought of himself so.

"He made an honest living, Edric. He didn't have to go begging."

So that's it. Breathing deeply through his nose, he tried to calm himself. "So what is it you're saying? I don't need to beg? Why don't I have an honest job like your sire?"

"I'm thinking maybe you were so used to not working you haven't got a clue as to what it's like."

"You calling me idle?"

"I'm not calling you idle." Her fingernail traced the rim of the cup before she suddenly slammed it down. Foam sloshed onto the table. "Maybe you are! It's only dogs what begs in the streets!"

"So now you're calling me a dog. That makes you my bitch, don't it?"

The bowl skidded forward when she swept her hands across the table at him. "Is that the way you make things better for yourself? Don't you want to think better *of* yourself?"

"I think of m'self just fine. It's you that don't like the way I am. Here I go and spend good money on feeding you when I don't have to. That's gratitude, isn't it? So what if I beg? I'm not fit for naught else. If your sarding father drove a cart, then good luck to him. Course he died just the same, didn't he? We all die anyway, don't we?"

Scandalized, Margery rose.

"Here. Sit down with you. I know what you're up to. You want to change me. Isn't that like all women! Well harken to this. I'm not changing. No matter what you or that bastard Azriel want to make of me, I am what you see and there's no use crying in your beer over it. And speaking of that, drink it! I damn well paid for it, didn't I?"

Some of the folk were staring again. *Well, let them stare!* It was not every day he was with a comely lass.

Margery smoldered. He urged her to drink again but stubbornly she kept her hands in her lap. "You think so good of yourself, eh? Then what of me?"

"Quit speaking riddles, woman. Say what you mean. My head hurts with all your noise."

"I'm asking what you think of me."

He took a sip and glanced at her from the rim. An embarrassed grin forced his lips into a curve. "You're right pretty at that."

"I don't mean that." Face paling, her lips went rigid. "I mean…what if I was no better than a beggar. What If I was a whore like you first thought."

He laughed and pushed at her shoulder. "Go on! You?"

"You thought so when you first met me."

"That's 'cause I'm a lusty man, like any man."

Dropping her gaze, she thumbed the rough edge of the table. "But what If I was?"

The seriousness of her expression failed to amuse like it did before, and Edric's smile eased. "I'm not playing this, Margery."

"It's no game, Edric." She sighed wearily. "A lad wants a woman for the moment, and then he's on his way. Even…even If she don't want him. It's coin, isn't it? It's better than starving."

A sickening feeling made him lower the bread in his hand. "Just drink your beer," he said quietly, darting his eyes away from her.

"Edric, did you hear what I said?"

Wriggling on the bench, he slid imperceptibly away. "I don't know what you're talking about."

"I lied to you. I'm saying I am a whore. I'm admitting it."

"Admitting what?" he said hazily. He could not look at her. "Are you mad?"

Her fingers touched his arm, but he pulled away. Something fisted his heart, stalling his breath.

Softly, the gray edge of her voice reached him. "It's true, Edric. I…I just couldn't tell you before. I didn't want to. You were so sure I was it made me cross." Shaking her head she stared at the table. "It was long before the baker took me in. I was all alone, starving, Edric. So young. It was only a few lads a long time ago and none since, and all in secret. Even the baker didn't know. I did penance. I asked forgiveness from God."

He concentrated on each breath, feeling it leave his lungs, and the slow process of drawing it in again. He listened to that, not her words, though they flitted past the sound of his breathing anyway.

"Well?" she asked meekly after a time.

"Well, what?" he sneered. "Have you made a proper fool of me, woman?" He could not catch his breath no matter how hard he heaved his shoulders. "*Haven't you never kissed a woman, Edric,*" he mocked. "*Haven't you never been tender?* Haven't you never been a fool!"

"Edric…"

"And what was all that talk of honest work, eh? Honest work. You'd not have me beg, but you'd spread your legs for any man what wants it."

She sunk back, hair blazing over one shoulder when she tilted her head. "I didn't want you to see me as a whore. But…" She sighed again, lip trembling. "Oh, what difference does it make? You're a beggar and so am I. And that's all we are, so why try to be anything else? You sing for pence and I work at the baker's, but sometimes we whore anyway."

"I'm not a—"

"Aye, you are. I thought you were like me, Edric. I thought I saw it in your eyes. That's why…" Quivering, her voice gave out for a moment before she swallowed and shook out her hair behind her back. "That's why I lied to you. It was nice just being a maiden again for a while with you."

Head hanging, Edric stared at the table, paralyzed by emotion.

Why was black no longer black and white no longer white? Whore or virgin, angel or madman. Beggar or— His shaggy head shook. Angrily, he bore into the money pouch and slapped two thin coins on the table. "Here's payment, then. Off with you."

"Edric…"

"I said off, woman! Be whatever you want, just not with me."

She bit her lip. "Go back to the village, shall I?"

"Do what you like."

She expelled an irritated breath. Coiled, her whole body trembled, poised to strike. He waited for it, relished it just so he could strike back. But her anger lost momentum. "I pity you," she said, voice exhausted, "but not the way you think I mean it."

He felt the table shake when she pushed herself away, felt her shadow recede and the scent of her disperse like a snuffed candle's smoke. The coins lay on the table where she left them.

Emptiness and despair shivered his shoulders and crept up his crooked spine. A weight pressed on his chest and he snatched up the cup of beer to drown it. Signaling to a servant, he secured a jug and poured cupful after cupful, drinking each down.

"Christ," he grumbled and hunched over the table. His reddened eyes surveyed the room and he wondered why he was even there until he suddenly remembered. "Azriel. That's what I'm doing here. Right, then. Let's get to it." He waved the innkeeper over as if he were the lord of the manor.

Impatiently, the red-faced man stood over him.

"Have you heard of a singer hereabouts?" asked Edric. "He's got a marvelous sweet voice. Golden hair, looks like a minstrel."

"I've not seen anybody like that," he answered.

Scowling, Edric drew up and grabbed his sleeve. "How about a beggar what thought himself too good for his rags, but what acted more like a lord?"

He sneered. "You mean like you?"

Edric did not need to think. His fist sailed toward the innkeeper's insolent jaw, making a loud crack. Eyes wide but insensible, the innkeeper hit the table sending all its contents heavenward. A woman screamed, and the other diners whose food catapulted away jumped angrily aside. A string of curses flew across the tilted table and Edric drew his knife, poised over the insensate innkeeper's body.

"Look what you've done, you damned cripple!" A drunken man pulled his wine-soaked shirt away from his body. He lunged toward Edric, but another man—faster and more agile—came at him from another direction and grabbed Edric's knife, knocking it from his hand.

It slid across the floor under the feet of more scattering men. A fist was thrown and Edric ducked, but not before another from his right caught the side of his face. The noise in his ear deafened and bright pain sparked in his eye. Unable to close his jaw, he thought for a frightful moment it might be broken, but it was only the pain preventing him from moving the muscles.

Blinded in one eye, Edric swung his arm out and felt his knuckles connect with flesh, cracking his own hand in the process. He shook it out with a grunt and quickly dismissed the idea of any more punches. But just then two sturdy-looking men bore down on him.

Edric dropped to the floor and crawled quickly under the broken table, looking desperately for his knife.

Hands grabbed his ankles and dragged him out. He clawed the floor but they managed to bring him into the light and haul him to his feet. With a man on each arm, he could not wrestle away.

The recovered innkeeper staggered forward, smacking his fist into his palm. Edric braced himself. "You come in here thinking you're as good as any man and throw me your stinking money, ordering folk about? Look what you've done to my place!"

Edric raised his eyes past the man's fury and spied the other angry faces. He well knew what was about to happen. He did not mind these others watching, for it happened so often before. But he was suddenly glad Margery would not witness it.

He was allowed only a moment of relief before a fist sunk into his stomach, and he retched up all the food he had so proudly paid for.

CHAPTER SIXTEEN

Hugh scowled. The pain in his gut forced him to lean over the high saddle pommel, pressing on the unrelenting tumor for relief. His fingers gripped the decorated leather until his hand whitened almost as much as his face.

Once they entered Evesham he dispatched Sebastian to go on ahead outside of town to the manor house. In no mood for an inn, he needed instead a good secure place to rest where Sebastian was free to mix up the potion the last physician gave him. He resisted its use because it made him woozy, but he now conceded to a pain growing too much to endure, and he desperately needed relief. Wine no longer satisfied.

He moved his horse through the town, trying to distract himself by its vitality. The townsfolk moved with speed and life, singing out their daily work with full-throated calls. The women were rosy and plump like ripe peaches. Even the dirt of their faces did not discourage his admiring their carriage and appearance. The smells of waste balanced on the thread of cooking aromas. He could almost feel the tread of workhorses straining to pull their loads over the ruts.

The animals and the people breathed vitality, the whole town seethed with it. It was almost as if he could suck a bit of it from them, soak himself in it and rejuvenate. If only it were so.

He raised his head to the manor house he could barely see beyond the hills. It was an old house of stone surrounded by its own fortified walls. He recalled that it was a comfortable place, though he had not passed this way for many years.

The slicing pain subsided to a rotting ache, and he was able to lean his arm on the saddle pommel and breathe again. He bobbed, watching a tall man stride in a long, unhurried gait before him. Observing for some time, Hugh wondered how the man could remain so unconcerned with his surroundings but so confident of his steps. He seemed to be just another peasant, cloak torn and full of holes, shoes muddy and scuffed almost through the leather, stockings sagging from lack of gaiters. His crown of bright blond hair gave his otherwise uninteresting form some appeal. Hugh's horse followed him through the narrowing lane in a lazy amble, yet the man failed to yield to the horse. After a while, it began to irritate.

"You there!" Hugh cried.

Unbelievably, the man continued onward. Was he deaf?

"You there! Hold!"

At last the man slowed to a stop, and casually turned. Raising a hand to shield his eyes from the sun, he squinted upward toward Hugh. "Yes?"

Amused, Hugh straightened and stared at the comely individual. Blue eyes considered him with calm indifference. Hugh slid his fist into his hip. "You have an insolent air about you, man. Do you know who speaks to you?"

Lowering his hand, the man slowly assessed. "A man. On a horse."

Hugh's eyes darted momentarily toward his two footmen who regarded the ragged man with intensifying irritation. "Yes. And any man on a horse is your better."

The stranger seemed to consider this news before angling his head with an impertinent lilt. "Am I to address you as 'my lord,' then? Is that what all the fuss is about?"

One of the footmen lunged and struck the man in the head with the butt of his spear.

The blond man jerked backward and fell to the ground. His trembling fingers nursed a bloody gash.

The footman leaned toward the prone man to deliver another blow but Hugh raised his hand to wave him off.

The man—who did not look half so insolent on the ground—peered upward when Hugh dismounted and stood over him. "Who are you, knave?"

"I am Azriel."

"Freeman?"

"A beggar, I suppose."

"You do not sound like a beggar. Your name again?"

"May I rise, my lord?"

Hugh stepped back and affirmed with an amused salute. "So now you call me 'my lord.'"

"That is as you would have it…apparently." Azriel cocked a glance at the alert footman. Rising, Azriel brushed at his tunic. Gingerly, he touched the side of his head and looked at the blood left on his fingers. "I am Azriel, my lord."

Hugh noted that Azriel stood at his same height, if not taller.

"I am an Angel of the Lord God," he announced, "though I am told it is not to be believed."

Hugh blinked. "*What* did you say?"

With an impatient snort, Azriel postured. "Is all the world deaf?" he muttered. "I said I am an Angel."

"Saints!" Hugh rasped. "I think we have found our man! Did you say you believe yourself an angel?"

"I did not say I *believe* myself an Angel. I said I *am* an Angel."

A chuckle rumbled up Hugh's throat and finally he laughed outright. "Bless me! Then we have need of your company, Master Angel. You have led us all on a merry chase. I am glad to see it conclude so peaceably." He turned to the footmen. "Please escort our…Angel…to the manor, my friends."

They lurched forward and grasped Azriel each by an arm. Roughly they dragged his unresisting form while Hugh mounted and followed behind.

Hugh settled by the large hearth fire at the manor while Sebastian carefully mixed his brew. "Where is our guest?" asked Hugh.

Sebastian brought the bowl and handed it to Hugh before seating himself opposite. "He is in the lower crofts, my lord."

"Did you meet him?"

"No. Is he our monk?"

Hugh gulped the sour liquid and sucked the cold air through his teeth. "God, that's horrible. Bring the wine jug over, Sebastian."

He watched the squire comply. Hugh recalled when he himself was that young and full of the vigor of youth. Sebastian was only now coming into the pinnacle of his strength. Why was it, he wondered, that wisdom comes so much later, when the body is too weak to appreciate it? In a way, he envied Sebastian. The lad would wed soon and start his own family. But always there were uncertainties; lands to protect, vassals to secure, poverty to stave off. And in between it all, he must keep his honor in tact while serving the king, not always an easy juggle. Sebastian would be able to do it. Hugh had confidence in him. It was just a pity Hugh would not be here to see it.

He shook his head and the cobwebs with it. So many miseries in the world: himself and this poor Mad Monk, thinking himself an angel! Hugh sighed. If only he truly were a heavenly being. Hugh was filled with many questions. What a cruel jest that this man believed himself to be the one creature Hugh wanted most to meet.

With a deep breath, Hugh downed the entire contents of the cup in one gulp. Pursing his lips in loathing, he held the cup out to Sebastian, who obligingly filled it with wine. After drinking, Hugh settled the goblet down on his thigh and rested his head back against the chair. "Let us hope this does the trick, Sebastian. Fetch me some food, would you? Give my regrets to our host that I will not be joining him tonight."

Bowing, the squire moved to leave, but stayed when Hugh raised his hand.

"I would also like you to send for this 'guest' of ours. I need to determine if he is *our* lunatic or some other."

"Yes, my lord."

Hugh closed his eyes for only a moment. *Only a moment to rest.* The potion began to surge through his system, sucking the strength from his limbs, but at least his gut no longer ached. The wine stewed him nicely and he smiled, feeling the warmth permeate his toes and under the furs that Sebastian had draped over him. He hummed softly, actually feeling good. He knew it would not last more than a quarter hour before the wooziness overtook all, but decided to enjoy it while it lasted.

The sound of leather soles at the threshold awoke him and he drew open sluggish lids.

With hands bound, the madman stood with a guard at his side. He did not appear menacing with his rumpled blond hair tinged with mud and dried blood. A stained and torn tunic hung in wrinkles down to his thighs. A dirty cloth bandaged an arm and red sores ringed his wrists where the ropes bound too deeply. He smelled to high heaven, but wore his dirt and stench like a regal robe.

"Come in. Let me have a look at you."

"My lord, why am I being detained? Did I commit a crime?"

Hugh eyed the prisoner and the guard, and then waved the guard off. "Leave us. Wait outside the door. I will call you if I need you."

The guard left and shut the door, leaving it slightly ajar.

Hugh lay draped on his chair like a rag doll. His extremities felt numb and, for once, he was perfectly relaxed.

The man regarded him with a penetrating glare.

"You do not know why we hold you?" he asked Azriel.

"No. Is it a crime to be an Angel?"

Hugh chuckled. "It could be, friend. So few would be

welcomed here, that is the truth of it." His brow moistened with sweat and he raised his hand to wipe at it. "No, you are here because it is said you are a dangerous madman. A mad monk, to be exact."

The man's face remained neutral. There was nothing revealed in the cold blue of his eyes.

"Does the name Brother Peter of Pershore Abbey nudge your memory?"

Azriel's eyes softened. Held tautly in bonds, his hands relaxed and fell forward. Lowering his face, he considered a moment before raising his head and shaking it slowly from side to side. "Poor Brother Peter. Such a lost soul."

"Aha! You know him, then?"

"I have heard of him."

A log snapped in the fire sending a shower of sparking embers across the floor. Azriel stared at their pulsating orange glow before turning to the hearth. Amber flickered across his face. His eyes, enthralled by the changing flames, never wavered. "Alone in his cell, he frets. He obsesses. Held captive by his cassock and his vows."

Hugh's lids drooped. "You seem to know quite a lot about him," he drawled.

"A monastery is for a stout heart and an even mind. It left Brother Peter mad, I am afraid."

Azriel's confused soul softened his mood. He was suddenly glad he did not have to hunt him down like a dog. "Brother Peter, your brothers are anxious for your return. They will welcome you."

Azriel turned his head in a slow, graceful arc until his gaze lighted on Hugh. "You think *me* this Mad Monk? No. I am not. I am an Angel in the guise of a human creature. If that makes me a madman, then woe to the rest of you."

A deep sigh drew up from Hugh's being. "The game is over, Brother Peter. You must return to your abbey."

"But I tell you I am not this monk."

Hugh nodded, eyeing the gold ribbon of light at the open door, and the guard's shadow beyond it. Stewed from the potion and the warmth of the room, Hugh knew he could not maintain this interview much longer. With regrets, he nodded his head toward Azriel. "Soon we will travel back to Pershore and show you. The secret will be discovered right enough, Brother."

"The secret of me, Sir Hugh, is that I am an Angel of the Lord, and my name is Azriel, not Peter."

"Forgive me…Azriel…but you do not look like an angel. You look to be a man who has been too long on the road."

"I know. But Angel I am."

Azriel's form seemed to fluctuate before the shimmering heat of the fire. Hugh ran a hand over his perspiring forehead again. A wave of euphoria followed by dizziness washed over him and he closed his eyes to it. *Damn this potion! Damn this illness!* When he opened his eyes again, he saw that Azriel had taken a tentative step forward. His golden hair fell over his brow, and he gazed steadily at the knight.

"You look to be a man with questions," said Azriel. "You now have a rare opportunity to ask."

Startled, Hugh stiffened and clumsily sat up. Fear engorged his throat, striking his voice momentarily from his lips. The ache sunk to his heart and began a furious rhythm. "Why do I look like I have questions?" he gasped.

"Every man has questions. But you, Sir Hugh, have need of…answers."

Confused, Hugh tried to clear his head. What was the man saying? All was becoming so hazy. The potion made it difficult to think. "What do you know of me?" he demanded, scowling.

Azriel shrugged, clasping his bound hands together before him. "Very little. But there is a cast to your face. I have seen it before."

"Are you, too, a physician?" laughed Hugh uncertainly. "I have seen far too many."

"No. Not a physician. Though were I in my heavenly state I could heal…if it were the Divine Father's will. Most often…it is not." Azriel's words and mellow timbre overwhelmed, and suddenly Hugh felt uncertain. The man's authority somehow seemed unquestionable, his answers firm and succinct. Perhaps, in an odd way, he did know the answers. Was it not said that madmen were closer to God?

"Why? Why must men suffer?" Hugh asked.

"As an example to others."

"But…some are good men. Oh, I am not speaking of myself. But it seems that God chooses by lot rather than reason."

Azriel smiled fondly and shook his head. "You are not thinking as God thinks, but as Man thinks."

"That is not an answer. That is a priest's rhetoric."

"It *is* an answer. I cannot help it if you do not like it."

He frowned at Azriel who seemed to grow larger before him. Was it the fire playing tricks on his eyes? Softly, almost timidly, he asked, "Do…many get to Heaven?"

"Yes. A surprising number."

Hugh leaned forward, afraid to ask but knew he must. "And…Hell?"

Azriel blinked slowly. "Yes. A surprising number."

He tried to think, to reorganize his thoughts into a familiar pattern. "Tell me of Heaven, then," he asked, licking his dry lips. "Is it a place, like a city?"

Azriel shook his head. His face wore a patronizing expression. "You must not think this, if you are to imagine the unimaginable. You see, God's creation is far more expansive than mere humanity can fathom. In Heaven, you are pulled free of yourselves, leaving behind your body, your old skin like laundry in a basket. Do you see? I know it may be difficult for you Little Creatures to fully grasp. You are so different from me."

"But…I thought Heaven was a place—"

"Not a place. Not exactly. Oh, such feeble terms!" Taut, his whole body seemed ready to shatter, to fly in all directions. Confounded by language itself, he tried and then abandoned speaking for some time. "It is emotion, love," Azriel went on at last, gesturing. "All bound into a unified presence of God. Does this make any sense at all to you?"

Almost, Hugh could put his finger on the concepts so alien to his perspective, but in his state of bleary consciousness, he thought it *could* make sense, that with dreamy deliberation, it did. He found himself nodding. "Yes. Yes, it does."

Surprised, Azriel eyed him critically. "Then you are a rare creature, Hugh Varney. A rare human. One who sees beyond the hardness of his mind."

Hugh's breath was heavy within him, so heavy it caused his shoulders to rise in agonizing slowness when he tried to breathe. These ideas were new and frightening, yet Azriel was so confident. "But can *you* tell me where…where…will I…"

"That…is not for me to answer. Rather, you must ask yourself where has your life led you?"

"You talk in circles! I need comfort, dammit! I need to know!"

Azriel frowned. "Have you no faith? Have you no trust in God? Do you not realize He has loved you and known you since before you were ever conceived? There is no greater love than that of the Divine Father for you creatures… How I envy you."

"Ha! An angel. Envy man? Envy is a sin, Brother. No wonder you are here as a sinful man."

Azriel's lips parted in amazement and he took an awkward step back. A sharp inhale curved his mouth. "Yes. I see. How interesting. These revelations come at the most awkward of times."

"It is an interesting but dangerous philosophy you preach, Brother Peter."

"Azriel."

The pleasant haze shrouding Hugh's senses began to fall away, replaced by vertigo and a disagreeable tingling of the skin. "But I know you are not an angel."

"And I know that I am not this Brother Peter."

"Then who is right? What is the truth?"

"Your truth is the truth of men. Mine is the Truth of the Divine."

Hugh touched his fingers lightly to his forehead just to make certain that in its numbness it was still there. What was taking Sebastian so long? It was time to send this poor soul back to his cell. Azriel's mind seemed to work in spirals. Hugh wondered how a man like Azriel managed to remain hidden for nearly a week. "What have you been doing all this time?"

"Begging."

"Ah, yes. So you said."

"And singing for food. It is not difficult to do."

"You sing, eh?"

"Most eloquently."

Hugh hid a smile behind his hand. Whatever this fellow was, humility was not part of it. "I am certain you do."

"Will you hear me?"

Shrugging, Hugh sat back. "If you so desire."

Hugh expected a decent voice full of more puff than substance, but when Azriel opened his mouth to sing, it threw Hugh back into his chair with its startling fullness of tone. It was a voice unlike any other. Hands aching, Hugh looked down to see his fingers gripping the chair.

The song ended and Azriel's face took on the placid tone of before. Hugh wondered if all that was said of Azriel was entirely true. It was difficult to believe he was a dangerous madman. Even though Azriel believed himself to be an angel, he sounded perfectly rational and calm. Where was the unsound behavior Hugh expected?

They regarded one another silently until Hugh politely clapped his hands to Azriel's singing.

The guard peered into the room a moment before slipping back outside again.

"With a voice like yours, I could be willing to believe in your angelic nature."

"It is a voice you will hear again."

Hugh's smile slid away. A chill seized his heart, squeezing. His eyes locked on the madman's. "You know I am dying."

"All men are dying."

"No. I mean…my time is soon." Why Hugh admitted it to this man, he did not know. It must be the potion speaking, he decided. His fear returned. He could conquer it for longer stretches at a time, but sometimes it scaled the fortress he built about himself, slipping past all the sleeping guards. He blinked at the man who seemed so sure of himself. Angel, monk…who knew? The calm that only came with conviction made Azriel's features rigid.

"If you are an angel," Hugh said softly, "maybe you know…when."

"Your Guardian Angel knows. I am not he."

Almost, Hugh rose from his seat. "Can you tell me nothing?"

"I have told you much already."

"Of my own death, dammit!"

Azriel turned his body from Hugh. It was the action of a man sidestepping muck splashed up from a ditch. "You creatures speak endlessly of Hell and damnation," he sneered. "Would it not be better to speak only of Heaven?"

Hugh sank back. How did it happen that Azriel took over the conversation? Hugh stared at the tight ropes around Azriel's wrists and suddenly thought of Jesus and Pilate.

"You do not have much time," said Azriel, sympathy in his eyes at last. His emotions flitted quickly from anger to amusement and now to empathy, yet the last was equally short-lived. "You will not see the end of the year," Azriel said smugly. "Does that make you happier to know?"

"I do not know." It was probably a guess. Hugh suspected it himself. If the tumor did not kill him soon, the pain would…or he would take a knife to his own throat to stop it. Surely this man, this monk, could see all this in Hugh's eyes.

Azriel smiled. "You see. You creatures are never satisfied. No doubt it is that which amuses and saddens our Lord the most."

"You are an unusual man."

Azriel drew himself up, somehow more regal even in his rags and bonds. "I am not any kind of 'man.'"

"And yet…" Hugh traced a design with his finger on the chair arm, focusing his eyes to steady himself. "You seem to know this Brother Peter rather intimately."

"There are certain souls of which we are aware."

"That is an easy answer." He rumbled an unpleasant chuckle. "And a cagey one. If that is true then you know where he is now. Tell us."

"I have no powers in this human guise."

Hugh snorted. Of course not. The fantasy was complete, crowded with all the answers to every query.

"I am like you now," Azriel went on. "I feel hunger and pain…and sadness."

"You make it sound rather dreary Brother—er, Azriel. Do you experience no happiness as a human? We do."

Thoughtfully, Azriel angled back toward the fire and moved toward it, standing almost too close. His finger played at his lip. "Yes. I have felt happiness. Briefly. There was someone…" He inhaled a shallow breath but released it in a long, exhausted exhale. It seemed to drag something of his strength along with it. "But bound up with all this happiness seems to be such uncertainty and grief."

"That is the lot of Man, my friend."

"Yes. Perhaps it is little wonder after all why you have no faith."

"What can help this lack, Azriel—since you would be called that. Here is your opportunity to help Mankind. Give us the answer. We are so very anxious to hear."

"Our Lord gave you the answer."

"That is rhetoric. And it is mostly for clerics. They are the only ones who read Scripture at any rate." Eyeing Azriel carefully, Hugh was slightly disappointed that he showed no signs of cracking his façade. "What of the rest of us, Azriel? What is the real secret?"

For a long time Azriel said nothing. He stood with his back to Hugh and gazed into the flames. The edge of his cloak gilded from the fire. When he turned at last toward Hugh, his eyes revealed a depth Hugh had not noted before. It made him shiver. They seemed to be old eyes, the same eyes in holy statues, in gold-flecked paintings, in wise men who lived longer than their bodies should have allowed. "The secret is…Hope."

"Hope?" Hugh asked, his voice hoarse. "What kind of secret is that?"

"An all-encompassing one. It is the source of love and renewal, and the vision of your own humanity. And it is knowing with all your being the promise of everlasting life. Do you see? *Can* you?" Azriel held Hugh's gaze like one who holds the rope of an ox, leading, urging…until it fell away, and he stared again into the engrossing fire. "Even a peasant can embrace so simple a concept as Hope."

"I see a great deal of debate with this way of thinking, Brother."

"No. It is as simple as it sounds. Why must you creatures make it so complicated?"

Hugh's hands curled over the chair's arm, gripping again with whitening fingers. "This is very hard, what you say."

"I do not recall our Lord saying it would always be easy."

Vertigo set in, and Hugh shifted forward, trying to hold on for a few moments more. Azriel became like a candle flame before the hearth, a single image of something unidentifiable, something bright. Hugh squinted, trying to focus. "Are you…truly an angel?"

Azriel did not move from his steadfast contemplation of the fire. "What do *you* think?"

The moment, tenuous like a wet thread, fell away and Hugh sat back, defeated by his own body. He closed his eyes to stop the room from swaying. "I…I think you are a very clever madman."

"Then that is your loss."

"Enough of this. Guard!" Immediately the footman appeared at the opened doorway. He held his spear forward, darting his eyes between the two men. "You are not an angel," Hugh said to Azriel.

"Am I not? Then nothing I said here was true. Was it?"

"Take him back to his holding place." Hugh did not watch when the guard manhandled him away and shut the door. Instead, he laid his head back against the hard wood of the carved chair, his throat exposed to the chill draft and the sudden upsurge of heated air from the hearth. He breathed, trying to do it normally. How easy it was to be captured by a madman's song and an even gaze. Other men were not as confident, yet their cloying was easier to believe only because one wanted to believe it. It was not often he met a man who held true convictions even in the face of disaster.

At last, Sebastian entered carrying a tray. "You brought it yourself?" Hugh said, "You are too good to me."

"I did not think you wanted many servants about just now, my lord."

"How well you know me. Though by such tender care you missed my interview with our 'guardian angel.'"

"Is it the monk, my lord?"

"Yes. He must be. Or else he *is* an angel."

Sebastian stopped, holding his knife up. A skewered fish dangled from the blade. "I am sorry I missed the interview if he caused such doubt in your mind." With a thoughtful expression, Sebastian continued filling a wooden bowl with pieces of fish, leeks, and sprigs of borage. Handing it to Hugh, he sat on the knight's footstool. "What exactly did he say?"

"Oh, Sebastian. Maybe my mind is too addled from that potion of yours. Or maybe the wine. But he said a great many things that made a lot of sense to me. Is it my state? Am I that fragile that even a madman's philosophy can enchant?"

"I…thought *you* were to question *him*, my lord. Did it become the other way around?"

Hugh laughed, enjoying the sound echoing in the smoky chamber. It relieved the spines of anxiety pricking him. With Sebastian's return to the room, all fell into a normal pattern again. It was the presence of Azriel that reeled him into befuddlement. "Bless me," he chuckled uneasily. "It was."

"'Be not forgetful to entertain strangers: for thereby some have entertained angels unawares.'"

Hugh grasped the fish in his fingers and lifted it to his lips. He smiled before stuffing it in. "You might be right at that, Sebastian," he said with mouth full. "Angels in cassocks with a madman's disposition. He may be right. If he is mad, woe to us."

"Shall I ready us to return to Pershore on the morrow, my lord?" Sebastian said it with such an unsure tenor Hugh turned to him and settled his bowl of food more comfortably on his lap.

"I do not wish to go anywhere tomorrow. Let us bide her a while. I must decide what this abbey is to do with this man. I need time for that and a good rest. Let them all wait."

"Yes, my lord."

"I know," he said fondly. "It delays your wedding announcement. But you waited this long. A few more days will not matter."

"Yes…Hugh."

Hugh laughed again, running the end of the leek in a yellow broth collected at the bottom of the bowl. He scooped up the still dripping leek and bit down on the end of it.

Sebastian smiled.

What was it Brother Peter said? Hope? There was no doubt that Sebastian was the hope of Hugh's family, but what of himself? Hope of an afterlife in Heaven? He pondered Brother Peter's words. Hugh considered himself to be a good man, generous, charitable, loving. His lands prospered, his servants lived well, his cattle and sheep grazed in abundance over the verdant hills surrounding his home. The abbey flourished. Did he do enough? It seemed enough. Only enough?

He chuckled. Brother Peter was right. Men made everything more complicated than necessary.

CHAPTER SEVENTEEN

Edric's face throbbed from pain. Laughter echoed loudly around him, but also drifted far off. His head rung like a bell tower, and one of his eyes was shut from blows. With what was left of his consciousness, he knew he need only wait it out, and the ordeal would soon be over.

"Here!" said a familiar voice. It was the voice that inflicted most of the pain, the innkeeper. "What's that in the bag?"

Edric's head lolled, but when he felt a rough hand behind his knee lifting the leg, terrifying awareness sputtered him to wakefulness. They meant his shoe!

Struggling, he tried to liberate himself, yanking with all his weakened strength to pull even a hand free. "No!" he whispered when he felt fingers at the ties.

"What have we got here?" wheezed the innkeeper. "A cloven hoof, maybe?"

Another hand secured the leg so Edric could not thrash, until finally the shoe was pulled off, the wrappings falling away.

Gasps and silence followed until expressions of disgust simmered through tentative laughter.

Out of breath from fear and humiliation, Edric felt Time itself come to a halt. He felt the tears at his eyes but was as powerless at hiding them as he was at hiding his shameful deformity.

They raised up the leg, shaking the sickening flesh. Sharp points of faces glazed by firelight and shadowed by smoke, leered out of the gloom. He closed his other eye. At least if he did not see their faces he might endure it.

With eyes closed he wished he could cover his ears. Muffled at least, he might be able to withstand the feelings of helplessness when they roughly paraded him about the room.

"Stop this!"

The world froze, petrified by the sudden masculine order chiming from above, like bells calling penitents to prayer. The hand clutching his hamstrings lowered the leg, and those at his upper arms loosened and drew back. With nothing upholding him, he dropped hard to the floor on his knees. He drew his arm up to his face, wiping the tears. His hand was wet with them until he realized that most of it must be blood.

He opened the good eye to his savior, and saw a monk bending toward him. Startled, Edric drew back, seeing only an indistinct, dark form. White hands reached for him to put back the discarded shoe. The monk drew it over the twisted foot and tenderly tied the laces.

A sob escaped Edric's lips but he stifled it by viciously biting down on his lips. The shadow of another monk loomed, and lifted his shoulders in an attempt to help him rise. He did not think he could, but he felt a vague sense of obligation and surrender. For them, for these gentle hands, he could do it.

"What is all this?" the monk's voice boomed again. "Do you call this sport? You should be ashamed of yourselves. You are all an abomination. Innkeeper! You of all people—"

"He started it, Brother Latimer. He come in with his high-thinking ways—"

"Enough! I can clearly see the difference between him and you."

"He caused damages."

"I think mostly your friends caused the damage."

"I want restitution or I'll call in the law."

"I should do the same to you."

"All I want is payment."

The monk looked down at Edric and grasped the pouch. He yanked it from the belt and tossed it to the innkeeper. "That should do it."

"That's all I got in the world!" Edric wailed. "You'll beggar me again!"

"Worry not, friend," said the monk quietly. "I will be your Good Samaritan and cover your expenses."

It's that sarding Good Samaritan again, thought Edric hazily. *I've got to ask Azriel what that means.*

Hands lifted him, but this time it was gentle and slow. Carried up the stairs, he was laid on something soft. It was like hay only feathery. They left him for a moment and he smoothed his palm over it, and he realized he lay on furs atop a pallet of straw. Struggling to rise, he knew he must get off of it before he got into even more trouble, but the monk returned and restrained him gently at the shoulder. "No, my friend. Please. You are hurt. Let me help you."

"But it's a mistake—"

"Indeed. Those rustics downstairs made it, trading sport for eternal life."

"You gave them all my money! How will I feed her now?"

"Her?" he asked, gently dabbing a cool cloth to his bruised face. "Is there someone with you?"

"I don't know where she is," he moaned.

"We will find her. Worry not. Do you remember your name?"

He almost laughed, thinking of the day he met Azriel, and asking the same of him. "Aye. It's Edric."

"Edric. I am Brother Latimer and this is Brother Herbert."

Latimer's tone was gentle and reassuring even though the tautness of his face did not seem to match the mood of his voice. Yet the expression was compassionate and nothing else was said or asked about his deformities. Edric relaxed slightly and then surrendered to the lushness beneath him.

Monks were never this kind to him before, or did he never notice? He seemed to question everything now that Margery put the notion in his head. Maybe all of his experiences prior to meeting Azriel were misinterpreted. The idea was hard to accept, especially after the mortifying events of the inn below. Did not his history include more of that than what the silent monks now offered him? It seemed so, yet the uncertainty tapped his senses like a twig in the wind tapping insistently at a shutter.

Latimer sat beside him, ringing bloody water from a rag. He dipped it anew in clean water and pressed its relieving coolness to his eye. He could almost open it now, and he stared at the other monk who did not seem to know what to do. He was pudgier and much younger than the other, with a whitened freckled face and bright ginger hair. It made him think of Margery, and he moaned aloud.

Latimer drew back. "Am I hurting you?"

"No, no. It isn't that. It's her."

"Your child?"

"No. A woman. It don't matter. She's just a—" He meant to say it, but it would not release from his lips. He could not think of her that way, lying with other men, submitting to them.

The monk worked silently for a time and then looked down at Edric's garments. "May I remove this shirt? It should be washed of this mess."

Edric shrank again. "You don't have to do that."

"But I am doing it. How are your ribs? May I move you?"

"It don't matter. It'll hurt no matter what's done."

Herbert moved reluctantly forward at Latimer's signal and they lifted Edric to a sitting position. He tried not to moan or cry out. They were being kind and it was so rare a thing, he did not want to alarm them by making them think they did him further harm.

Latimer pulled off the overtunic and handed it to Herbert.

Appalled, Herbert grasped it with two fingers and carried it away, disappearing into an outer room while Latimer laid Edric down again.

"I…I have to admit something…or…I reckon it's a confession."

Latimer's dark eyes encompassed Edric, fluctuating between compassion and a struggle with something Edric could not quite identify. "I am not a priest. I cannot accept your confession."

"No, I don't mean that. I mean that I never been treated so nice by your like. I'm a beggar, you see, and it isn't always monks like you what give out at the almoner's door."

Amusement glittered in Latimer's eyes when he poured a portion of ale from a jug into a horn cup, and offered it to Edric. "Drink this slowly."

"It's just that I never thought too good of monks. I…never said much of a kind word to them. I reckon that's a sin. I never much thought of sins before. Too many other evils to worry over."

"Take this. You need something back in your stomach."

Latimer's arm encircled Edric and lifted him enough to bring the cup to his lips.

"I paid for that meal!" Edric rasped. "That whoreson of an innkeeper!"

"He was unnaturally cruel. I have never seen the like. But you must calm yourself and drink this."

Edric struggled upward and took the cup. His belly hurt as if it were trampled—and for all he knew it was—but he gingerly drank. It tasted good and also served to get the taste of sick from his mouth. He licked his lips. "I've had crueler." But he was glad Margery had not seen it.

Latimer moved across the room, clearly ordering the younger monk to this chore or that one. Edric laid his head back into the softness and stared at the ceiling. Opening the other eye, he was relieved he could still see.

"Why were they taunting you?" asked the younger monk. He stood aloof, not willing to approach closer without Latimer's prompting.

Edric lay on his back, taking inventory of his muscles and bones. He wanted to be on his way shortly. He hoped they were not soaking his shirt. Just a quick wipe would make it as good as new. "There's little excuse needed. I was only asking about a friend."

"I have scrubbed out the shirt. It is not too wet," said Herbert, returning to the room and draping it before the fire "By morning it should be dry enough."

"I can't wait till morning! I've got to be on my way now."

Latimer gestured gently toward the bed. "You will do no such thing. By the grace of God we found you and we shall nurse you until you are well."

"Why bother with my like? Your kind never took me in before? What of all the times I was starving or freezing in the snow? I was never taken in then."

Latimer's face was stony. "When you asked at these monasteries, what did they tell you?"

"Asked? I never asked."

The monk laughed. It was a coarse sound from a face that seemed to crack with the unfamiliarity of it. "If you never asked, how were they to know you needed such assistance? 'Ask and it shall be given you. Seek and you will find.'"

"Is that Scripture?"

"Yes."

"'Seek and you will find,' eh?"

"Yes."

Considering, Edric recounted in his mind the many times he begged at the almoners' door and did not once ask for more than they offered. There were even times when they looked like they might invite him to come in by the fire, but he had quickly escaped. Was it really his fault? He eyed the monk returning to his other duties in the room. The ridiculous notion almost took hold, turning over on itself. How could Edric's lot be his own fault? *That sounded more like some fool thing Margery would say. Or even Azriel.* His own fault!

He turned his head. The soft fur touching his cheek reminded of Margery's caressing fingers. "I'll…I'll have to go and look for her."

Latimer walked patiently from his place by the fire and stood over the bed.

Panting with the effort, vowing to take his time, Edric struggled to a sitting position.

"Stay where you are, Edric. I'll send Brother Herbert to find her."

Herbert blanched. "Brother Latimer!"

Latimer did not spare Herbert a glance. He merely cocked his head in Herbert's direction. "She is probably hovering outside nearby. What does she look like?"

"She isn't there. Don't bother."

"It is no bother. And it obviously troubles you."

"She's just a—" Still, he could not admit it aloud. Clamping his lips, he accepted a wave of pain.

"What is her name?"

"Margery," he said harshly, clearing his throat to hide his embarrassment. "She's…she's got ginger hair and a feisty attitude. You can't miss her."

Herbert nodded uncertainly, cast an unhappy look at Latimer, and hurriedly left.

"I take it she is not your wife," said Latimer, barely taking notice of Herbert's departure.

Edric blushed. Were his sins written across his forehead? "No…but…tell me, Brother. If you were a woman, would you marry a cripple?"

"Well, I can hardly be a judge of that."

"It don't make sense, that. A woman what could have any man she wants, settle for a cripple? Something isn't right in the head with a woman like that."

"It is not the head. It is the heart."

Edric waved a hand in dismissal. "No one would be that senseless for love."

Latimer suddenly looked away. "Much can be sacrificed for

love."

Sobering, Edric quieted. "I suppose you gave up all for love of God, eh? Why'd you do it?"

Latimer took a deep breath and paced slowly beside the bed. He stopped at Edric's feet with his back to him and his eyes toward the shuttered window. Slats of light angled through to the floor.

Latimer turned, covering Edric with an enigmatic glance. "When I was young, I did not understand the world. It moved so swiftly and with no direction. A scramble for this piece of land and that one; marry this one for gain or this one for prestige. We hurry through life, and do not know where we are going…or why. I wanted to slow down, to breathe. In God, I could do that."

Edric frowned. Give up all for God? To Edric, God seemed absent most often in his worst times, when it was cold or when he hungered…or when knaves thought it sport to beat him. What did this monk know that Edric did not? What did Azriel know, who mooned like a lost lover over the Almighty?

"That don't answer much," said Edric. "A man can't slow down if he's got to eat or feed a family. God isn't going to do that for him."

"The Lord will provide. He provides for me and my brethren."

"Forgive me, Brother, but isn't it the servants who farm your land what provides for you?"

Edric saw Latimer's patience wearing thin. Perhaps these were discussions better left between clerics. He supposed Azriel could tell this monk a thing or two. A lump of misery stopped his throat when he thought of Azriel. Edric missed him. There was no reason in it, but he missed him just the same.

"That is not exactly what I meant," said Latimer. "It is difficult for you, I know, to understand it all. But know that it is so. You must have faith."

Edric dropped his hopeful eyes. It was all the same. He heard it a thousand times before. Have faith and all would be well. It seemed to be an awfully weak God if He could not provide more without faith, Edric reasoned. Faith had somehow twisted Azriel into a fantasy so real he could almost make others believe in it. He knew more of angels and God than Edric surely did. Maybe even more than this monk.

"God and His angels," Edric muttered. "I reckon you believe in them. Angels, I mean."

Latimer nodded distractedly. He sat on a stool while his hands graced his lap, more statue than man.

Edric sat up and pried open his swollen eye. "What are angels like, Brother? I mean…if a body were to believe in them."

"'Are they not all ministering spirits sent to serve, for the sake of those who are to inherit salvation?'"

"Angels serve men? I thought they served God?"

"God is always served first. Serving Man serves God."

Edric chuckled, shaking his head. "That's like rocks rattling in a barrel, Brother. It's only noise."

"I am serving you," Latimer explained carefully, "and in so doing, serve God. 'Love thy neighbor as thyself.'"

Edric laughed louder. "That's all well and good, Brother, but it don't happen that way."

"That is why the gates of Heaven are closed to most."

Latimer glowed with authority, but it hung loosely about him, like it was pinned on. It reminded him of Azriel. "Do…do angels come to earth, then? Talk to folk?"

"Of course. There are many instances in Scripture where this occurs."

That was not the answer he expected. It puzzled him further. Much of religion puzzled him. "Can an angel…look like a man?"

"That is frequently how they communicate God's desires to us."

Edric considered further until a bright thought spread a smug smile on his face. "But *they* got wings!" he chortled, pointing his finger at the monk.

Latimer's lids hovered low, cloistering his thoughts. "Something like wings, I imagine. But you must remember they are *not* men. Only in the *guise* of men."

That did not satisfy either. If anything, it made Edric more out of sorts. When he looked again at Latimer, the monk was studying his gnarled foot safely encased in its shoe. Latimer almost made him forget he was different, talking with him and sitting beside him like any other man.

When his glance rose at last to Edric's, they locked eyes.

"Tell me," said Latimer smoothly. "Do you, by any chance, play a reed?"

"Why?" he asked suspiciously. "You want music?"

"No. It is just… Never mind. It matters little now." Latimer frowned suddenly. His patience seemed to have come to an end. "You must rest," he said in dismissal.

Herbert reappeared. He apologized to a disinterested Latimer for not being able to find the woman, but it was Edric who sourly replied, "If she had any sense she'd be on her way home. It was foolish to bring her."

Both monks stared at him, trying to discern what he meant, but Edric turned away first. He did not want to think about Margery but it was harder not to. He fancied her, her face and demeanor, her ambling walk. He thought there might have been something special about her, but she turned out to be like every other woman he ever met.

He would leave in the morning, no matter what these monks said. He just wanted to get far away from this god-forsaken town.

And Azriel? *Azriel be damned!* Why should Edric bother with the likes of Azriel anymore. The madman was probably better off on his own. It was not always safe to be with Edric. Maybe Margery finally figured that out.

Herbert spoke softly to Latimer, pulling the reluctant monk aside. "While I was out, I heard news that Hugh Varney was in Evesham. I also heard he has apprehended a man who claimed to be an angel!"

Edric cried out when he twisted around. He forgot about his bruised side. Herbert spared him a glance, but Latimer yanked on the monk's arm and demanded, "*What* did you say?"

"It is said Hugh Varney found a man who claimed to be an angel. Obviously a madman. Is…is this our Brother Peter?"

Latimer's face—so stoic in its rigid control—collapsed. "It sounds very like him. Evesham, you say?"

"Yes. They have him captive."

"Is he hurt?"

"They did not say."

"Are they returning to Pershore?"

"They did not say."

Grasping both Herbert's arms, Latimer glared into the younger monk's face. "Just what *did* they say, Brother?"

Herbert shrank back, trying to free himself from Latimer's tight hold. "J-just what I told you, Brother Latimer."

Slowly, mechanically, Latimer's face mellowed. He released the monk and even smiled, but there was little humor in it. "Very well, Brother. Then as soon as we might, we must go on to Evesham. Rest now. Our guest also needs his rest," and they glanced again at Edric.

Edric breathed hard, trying to absorb all he heard. Brother Peter? Was that Azriel's real name? It must be him. There could not be two out there who thought themselves angels. But who was this Hugh Varney? Latimer's reaction might be comical if he were not so frightened.

Azriel was being held captive. Edric was not certain what happened to madmen but it probably was not good. If Latimer feared the consequences then there was probably much to fear. Edric hunkered into the fur, forgetting how luxurious it was. He would definitely leave by first light. Something needed to be done about Azriel. Just what, he was not certain.

CHAPTER EIGHTEEN

Latimer feigned sleep while the lame man grunted into his damp shirt. The scant light of false dawn crept in behind him, casting a crooked, darker shape against the far wall. The deformed creature was in much pain. Latimer could tell that even from his own place on the floor before the fire, but these peasants were hearty stock, more like oxen than humans, and recovered from even the most abominable afflictions. This one would no doubt be begging in the street come sunrise. But just to assure escape, Latimer had left his own flattened money pouch in clear view on the table.

Curiously, Latimer watched Edric peer toward him and Herbert. Herbert snored and moaned in his slumber, but Latimer mimed perfect repose. Under his cowl, he could appear asleep and still spy the room. He saw Edric grasp the pouch and a knife, sliding them carefully across the table and into his awaiting palm. They made no sound.

Astonishing, thought Latimer. *Such accomplished larceny*. Amazed, he further noted how Edric made no noise when he dragged his limp foot over the floor, and even opened the door soundlessly.

Once Edric was gone Latimer sighed. His obligation to him was now relinquished. They were free to hurry to Evesham.

He had acted in charity toward Edric and in so doing God

rewarded him with information about Peter. Latimer had seen men with worse deformities than Edric, but the treatment Edric endured at the hands of these barbarians was exceptionally cold-blooded. He was glad to stop it, while at the same time amused by Herbert's reaction. He wondered what made the man become a monk in the first place. Nowhere else to go? Like Peter?

Peter was a gangly thirteen-year-old when he came to the monastery. Stoic, he had accepted his new fate. A bastard had little choice, but Latimer knew he was one of the lucky ones. He was educated in his sire's household and so his advantage over the others at the monastery was immediately apparent. Controlled and aloof, Peter was absorbed by the library and its works, yet managed by his force of presence to gather a cadre of oblates who wanted merely to be within his enigmatic sphere. Once he knew there was nowhere else to go, Peter consumed himself with study and became the model monk to which all the others aspired. Including Latimer. Latimer was the same age as Peter. The fifth son in a steward's household, Latimer found nothing of the world to entrance him. Together, he and Peter made sense of their lives, enriching themselves through mutual pursuits. He could not remember a time when together they were ever anything other than intrigued by their lives, diving into each new area with the joy of a dolphin in a glittering bay.

Yet here was Herbert, dull as an unpolished mirror. The wood mouse, fearing anything new or foreign.

Latimer nestled lower in the straw, worrying at the frayed edge of his sleeve. How were they treating poor Peter? Was he hurt? He wanted so much to leave him in peace that this new imprisonment tore at his heart. If it must be so, Latimer would go to him and offer what comfort he could.

Without disturbing the sleeping Herbert, Latimer rose and crept through the yawning door. Too agitated to remain still until dawn, he wandered down the narrow stair and into the hall where the coals from the large hearth rimmed other slumbering travelers with an amber haze.

Secure in the archway's shadows, Latimer scanned the room's stillness and inhaled the stale, musky odor of men in smoky clothes. Sunrise was still an hour away. Impatiently, he sighed and rested his head against the jamb. The room closed in. He pulled at his collar, loosening the laces at his throat, but it was not enough. Carefully, he stepped over the piles of snoring men and went outside.

He immediately rejuvenated in the fresh, wet air and strode toward the stables. The shuffling and snorting of the sleepy beasts reminded him with a rueful sneer of the men lying in repose on the inn's bottom floor. *Animals, all of them.* He recalled the laughter and celebration when he and Herbert carried Edric up the stairs. The fools continued their revelry, not one of them contrite at their behavior.

Disgusted, Latimer meandered behind the stable to the privy and attended to his bladder. The sweet hay smell of horse droppings briefly filtered out the stench of human excrement issuing from the hole in the bench. What a wonderful metaphor for humanity, he mused. Even the excrement of the beasts smelled better than that of humans. After all, it was what came out of a man that was most foul, not merely his backside, but out of his mouth and his mind.

He rounded the corner and slipped into the stable, running his hands along the rough-hewn paddocks. The hay smelled fresh and fragrant, the animals pungent, but clean. His horse recognized him and nickered before shaking its head, the metal rings of the tether clinking softly. Latimer wandered toward him and reached his hand out to stroke the blaze down to the wet velvet of the horse's nose.

He was sorry he hadn't found Peter first. Now that Sir Hugh held him, what was Latimer to do? He could, at least, convince Sir Hugh not to hurt the monk. He might even devise a way to allow him escape. Subterfuge was not outside his experience. Latimer's words could lull the knight into relaxing his guard. It was worth a try. They must not delay and get to Sir Hugh's party before they returned to Pershore. Or better yet, Latimer could wait until Peter was safely ensconced at Pershore and release him there. Might that be easier? But then it would all happen again.

With a sigh, he stroked up the animal's face to his cheek and rubbed. The horse huffed at him.

"More charity, Brother?"

Latimer spun, focusing his eyes on the silhouette coming from a paddock. The figure lurched toward him, and Latimer pulled back, drawing a fearful breath. The smell of wine belched forth before the shadows dropped away and he recognized the innkeeper far into his cups.

"Can't leave stupid beasts alone, eh?" he slurred.

Latimer relaxed, though remained cautious. "You are not a one to speak on such a subject." He stepped forward, but the innkeeper's large hand planted itself on his chest, stopping him.

"First it's arrogant cripples, now it's arrogant monks. What's this town coming to?" He lifted a wineskin to his lips but most of it ran down his bruised cheek when he tried to drink. With his other hand, he secured his loosened breeches.

Latimer stepped away, but the drunken man scowled and lurched forward, pushing at Latimer with curled knuckles. "What's the matter? Don't like that? That crippled friend of yours liked it even less. What you go and befriend a beast like that for? Beasts." He belched again and staggered forward, resting his outstretched arm against a paddock. "Beasts and lunatics, eh? They're all over the sarding shire. Evesham's got a lunatic, so they say. They should toss 'em all in a big pyre and light it up! A right glow that would make!"

Tensed, Latimer's eyes narrowed. "Your immortal soul is already in the gravest danger," he said icily. "I would not venture to add more to an already stained existence."

"Stained? How's this for stained?" Whirling, he suddenly shoved the monk. Unprepared, Latimer reached, but found nothing to grab hold of before he lost his balance and landed on his backside into a pile of horse droppings.

Bellowing with laughter, the innkeeper crouched and slapped

his thigh. "You're nice and meek now. There's some prime earth there to inherit! You can give some of it to that cripple you harbor. You think that's a twisted foot? I think it's a cloven hoof, you just can't see it for yourself!"

"You are a loathsome man," Latimer hissed, slowly rising to his feet.

"Aye, that I am. But I know something about you, too, Brother. Something your little cleric friend let slip." He giggled unpleasantly, and put a finger to his lips, making elaborate shushing noises.

Latimer frowned, shaking out the sticky mess from the back of his cassock. His collar grew hotter with each slurred word. "I am warning you—"

"Warning *me*? That's a laugh. You must like to laugh yourself, eh, Brother? You like them cripples and lunatics. That little monk friend of yours said as much. You're looking for a madman, aren't you? And he's a monk, isn't he? That's what he said, right enough. Once he spilled it, he told the whole thing. I'm thinking it's that one what they found in Evesham. Wouldn't that be a tasty morsel to share around the hearth?" He chuckled, rumbling an unpleasant sound in his throat. "You monks. All so pious. Pushing us honest folk about. What's it to you if we want a bit of sport off some cripple? That's you, it is. A sarding cripple. That's all monks, isn't it? What do you do up there in your rich little cloisters? All you *men*!" He laughed. "And now lunatics!" the innkeeper went on. "I think the good people in this shire should be told. It isn't right to let them feel all safe and snug in their beds when madmen and cripples are allowed in their midst. 'Course…" He tilted the wineskin up again and slurped the last of it. "I'd be inclined to keep these terrible tidings to m'self if a body could see his way to line my purse."

Appalled, Latimer shrank back. "You…you want me to *pay* you for silence?"

"It's only fair. Should it let slip, the whole town's liable to stone the two of you…as well as your pet cripple. They wouldn't much like all the lying you done."

"This is monstrous! What do you take me for? I am not a wealthy lord—"

"That monastery of yours isn't poor, Brother. You look well-fatted to me."

"That is God's money, to be used for His servants! Would you swindle God Himself?"

"God don't need the money, does He?"

Furious, Latimer's eyes would not focus and he blinked to clear them. There was no memory of grabbing the shovel, only that it was there within reach and that the innkeeper's gargoyle face leered at him and cackled that abominable, drunken laughter. *That stupid Herbert! How could he have let something like that slip? What a fool! What an idiot!* And to allow this man to discover it for his own merriment was too much to take.

"A secret! A secret!" the innkeeper sang, dancing in a circle. "Shall I tell them there's mad monks everywhere?" He laughed, amused by his own jest. Dancing giddily, he spun and turned viciously toward Latimer.

The shovel's spade slammed into his face and stopped him cold. He cried out, like a child's wail, and dazedly staggered from side to side. Another hard blow forced him to his knees, and yet after another and then another, he could no longer make an intelligible sound except for gurgling and a prolonged whine. The shovel slapped his head again with a meaty sound followed by a crunch. One last blow over the dented head yielded no more than another wetter crunch, and then a halo of blood widened under him into the straw.

The horses whinnied nervously, shuffling in their stalls. The wooden shovel clattered to the floor and Latimer's face lengthened in horror. Breathlessly, he stared at the lifeless form on the stable floor and then at his own hands. He lurched toward the entrance in a panic.

"What have I done, what have I done? Oh, gracious God!" He wheeled about and stared again.

It was true. The man—the *body*—now lay as he left it, as he had pummeled it into the floor, the shovel lying beside it. His quivering fingers reached for his mouth. "No, no, no, no…" He must stop his lips or he would surely scream, he told himself. Clenching his eyes shut, he tried to breathe. *I must calm. I must.* Images flashed through his mind, becoming confused with that of Peter's fist crashing down at him, striking and striking…

What have I done? I am a man of God! What have I done?

He breathed again, willing himself to calm, to slow his heart to a normal rhythm. Gradually, his breath decreased until he was able to reopen his eyes.

The body lay crumpled and dead. The horror receded and logic rushed in to replace it. Latimer rubbed his numb hands and strung ragged thoughts together, each one like a prayer bead. *A murder…a terrible sin…and yet, a miserable, foul-tempered creature, more animal than man…A blasphemer! He would have told about Brother Peter. I never would have a chance to help him…Necessary…A righteous war, then. Him against Brother Peter. Yes. Yes.* He leaned on the wall for support. His legs felt weak and numb.

The edge of his eyes flared, running red veins into his sight, but on turning, he realized it was the sun rising, sending spikes of light outward. Morning. They needed to leave anyway. He would get the horses ready and tether them outside. He would have to hide the body. He was certain murders were committed all the time and some murderers were never discovered. It was a shame, but since he was a man of God he knew best how to atone for such a crime. He would do much penance. Yes, that would satisfy. Grievous penance.

Stepping over the sickening corpse, Latimer found the horses and their tack and proceeded to prepare them. It was harder leading them over the body, for they were reluctant to go near it, but after throwing his cloak over their eyes, he was able to lead them one at a time out to the courtyard.

When he returned, he stared at the corpse. The sun was climbing faster and servants would soon be about. He must hurry.

Grabbing the man's ankles he lifted, but the dead weight made it difficult. Panic started to rise again, and he pushed his straining muscles harder, heaving the man along the floor into an unoccupied paddock. He tossed hay over him, picked up the deadly shovel again, and moved the hay about on the dirt floor to sop some of the blood, then redirected the bloody straw into the paddock. Scooping horse droppings from another paddock, he splattered it against the place where the blood pooled, effectively hiding it. Only the horses knew where the murder had been, and they mutely stared at him with dark eyes and a shuffling step.

Reaching the entrance for the last time, he paused.

Did he hear a whimper? It was a soft sound, but surely not from the dead man! Latimer turned, straining his ears again, but did not hear it a second time. Scanning above to the hayloft, he saw no figures against the filtered sunlight, no movement from any other than the beasts. It was his fear manifesting, that was it. He hurried away and back into the inn. Herbert would have to be awakened so they could be quickly on the road.

CHAPTER NINETEEN

Hugh lay awake, watching the bed curtains sway from the warm heat of the brazier. He delayed moving on to Pershore partly because he felt weakened, and also because he did not quite know what to do with the madman.

An unusual man. Brother Peter did not foam and rave like other madmen. Brother Peter could be anyone. He could even be what he said he was, he mused, except that it was impossible. Yet why *not* possible? Did not Scripture say that angels walked among men: 'Be careful to entertain strangers for you may entertain angels unaware.' But no, thought Hugh with a cautious shake to his head. This was certainly Brother Peter, the Mad Monk of Pershore Abbey. Who else could he be?

An angel. Could one reason with an angel? Even...bargain? Hugh could accept his own death at any other time in any other way, but surely not like this. If he could parley with him...

Inhaling sharply from a fiery ache, all his notions stopped short. The pain had grown steadily since sundown and even with Sebastian's potions and wine, nothing seemed to help. To pass the time, he had prayed for a while, but the throbbing ache soon made concentration impossible. Was it delirium forming such convoluted thoughts about that man below in the mews? Was it something in

Brother Peter's eyes?

No, it was only the numbing potion that made Peter appear otherworldly, Hugh decided. Undoubtedly Brother Peter was an enigmatic individual and the potion mixed with wine only intensified Hugh's already strange mood.

Craning his head upward, Hugh made out the outline of Sebastian curled on his pallet. It was not fair to disturb him. He had his own concerns.

All at once, Hugh jerked into a curled position, groaning. *Oh blessed Savior!* How it hurt! Gritting his teeth, he huffed, billowing his cheeks. He tried, but could not suppress the moan that released in a grunt.

Sebastian stirred and rose, staring over him sleepily. "My lord?"

"Oh, Sebastian!" Clutching the bedclothes seemed to help, but only briefly. "Oh God! I shall go mad!"

"My lord!" The gentle presence—blurred by flashes of pain and flickering light—hovered over him. Hands caressed his moist brow, trying to soothe, but it was of no use. Hugh shot out of bed, clutched his side, and paced the room, grasping the bedpost and then a coffer. "God help me!"

"I will fetch a physician!"

"No! Sebastian, no. They will only bleed me again and it does nothing to relieve the pain. Talk to me. It is so lonely and dead at this hour of night. Only spirits walk now. Shall I walk with them? It seems the only remedy."

"Lean on me, my lord."

"And so I always have," he whispered, resting a shaky hand on the young squire's shoulder. Limping with the pain, he paced the floor, the only sounds Hugh's labored breathing and shuffling footsteps. No words passed between them, until Hugh gasped a sob that he quickly inhaled, chagrined. "Talk to me," he rasped. "Keep my mind from death. It craves me, Sebastian. I feel its claws."

"It will not take you, my lord. Not now. I am here and have my sword."

Hugh tried to laugh, but it choked on a twinge. "Will you fight off death with a sword, young warrior?"

"For you, my lord, anything!"

"The Angel of Death will not be so easily abused. Do you think to trifle with divine forces, Sebastian?" A strained chuckle sputtered from his lips. "The Lord is the giver and taker of lives…though I have taken enough lives in my day. Sebastian, is this why I suffer now? Does the Almighty punish on earth?"

"Surely not you, my lord."

"Every man. Dreadful, dreadful deeds am I guilty of, Sebastian. I wish I knew—Oh God!" Crumpling, he clutched the bedpost, resting his head against the carved wood. "Get a physician…and a priest, Sebastian."

White-faced, Sebastian moved quickly to comply, grabbing his cloak from where it lay strewn on the coffer.

"Wait!" cried Hugh to Sebastian. "Get that monk instead."

"What? My lord, not the madman!"

"Yes, yes, him!"

"Would not a physician be better—"

"I have no time to waste, Sebastian! Jesus mercy, get him!"

Mute, Sebastian whirled the cloak over his shoulders and scrambled down the passageway, the scraping of his shoes dwindling.

Hugh dug his fingers into the wood and wrapped his arm around the post before hauling himself upward again. He leaned against it and waited. If he stood in a certain position, it did not seem so bad. He could even take a deep breath without the pain intensifying. Flattening against the post, the raised carving digging into his hip, he breathed, ticking the time away in his head. Shadows were deeper in the dead of night. Even the air seemed to hang in putrid mourning, musty, motionless, and thick. "God is with me," he murmured. *Then why am I so frightened?*

So still was the manor that Hugh heard them from quite far off. He counted each footfall, playing a game with himself to guess which one was Sebastian's and which the monk's. The faster one would be the squire's, he reasoned, and the slow, steady gait that of the monk's. The monk was certain of himself, as certain as his madness was a certainty.

Azriel entered first, followed by Sebastian, whose features were grayed by worry. Azriel stood before Hugh, resting his bound hands before him peacefully. His eyes, dark crystals, pierced the gloom and captured Hugh's desperate gaze. "Sir Hugh," he said with a nod.

"Brother Peter."

Azriel stood immobile, like a stick of furniture. Hugh closed his eyes. He wondered if he was making a mistake. Sebastian must think him as mad as this monk. "Brother Peter—"

"I must interject again, Sir Hugh, that I am not Brother Peter."

"Would you prefer 'Azriel,' then?"

"It is my preference and my name."

"Very well." Now that the man stood before him he began to feel foolish. Somehow, only minutes ago in the throes of so much pain, it did not seem foolish.

"Is there something you require, Sir Hugh?"

"Require?" He smiled sadly. "I require peace, Azriel. And the need to know."

"You have already asked many questions of me. What else do you have need to know?"

Shadows that would hardly garner interest by day suddenly took on sinister intent at night. They wavered, like a venomous spider hiding in a corner. The brazier's faint glow made it worse and Hugh asked for a candle with a tremor to his voice. Sebastian hurried to light one and the horror of the corners opened into nothing. Hugh glared at Azriel, suddenly angry at his own helplessness.

"Are you the Angel of Death?" Hugh blurted.

Surprised, Azriel cocked his head. "No, Sir Hugh. I am not he. But he hovers."

Sebastian struck Azriel on the side of the head. "How dare you!"

"Peace, Sebastian," whispered Hugh. "Is it not true? Especially at this hour?"

Azriel mildly rubbed his temple, ignoring the smoldering Sebastian. "This is the hour he favors, Sir Hugh, but tonight is not your hour. Is that what you wish to ask?"

"No." He caught Sebastian's wary stare, bouncing from Azriel to himself. "Sebastian, would you please leave us?"

The squire shoved Azriel aside. "My lord, is that wise?"

"He will not hurt me. He…cannot."

Wincing, the squire acceded and carefully backed out of the room. "I shall be right outside this door, my lord. Should you even whimper, I shall hear."

Azriel's smile was broad when the door clicked softly closed. "He is loyal. You should be grateful."

"Have I anything to fear from you?"

"I am a madman, by your assessment. *Have* you?"

"I will untie your hands if you give me your solemn oath. Do you swear by God?"

"I will not swear by God," Azriel sniffed indignantly. "My no means no and my yes means yes."

"Then…do I have your word you will do no mischief?"

"You have my word."

Hugh smiled. "Good enough." Hobbling forward, he retrieved his belt and withdrew a dagger. He gestured for Azriel to approach, and he did so with arms extended forward. Hugh slipped the blade behind the ropes and sawed until it cut through. Azriel rubbed his wrists and slipped the ropes free, letting them hit the floor. Again his gaze rested on Hugh's, a quizzical shadow arching a brow.

Bringing a shaky hand to his gray-salted beard, Hugh stroked it, thoughts racing. "I brought you here…to…to…well. I will be damned if I am not certain why I brought you here."

"Certainly not to damn yourself."

"No." Hugh slumped to sit at the edge of the bed in the shadows cast by the bed curtains. In the obscuring shade of anonymity, he could speak of these things. "I do not know. I do not know what I believe anymore. I am on the threshold of death, and I fear."

"Why?"

The stranger's expression was one of deep curiosity. "Most of us do, you know. Fear of the unknown, of further pain, of loss."

"But death is none of those things."

"It is *all* of those things!"

Blinking, Azriel studied him for a long, silent moment. "You struggle to fend off that which is an inevitability. Why?"

"Because it is death. Surely you fear it too."

"No. Because I know what is beyond it."

"What? Tell me."

Breath trembled on Azriel's lip. "God," he whispered

Disappointment and foolishness bruised Hugh's pale cheek, and he shook his head, thrusting a hand into his gut to squeeze at the throbbing tumor. "I do not wish to die this way," he grunted. "It seems that there must be something a man can do."

Azriel refused to aid him with suggestions. He stood aloof, a stone.

Angry at his silence at first, Hugh grew frightened at a mood he could not decipher. "There is something about you," Hugh whispered. "Am I, too, losing my mind?"

In the corner of Hugh's eye, Azriel stood, unmoving. "I am a desperate man, Azriel. Tell me—with all the sanity you can muster—are you something...*more*? Are you what you say you are?"

Azriel straightened, and in the scant light of the brazier and single candle, he also seemed to grow from a slight form to something much larger. Perhaps it was his shadow stretching wide across the wall behind him creating this illusion. "Sir Hugh, I tell you from the depth of my being, that I am an Angel of the Living God, His Messenger, His Servant. Look beyond what you see, Little Creature," he whispered, eyes round and wide. "Look beyond the ether, and behold that which is divine."

Clutching the bedclothes in a white-knuckled grip, Hugh shrank back in sudden fear. Not at the bedraggled beggar who stood before him, but at words so forcefully spoken that they hung in the room, hovering above the smell of old smoke and the lingering aroma of burnt mutton. The voice, the manner. Certitude without the hint of delirium bore through Azriel's words, yet it was also something in those very words: 'look beyond the ether'; the same words Hugh himself pondered.

"I long to do just as you say, 'to see beyond the ether.' To understand the very nature of Heaven. To…to bargain with you…for my life."

Azriel's expression widened in amusement. "Bargain? How extraordinary."

"Are you an angel or not!"

"Go on. I find this fascinating. Just what would you bargain with?"

Grimacing with discomfort, Hugh concentrated on Azriel's pale face. "Whatever it takes."

Azriel consumed himself in fitful laugh. "You creatures *are* amusing. 'Too high is the price to redeem one's life.'"

"Then what is there for us? Submission?"

The laughter stopped abruptly, and Azriel spun, staring at Hugh down his nose. "Submission? You say it like a curse."

"It is a curse! We are men—weak, yes—but men, nonetheless. We know nothing but this life and its ties. Should we submit helplessly—even to disease—without a struggle? How can one live only on faith?"

Angry, Azriel loomed. "Why can you not believe? Is the eye the only witness? Do you not feel love? Can this be touched or seen? I cannot place faith in your hands like a platter!"

"But an angel, so incorporeal a thing." Hugh nodded vaguely, tiring, "I have touched you, Azriel, loosened your bonds. You are as solid as I am!"

"How does that change what I am?"

"I do not know, dammit! All I want is compassion!"

Azriel sneered. "Your Heavenly Father has enough for you."

"But what of you? What of *your* compassion? If you are close to God, an angel as you say…"

"Compassion! I…" His certainty seemed to shrink. Azriel's eyes darted back and forth. "I do not know," he said pensively. "Perhaps…it *is* lacking in me. I do not know."

Hugh had stoically accepted men begging him for mercy, seen their bowels loosen, watched them disgrace themselves before him and his steel. But he shrank from the naked exposure in Azriel's eyes. "Are not all angels to have compassion for Man?" he asked softly.

"I do not know!" Azriel's hands wrung one over the other. "I was close to the Inner Circle. I had no congress here. That was the task of others. It was not my assignment!"

Surprised, Hugh echoed a smile. "You are frightened. Just as much as me." It gave Hugh visceral comfort to see such astonishment on Azriel's features. It wiped that condescending smirk from the madman's mouth once and for all.

Azriel stared past him, each breath raising his shoulders. Coldness seemed to descend on him and he closed whitening fingers over his forearms. His face—waxen and pale like the flickering tapers in the room—lengthened and reconfigured, melting into vacancy. "Yes," Azriel answered harshly. "I am frightened."

"And to think I came to *you* for help." Hugh dropped his head. "I do not know what I truly believe. A monk, a man of faith." Bright pain, an agony like a blade twisting into his flesh, doubled him, and he crushed his fist into his mouth, biting so hard his knuckles ran red with blood. "I do not know what you are and I do not care! But can you heal me from this suffering? For the love of God!"

"My love for the Divine Father knows no bounds, Sir Hugh," he said woodenly. He drooped. It seemed his arrogance alone could no longer sustain him. "And were I instructed, I surely would heal you. But as I said before, I am in this helpless form, powerless to do His will. I…I cannot even hear Him."

Sucking the blood from the back of his hand, Hugh eased back and regarded the man. "You cannot hear Him? A poor angel you, friend. For there are times when even I, a dreadful sinner, can hear God's voice."

For the first time, Azriel moved and walked very slowly to the iron brazier on its stand. It basked the under curve of his cheeks and enlarged his square chin with yellow-orange brilliance. "What you say is true," he said softly. "I know it is. I have heard this before. Why then is His voice denied *me*? What have I done? How have I offended? O gracious and loving Lord, how can I repair myself when I do not know how I have breached Your love?" Bright, pearly tears suddenly appeared at his eyes and rolled down, angling inward toward his chin.

"Enough!" Hugh swatted the air with his hand and instantly regretted it. Choking with agony, he steadied himself and spoke with a pain-roughened voice. "I want to know. I need no madman. I need an angel! Are you an angel or not?"

Unexpectedly, Azriel threw back his head and laughed. Hugh flinched at the unnatural sound.

Azriel wiped a hand across his face. "Yes…and no!"

"What sort of fool's answer is that?" Hugh barked.

"Not a fool's answer. A philosopher's one." Turning, Azriel's face gleamed with wiped tears.

Hugh drew back, shamed. "I only wanted help. I only wanted to understand…"

"And you ask *me*? I might as well *be* mad. I am as useless to you as I am to the Divine Father." Gravely, Azriel stared at the floor, hands curling into fists. "You want answers? Here is an answer. You will die. All men will die. Accept it. You, at least, have a future after death." His body stiffened. Raising fingers to his scalp, he raked them through the lank hair, fanning out the dirty locks in a flaccid coxcomb. The white skin of his fingers, reddening at the knuckles and joints, stretched taut, revealing each dip and mound of the bone beneath. "But what of *me*?" he cried. "There is no help for me! I am doomed to wander this earth…Oh God! Edric was right. This *is* Hell!"

"*Sebastian*!"

Instantly, the squire appeared, dagger drawn. "My lord?"

"Take Brother Peter back to his cell!"

"So," Azriel said tremulously, raising a distorted face, cheeks still wet from weeping. "I am 'Brother Peter' again? O ye of little faith. A poor excuse for an Angel am I, but Angel nonetheless."

Hugh heard his words but refused to look at him. He waved Sebastian on, and out of the corner of his eyes saw the squire grab Azriel's arm and walk him to the doorway. He could tell Azriel was staring at him, that his face was poised in his direction, but still he refused to look.

Trembling, Hugh's fingers crimped into fists, but instead of steadying his hands, they trembled all the more.

CHAPTER TWENTY

Edric's whole body ached and his eye throbbed. He had escaped with few scars, the biggest one being to his pride, but he had sacrificed that often enough. Thankfully, Margery did not witness the spectacle, yet he caught himself trying to discern why it mattered. A twinge inside his chest stopped his breath, but he owed it to one of many punches in the stomach.

The lane lay empty. Only the rutted street and the dim, blue promise of sunrise crossed his view. A cat's dark silhouette trotted across and disappeared. Lazy smoke from many smoldering hearths lolled over the thatched rooftops and trickled over the eaves.

He spent a little time looking for Margery—just wanting to say good-bye and good luck—and chanced by the inn yard again. Someone had left horses tethered there. He decided it was probably those monks. They sounded anxious to be on their way, but he did not want them getting to Azriel before him. Not until he talked with him.

He took a deep breath and grabbed the tethers in his fist. It was likely the most foolish thing he had ever done, but it somehow did not matter anymore within the haze of despair that encircled him. Grabbing onto the horse's mane, he pulled himself clumsily onto its back, settling on the unfamiliar seat.

He tried to remember what Latimer had called Azriel. Brother Peter? So that was his real name. *I knew 'Azriel' was a fool name.* The piebald horse huffed and bobbed its head. The shaggy chestnut cantered behind on the lead Edric clutched in his hand. "Hurry, horse," he said to the piebald while he bounced along with its quickening gait. "I'm no horseman so I'm leaving it all to you." The horse trotted faster, and Edric lurched forward, gripping the mane again.

He left town quickly and found himself heading south along the road, making good time, but though he tried to keep the notion at bay, the idea that he had stolen horses finally overwhelmed. He could be hanged for this. Was Azriel worth it? Was anyone? "I'll return them," he said with a shrug that did not pacify. "No one will know." It made him dig his heels viciously into the beast's warm flanks, dragging the other behind with hurrying steps.

Soon he felt the strain on his haunches. Always assuming riding would be easier, he did not realize how it would affect his bent spine. He was moving faster, though. He was taller, too, and once he gave himself over to it, could appreciate the view. No wonder lords and knights felt so important, he mused. A body looked up to talk to a man on a horse. He chuckled. *No wonder no one rides pigs.*

How did *he* look astride? Thinking of it, he straightened, feeling taller and more rigid. He supposed he did not look so lowly anymore. *I'd like to see the look on that innkeeper's face now!*

Remembering the innkeeper sobered him, and he sank slowly to his normal posture. Here he was on a stolen horse, and for what? "Brother Peter. A monk. A sarding monk. I suppose we're even, then. I helped you, and one of yours helped me. So why am I bothering?" From the monks' conversation, it sounded like Azriel would be taken back to the monastery after this Hugh Varney was done with him. He was a monk, after all. That was where he belonged.

He readjusted his seat, trying to find a comfortable spot. If that was where Azriel—no—*Brother Peter* belonged, then why had he run away in the first place?

Edric yanked on the reins and the piebald stumbled to a halt, complaining grievously over the bit. The chestnut ambled to a stop behind Edric and lowered his head to nibble on a dandelion. "What the hell am I doing? He don't need rescuing. And here am I, now a horse thief. They'll hang me, and not a soul would give a damn."

A raven's gravel-call rambled along the copses, bouncing from tree to tree. Even though the sky opened wide into a dome of lavender blue, Edric felt it converge like a roof falling in on him. "Brother Peter. I liked you better as a half-wit angel. Now you're just another one of *them*." A guilty flush reddened his numbed cheeks. He supposed that was not entirely fair. Those monks saved him and here he was, with their money in his purse and their horses under his rump. So much for gratitude. Maybe he should just keep the horses or sell them. He owed no one anything. It was about time he got something back. "'Ask and you shall receive,' eh?" It was a foolish thing to do, stealing horses. If he was to go on, he would have to move off the main road. "Azriel, you bastard. Look what you made me do." Since he had met the madman everything had fallen apart, everything he understood his world to be. New feelings and expectations rattled about in his head where they had no right to be. Feelings of friendship, of Margery…

An ache began in his throat and sank to his heart. Memories of her tingled his lips with the recollection of her mouth's sweetness, his fingers with stolen caresses. Why did she do it? Why come with him all this way if there were not something on her mind? Might it simply be the odd tale to tell her grandchildren someday? 'Whatever happened to Edric the beggar?' she might ask herself, but not truly care about the answer.

Edric reached into his shirt for his pipe, but the fingers touched something unfamiliar. Pulling forth only half the reed he stared slack-jawed and horrified. "Those bastards!" Staring at the broken pieces in disbelief, willing it to repair itself before his eyes, he stiffened. "Christ!" Rising in the saddle, he heaved the broken instrument far into the underbrush. "Christ's bones! Whoreson!"

His voice echoed across the lonely plain until he fell into a debilitating silence. What was he without his music? He was truly silenced. His tongue might as well have been cut out. "Bastards! Bastards!" he muttered, shattered. What was the use, then? Why even bother with finding Azriel? What were they to each other, after all? Brother Peter would surely be all right. He was going home, was he not? After all, what could Edric truly do for him? Perhaps it was best to go back…

It niggled and tapped in the hollow places of his mind, that expression Azriel wore at the bonfire. His cheeks had flashed with golden reflections from the jumping flames, and his eyes had opened into the depth of him, exposing misery. He called Edric his friend. The words resonated, rich and smooth like the tenor voice of the man himself.

Starlings interrupted the silence and began their own chorus before taking wing and their music with them. Edric watched them distractedly. "Ah hell," he muttered. "I've never been no one's friend before. What he have to go and say that for?"

His glance drifted from the tiny specks the birds became and settled ahead. The horse, with its weight and strength, moved uneasily beneath him in his hesitation. The road veered ahead to his left while another smaller horse trail trickled off the main route and through several fields.

A rueful smile yanked up the corners of his mouth. If he survived this, it *would* be a tale to tell someday.

Deciding, he kicked the horse's flanks again, and the two beasts trotted quickly over the main road before settling into an orderly cadence. They followed the road while it dipped, meandered, and narrowed. Edric's mind fell into a solemn reverie. The loss of the pipe saddened him. It was a waste, but he could make another. Stealing the horses…well. He would find a solution to that eventually. Margery…

The sigh he released tumbled away on the wind. She was clear in his mind's eye. Lovely plump cheeks, especially when she smiled, with dewy skin freckled by sun. She had good teeth, too. It was a pleasant smile, more so because, for some reason, it was often directed toward him. Maybe she was only laughing at him—but no. He could well tell when she mocked…and then he laughed at himself. He really didn't know her at all, and yet it seemed as if he had known her a long time. He thought of her lips, smiling, kissing, nibbling on him. He liked kissing her.

But then he remembered where she garnered her skills.

What was the use in thinking of it? Grasping his groin, he tried to squeeze the ache away, but a bump in the road did the job for him and he held on with a wince instead.

Squinting up the road he noticed a dark figure swaying with trudging steps. For a moment his heart pounded, thinking it might be Azriel. But the measured amble and stooped posture soon belied that.

The man kept to the verges, walking stiffly and dragging his feet, each step an effort of will. Eventually, Edric came abreast of him. The man raised his dirty palm reflexively to the horseman, not even looking at who rode, but hoping for alms nonetheless.

At any other moment in his life, Edric would have thought this the height of amusement, a beggar begging from *him*! But he did not find it so amusing now. Horrified, he realized this was a glimpse of himself; ragged, aged beyond his years, and devoid of hope. "Christ!" he breathed. Dragging on the reins, he stopped the horse.

Too weary from fear but wary just the same, the man stopped and looked up at Edric with the cringing attitude of one used to being beaten down. For a long moment, Edric and the man regarded one another. The beggar's eyes were sculpted deep within gray holes, and his cheeks were drawn almost as deep and as gray. Life hung heavily about him like the musky molt of a draft horse, dangling, threatening to dislodge with a mere breath.

Eyes burning, Edric studied him, from the cloth-wrapped feet to his splayed, greasy hair. The monk's pouch at Edric's own hip felt heavier and he found himself grasping for it. Taking out two coins, he held out his hand. He waited with gritted teeth for the man to approach. Stubbornly, he decided he would not throw the coins. It was humiliating to have charity tossed so carelessly like rubbish.

But the man, confounded at the windfall, did not approach. Edric cleared his thickened throat. "Come, man. I'll not throw it. I'm giving it to you man to man."

The beggar stared up through grizzly brows and a dirt-etched face. "Man to man?" His voice was a wispy crackling of old leaves.

"Aye. Take it, curse you!"

Like claws, the fingers curled and scraped into Edric's palm, scooping up the coins. "Thank you, sir. Bless you, sir."

"I'm no 'sir,'" Edric grumbled and kicked the horse's flanks, spurring swiftly ahead. He did not look back.

Nightfall swept in behind Edric when he finally rode into town. He did not need to ask, for talk buzzed in the street of a mad monk kept in the manor house a few miles from the town walls. Even hungry and exhausted, Edric could not rest until he devised something, and so urged the horses a little farther and tethered them safely in the woods below the manor.

The rising moon lit his way. He ambled around the manor's perimeter and wondered about the security of the rest of the stronghold. He knew from experience there was always a way in. Kicking the tall grass nuzzling the wall, he soon found it. A section of blocks dug out or fallen away, hidden by thickets. With a grunt, he managed to squeeze through and found himself in a courtyard below the stables. Against the walls and standing in the shadows, he was able to observe the empty quadrangle without giving himself away.

He knew under the skin he was afraid, but it did not obstruct his ability to proceed. It was familiar after all, like stealing into a barnyard, or slipping a sausage into his cloak while a shopkeeper's attention lay elsewhere.

Taking in the sight of stable and lowing horses, feed stable, and smoking brazier, Edric tucked it all in his mind, and inched forward behind the paddocks and into the unprotected archway of the main building.

Peering down a shadowed stair, he heard the distant ghost of echoes and a whisper of conversation. Azriel must be in the lower crofts. Where else would a prisoner be kept? Instead of creeping downward, he moved upwards along the stone stairwell, keeping eyes and ears peeled. The stairwell grew lighter, and he came just barely within the nimbus of an oil lamp in its niche. A wide passage extended before him. Casks and bundles were piled along one wall, perhaps ready to be taken below. A half-eaten loaf of bread and a jug and cup sat on a wooden tray on a table, and though it sparked his own hunger it also gave him an idea.

Listening and hearing nothing in the outer passage, he limped quickly forward, took the tray, and grabbed another oil lamp from its niche across the room. He found the doorway again and hurried down the stairs. Reaching the courtyard, he set the tray down. Only horses moved within the stalls and he gave an apologetic shrug to them when he meandered toward the grain stable. "Sorry, horses. But it must be done." He set the fire from the lamp to the hay and watched it smoke and smolder before an amber flame of its own jumped to life.

Heart thumping, he retrieved the tray and headed quickly down stairs, playacting like he belonged there. He stepped into another passage and heard echoing men's voices. A dank smell of mold arose and he pressed forward looking around, and caught his breath when three men playing dice noticed him.

"Here! What you want?" said one, rising.

Edging forward, Edric scowled. "I got food for the prisoner and I been all though this sarding place trying to find him, so don't give me no words."

The scruffy man in a leather tunic eyed Edric without expression. "As you will. He's down here." Edric followed the other, trying to control his terrified breathing. The man pulled a ring of keys from his belt and unlocked the wooden door to one of the mews. He stood aside for Edric, a fist at his hip.

Edric paused. "Is he dangerous?"

The man smiled. "He isn't dangerous. Thinks he's an angel."

Edric made the effort to laugh. "What nonsense," he said before moving inside and ducking under the low ceiling. He looked back and noted the door left ajar. Raising the lamp, it glowed wetly on the walls in the low tunnel, and he held it higher, cursing when it hit the ceiling and flickered. Pushing it forward instead, he walked carefully, fearing to fall down an unseen hole.

Suddenly, the light cast forward onto a stone wall. A man lay stretched out on the hay-strewn floor, his back resting against the moldy stone.

"Azriel!" Edric hissed.

Azriel glanced up. His blue eyes rounded with joy. "Edric! God be praised! What are you doing here?"

"Be still, will you!" Swinging his head over his shoulder, Edric stared worriedly at the distant opening. "I come to rescue you. Damned if I know why."

"Edric." Azriel blinked. His features softened. "I am touched. Truly. That you should come for me. I thought you decided to leave me on my own."

"Aye. I thought I did, too, but…well. You're not fit on your own. And God knows what they do to lunatics in monasteries. It just wasn't right."

Smiling enormously, Azriel laughed and clapped his hands together. "How fitting! This time, Edric, *you* are the Angel and I am Saint Peter!" He postured melodramatically. "Where will you lead me?"

"I got some horses outside the walls."

"Where did you get horses?"

"Never you mind. We'll be able to escape in a moment."

"Edric! Did you steal them?"

"What does it matter? We'll be getting out of here."

Azriel sat back down and crossed his arms over his chest with a pout. "I shall not use stolen property."

"Don't be a damn fool, Azriel!"

"The saints never relied on stolen property."

"Well you aren't an angel and I'm no saint! So let's go!" An outcry filled the halls and suddenly men scrambled about, shouting. "That's it, Azriel. We got to go now!"

"Now what have you done?" he asked, slowly rising.

Without replying, Edric grabbed Azriel's arm and tugged, running with him through the dark mew, out into the passage, and up the stairwell. "They won't notice us in the melee," he panted. "Go! Don't wait for me! I'm too slow."

"Do not be absurd," he said casually over his shoulder. "Of course I shall wait for you. I am grateful. You see, I have learned something."

"Oh, be still and go, will you!" he rumbled under his breath, shoving Azriel upward.

Reaching the opening, they were shouldered aside by men carrying buckets of water to douse the inferno. Horses whinnied wildly, while grooms tugged on their taut leads to pull their straining silhouettes forward. The air was thick with black, choking smoke. Azriel turned, grasped Edric by the arms, and looked dolefully in his eyes. "You did not do this, did you?"

"You want to go back in that hole?"

Considering a moment, Azriel finally shook his head and waited while Edric pressed on before him. The panic the fire aroused effectively hid their escape, and while Azriel struggled to fit through the crevice in the wall, they remained undetected.

Breaching the hole, they both tumbled down the earthen mound, stopping with a thump in the ditch at the bottom. Edric rolled to his feet with skill that even surprised him. He ran headlong into the woods, finally relieved to hear Azriel's footfalls behind him.

CHAPTER TWENTY-ONE

Latimer stumped up the stairs and threw open the door. Roused, Herbert jarred awake and sat up. "Who is there?"

"It is only me, Brother." Quickly, he stuffed his extra clothes into a chest and hefted it up. "We must make ready to depart. I have saddled the horses. I have decided to hurry back to Pershore."

Herbert made no move from the pallet. Herbert's reticence after so much questioning began to irritate Latimer and, fit to be tied, he reeled toward the younger man. But Herbert's face no longer wore that mask of an easily managed neophyte. Latimer pulled up short and lowered the coffer.

Herbert's pink face scowled. "I thought we were going on to where Brother Peter is."

"I have decided against it," he said.

"*You* have decided?" Herbert slowly shook his head. "You have been deceiving me, Brother. For days I tried to deny it. But I am no complete fool. You prevaricate with your voice. You are lying to me, and you have been for some time, have you not? How long, Brother? Since a sennight? Since the day we left?"

"What a preposterous notion."

Rising at last from the pallet, Herbert roughly brushed the loose straw from his cassock. "'No,' I told myself. 'Brother Latimer's ways are just not my ways. I should learn from him.' But the more information I uncovered the more you tried to cover it again. I do not believe you want to find him." Herbert raised his trembling chin defiantly. Latimer would have been amused if the circumstances were not so dire. "What I do not understand is why," said Herbert. "Perhaps you should tell me."

"Herbert! Really! I thought you learned the proper respect for older more experienced brothers—"

"No more of that, Latimer. You use my youth against me. I…I am not that witless," he said with a blush. "Or as naïve as you think. You left your coin pouch out so that beggar could not resist taking it. You wanted to rid us of him. *After* you heard where Brother Peter was."

"Nonsense." How insufferable! That this whelp should dictate to him! "You do not understand—"

"I understand you are deliberately disobeying your superior. Abbot Gervase ordered us to find Brother Peter."

"I know Brother Peter best, after all. Some orders must be questioned—"

"No!" Herbert stomped forward, glowering. "We are holy brothers! We do not question. You, above all people, should know that!"

Nubs of sweat sprouted on Latimer's face. Confusion—a dark and swirling mist in his head—transposed Herbert's piggy features with the red and bloated ones of the murdered innkeeper. "It is folly for you to question me," he said vaguely.

"We must go on to Brother Peter and discover the truth."

"Where has your backbone been all this time, Brother?" Latimer rasped. "Only now you find your courage?"

"Yes. Yes, I found it at last." Herbert stood unsteadily, mustering himself before blurting, "Are you *too* insane? Is that why the subterfuge? Good God! Is all of Pershore Abbey mad?"

Mad? pondered Latimer. The face of the innkeeper, head dented and bloody, rose again in his mind. Latimer tried to dismiss it, pushed it away with the flat of his hand. A vague sense of impending disaster hovered just over his shoulder. He tried to direct an icy scrutiny at Herbert, but Herbert resisted. Latimer's stare soon fell away. "If you would go on, you had better do so quickly."

"You are going with me."

"No."

Herbert's exasperated exhale puffed his cheeks. "Brother Latimer!"

"Go on," Latimer said, moving toward the window. He pushed open the shutter and inhaled the stench of the privies below. "I do not need you."

"I will not go on without you!"

"And I will not go with you." Depleted, Latimer leaned against the wall and glanced below, watching a gruff man walk with long strides toward the stable from the privy. The man reached the courtyard and was nearly up-ended by a women darting madly from the stable. She screamed when he caught her wrist, and she twisted on its tether like a snake coiling about a stick. Wild red hair spiked with straw hazed around her head, glinting in the sunlight. Her hysterical babbling shrieked throughout the courtyard, arousing others who opened shutters and leaned out of the windows.

She turned once toward Latimer's window, and instinctively he pulled back away from the sunlight. The gruff man pulled her toward the stable, but she shook her head vehemently while he dragged her forward. Scratching at the man's wrist, she had no choice but to follow into the shadows where they both disappeared.

Herbert droned on. Latimer listened with only half an ear and instead watched the muffled drama below.

Another man came running, joined by another and soon men and women gathered at the discovery in the stable. The gruff man returned with the red-haired woman in tow. Latimer watched dispassionately when they forced her into the inn. Once inside he could more clearly hear their incriminating shouts from below.

"What in the name of God?" said Herbert. The noise stopped

his tirade and he hurried toward the door and yanked it open. Latimer stood still while Herbert left the room and peered downward from the dark landing. Herbert's face blanched until he finally turned pale eyes toward Latimer. "The innkeeper's been murdered!" Herbert rasped. "They have the culprit. A woman it seems. Should we…should we help?"

"They have the culprit," Latimer echoed. His foot slid forward. "Yes. Why not?" In a haze, Latimer followed Herbert down the creaking stairs and stood against the wall while the inn exploded with confused shouts and accusations. The frightened red-haired woman cowered in the midst of it.

A few people noticed the monks and rushed them. "A murder!" a man cried. "She's murdered the innkeeper! He lies dead in the stable!"

Latimer raised his hand, taking the position of authority back from Herbert, who seemed anxious to relinquish it. "Peace, peace all of you. Someone explain. Tell me."

The ginger-haired woman panted, and she stared at Latimer through her sweat-drenched strands of hair. Though her eyes enlarged when she saw him, her lips remained stubbornly shut.

The gruff man who found her, stepped forward. "I was doing my business in the privy when she came out of the stable, running."

Latimer turned to her, examining her curvaceous form without emotion. Her dress was muddied and stained, her hair mussed and speckled with straw. "What were you doing in the stable?"

When she raised her eyes at last, Latimer inwardly cringed. Like an animal, her glare bore into his. It was she who made the sound he heard in the stable. She had been there all along. Was she with the innkeeper in some sinful embrace?

Strangely calm, he awaited her reply. If she denounced Latimer he would simply deny it and declare her the lying whore she was. There was no fear in him.

"I…I was…sleeping." Snorts of disbelief made her lower her head again. "I was!"

"Did you kill the innkeeper?" Latimer asked, curious of her reply.

"No!"

"She's lying!" cried Herbert, caught up in the mob.

Latimer eyed him mildly. He stepped back when Herbert pressed forward, his righteous indignation condemning her for him. Herbert preached of Satan and evil spirits coursing through her sinful body, while Latimer wondered.

She glared again at Latimer, ignoring all the others. *Why does she not speak? Is she afraid? Does she know it would do her no good? A clever woman, then.*

Roused from his musings long enough to hear that their horses were missing, Latimer stiffened. They spoke of the crippled man who was with her and how he must have stolen the horses, killed the innkeeper out of revenge, and then left her here to suffer the consequences. Angered suddenly at the missing horses, Latimer interrupted Herbert and leaned forward. "You are Margery."

More frightened, she shrank back. "How'd you know my name?"

"Edric has our horses, has he not? Where is he?"

"How do you know Edric?"

"*I* am asking the questions," he said, moving stealthily closer. "Where are the horses?"

"I don't know. I don't know naught!"

"It was that cripple what murdered him, then," another man said. Latimer looked at him, recalling that this man was one of the many who helped to throttle the unfortunate Edric. "And she's helped him."

The first man who found Margery stepped away from the crowd. Latimer did not recognize him from the mob. "I've heard the bailiff is in Evesham. I'll ride on there and fetch him. He'll decide what to do with her."

The crowd agreed and the man headed for the door with their shouts of encouragement. Herbert glanced triumphantly at Latimer, but said nothing.

Latimer turned from him and watched the man depart with a scowl.

CHAPTER TWENTY-TWO

"There were these monks at the inn," said Edric, finding a comfortable spot in the dead leaves. His feet wriggled warmly before the campfire.

The two of them had traveled far before fatigue forced Edric to make camp. He hoped they were deep enough into the woodlands to stay undetected for the night. "And they were talking about a monk what escaped from their monastery. They said he was mad."

Azriel sighed deeply. "And you, too, think I am this monk?"

"Well aren't you? Who else could you be?"

"I told you—"

"Aye, aye. You're a sarding angel."

"Brother Peter is far more dangerous than me. It is his madness, you see. He fears even that." He laid his head limply against the dark oak bark and sighed. "And so he has become more and more muddled."

A prickle of discomfort ran down Edric's neck. "You know an awful lot about someone you aren't," he said cautiously.

Azriel's mood subdued while he regarded the flames. "You would be happier were I this monk, would you not? *That* you could understand." He shook his head, gritting his jaw. "I am an Angel, Edric, and to that I shall return when my punishment is over."

Regarding Azriel, Edric wondered for the umpteenth time why he bothered with him. "I got them horses from your friends, Brother Latimer and Brother Herbert. Those names sound familiar?"

Azriel looked like he might comment, but at the last minute his expression fluctuated, and he shrugged sluggishly against the textured bark. "I assume we shall be returning the horses to them."

"In good time. Monks and priests, eh? Now *they* can afford horses. No wonder they're always spouting how God provides. He provides for them right enough."

"He provided for you as well."

"'Course I had to steal them first."

"Do not remind me. I am certain I shall receive more punishment for acceding to this."

"Don't worry. If God cared so much what I done in me life, I'd be worse off. Course I can't get much *worse* off." He scratched at his head. "I'm just as poor as I've ever been. When did I ever get charity that wasn't begrudged?"

"Perhaps those other monks you met are merely poor examples. There are many more who—"

"Harken Azriel—or whatever your name is—*I've* lived this life. You haven't a clue up in your tower—"

"Up in my tower," he said vaguely. "An interesting metaphor. Perhaps you are right. Could this be why the Divine Father has sent me here? To learn to have pity? I have been too far away from his Little Creatures…up in a tower, as you say."

Edric sat up, throwing a stick angrily at the sizzling fire. "I don't want your pity!" With exasperation, he kicked ineffectually at the stoic flames. "A little dignity, is all. That I should not die in the mud. That I should not hunger while you throw your leavings to the dogs. That you should have too much while me and my like have naught. That's all we want. Is even that too much to ask? So much for your God."

"Edric," he said, squirming. "You must not blaspheme."

"I'll tell you what blasphemy is. It's treating men like dogs just because their foot is twisted or their back is bent. Do you think I wouldn't want to love a woman or have a babe on me knee? I'm a man!" His throat warmed and he whipped his face away into the shadows. "Ah, the hell with you!"

"Mercy, Edric." Azriel leaned toward him, his fingers tangled together in a prayerful gesture. "Never say that! Not to me!"

"Stop it! I'm tired of your angel talk. It sickens me. Go on. Go back to your monastery and your safe little cell. Go back to your own little world and leave me in peace!"

The crackle of flames and the snapping of burning twigs filled the pause. Azriel sat back. Firelight flashed along the planes of his face. "I cannot," Azriel said softly. "You know I cannot until the Divine Father wills it."

Sighing deeply with exhaustion, Edric flattened himself against a tree. Azriel's mood softened him, gently reminding why Edric came after him. "Well, why not a monastery?" he said, calming. "Wouldn't that be closer to God and all?"

"I do not know. What has happened to my judgment? Perhaps you are right. But it does not feel right to go to a monastery." Azriel ran his fingers over the sheen of sweat on his brow. "Some of the things Sir Hugh said disturbed me. Is it selfish of me to say that I prefer to be with you?"

"Who? This 'little creature'? Since when did you start liking us?"

"I have grown used to *you*, at least."

"'Used' to me. That's a far cry from loving us. Aren't angels supposed to love what God created?"

Azriel froze. Astonishment welded his face to a permanent expression of horror. "That is what Sir Hugh said, too. Edric…you…you do not seem to understand how astute you are."

"Oh, now that's it!" Edric marched around the fire, and pushed up his sleeves. "I don't like it when you call me 'little creature,' but I'll be damned if you start calling me 'astute'!"

Azriel suddenly laughed. "No, no. I only meant how wise you are. Truly."

Edric stopped short. "Me? Well...aye. I've been around, you

know." Azriel's weak laughter petered out to a gentle chuckle. Feeling foolish, Edric moved back to his place and settled in again, hoping Azriel would do the same.

"What happened to you while I was gone?" Azriel asked.

"Don't you believe in sleep, Azriel?"

"I merely wondered."

"Lots of things happened. Too much to say now."

"Yes," he said thoughtfully. "There is much you do not say. What of Margery?"

Somehow, Edric knew Azriel was going to ask, but being forewarned did not help the ache in his chest when thinking of her. "Nothing," he answered sourly.

"It only seems…well. Never mind."

"It isn't like I need her. I've gotten along without her like so far."

"You are not a very good liar."

Edric rolled back over. "You're the master of it, aren't you!" He meant it to hurt and hoped it did. "'Azriel'! I knew that was a fool name. You can call yourself Robin Goodfellow for all I care, but don't be calling *me* no liar! At least I know what I am."

"I do not lie," came the familiar refrain, followed by the more familiar and wearying, "I am an Angel. We do not lie."

"As you will," Edric sighed. For a long time, Edric grew quiet, melting into the solemn stillness of the deep night. Even Azriel seemed to have calmed, but where before Edric felt fatigue, he was now filled with crushing sadness. He did not mean to say it aloud, but it spilled from him nonetheless. "Why'd you have to mention her? Did you know she was a whore?" The night settled on the word, stretching it to a single taut note. "She lied about it. To me."

"She did not want you to know."

"'Course she didn't want me to know! I'm not a lackwit. But…why?"

"It seems obvious. She is disposed toward you."

"And you're a madman what don't know it," Edric muttered. "And *you're* giving me advice."

"When you left her back in the village…"

"I didn't leave her in the village. That is…she came with me...in search of you."

"She went with you? Edric!"

"That don't mean naught!" Azriel's chuckling heated Edric's ears with embarrassment. Why was everyone treating him like a spring fool?

"Edric, why would a woman lie to you about her past and then journey with you on a perilous quest if she did not care for you? As little as I understand of human nature even this seems obvious to me."

The clouded thoughts parted just enough to allow a ray of hazy light to glimmer down on Edric's hopes and desires. "That…don't make sense."

"Of course not! Nothing you Little Creatures do makes sense."

"She fancies me?" Nodding, Edric rolled to his back, glancing up at the glittering stars before frowning with a new set of thoughts. "A man don't know what to do with that." Edric felt better with this revelation, pleased even. But regret soon squelched the tender feelings. It was a lost opportunity now. She was back in her village and he was God-knew-where. Best to forget what was behind and concentrate on what was to come.

Azriel's presence began to soothe again. Quiet drifted over both men and with it, a sort of peace. Edric began to doze.

"Edric."

Azriel's voice startled, but its soothing tones wavered pleasantly in the firelight.

"What is it, Azriel?"

"What…what is it like?"

Drowsy with exhaustion, Edric sank into the duff, mingling with the dead leaves. "What is *what* like?"

"You kissed her, did you not?"

Frowning, Edric raised up just enough to stare at Azriel's vague figure. "Aye?"

"Well…what is it like?"

"Haven't you never kissed a woman?"

Azriel rose indignantly. "No! Certainly not!"

Edric smiled a moment remembering those long nights of smoky passion with Margery. An aching heart dragged his smile downward. "I…I don't want to talk about it." He hunched onto his side and turned away from Azriel.

"But I am curious." Azriel scooted closer to Edric. "It is not likely anything *I* will do, and quite frankly I never much thought about it before. Why do you touch lips?" Azriel's fingers reached for his own lips, wondering.

Edric shrugged into the dead leaves, hearing them crunch beneath him. "I dunno! That's what a kiss is, isn't it?"

"But why do it? Is it necessary for courtship?"

"Courtship," he sneered, yet the idea was not now so far-fetched. "Well...a woman…you just want to take in all of her. And…bah! I dunno!" Margery's image, her scent, played on his senses and he could feel her beside him. "To taste her lips, to inhale her breath…it's like taking a part of her into you, see?"

Azriel's eyes danced with each utterance. "Is it like the Holy Ghost?" he asked.

Scandalized, Edric barked out, "No!" It seemed blasphemous at first, until he considered it from Azriel's point of view. "Well…how should I know? It's like…a man and a woman."

"'And the two shall become one flesh…'"

Edric nodded. "Aye. That's it. You've got a way with words."

"They are not my words. They are God's in Scripture."

Twisting, Edric squinted at him. "Truly? God said that?"

"Yes. And much more."

Edric sat back and shook his head. "Why should God care so much? Look at us. We're a proper mess. If I were the Almighty, I'd throw up me hands and say 'good riddance to the lot of you!'"

Edric watched Azriel nervously tap his fingers against his chest. The firelight gave him a more wraithlike quality, as if he might be blown away with a mere breath. "Yes," he said slowly. "I myself did not desire to be a helper of Man."

"Truth to tell, Azriel, I don't blame you. If I were an angel, I wouldn't want to help us neither. We're all a bunch of ungrateful bastards with naught good on our lips for nobody."

Azriel stared at him silently for so long it grew uncomfortable. Azriel's face, sketched only faintly by firelight, revealed nothing of his feelings. Finally, Azriel said, "I used to believe that. When I first met you, I thought all my views were confirmed. You certainly looked like the sort of creature I came to conclude Man was."

Edric squirmed, not certain if he were being insulted. "But you changed your mind?"

"Yes. Because *you* changed."

"What? Me? You're mad."

"No. You hated life, your fellow man, and God for making you what you are. But Edric, from the first moment I met you, you did all you could to be my good neighbor, my good—"

"—Samaritan?" Edric finished. "I didn't want to, I assure you."

"Yet you did so anyway. And you continue to do so." He frowned. "I…I think I was…*wrong*."

Edric's barking laugh rang out into the night, startling a sleeping bird above. "God's blood and bones. *You* were wrong! That's something I never thought to hear."

"Do not begrudge your humanity, Edric," Azriel said quietly. "You have little, yet you give so much. It is a puzzle to me. And I thought I understood all."

"Ah be still, will you. You're making me skittery again. All I want is to figure out what we're to do now."

"If you like, we can go back in search of Margery."

Edric frowned. "We can't go that way," he said sharply. "If you're near Pershore, they'll grab you."

"I appreciate your concern, but since I am not this monk—"

"Azriel, this is Edric, remember? I took you out of the mud, didn't I? I well know who you are."

Azriel shook his head gently. "Poor Edric. You truly do not."

With a sigh, Edric lay back. "You will have your fantasy, won't you?"

"And you will have yours," the other said under his breath.

"Well, it's witless, is all. Too risky going back."

"I do not fear their accusations. I am, after all, an Angel."

"No you aren't! You're this monk, and they'll lock you up…or worse."

"Worse? Than being here? I doubt that." Unexpectedly, his shoulders drooped. "No. That is not entirely fair any longer. I must…readjust my thinking." He brooded, watching silently while the campfire dwindled to little more than a glow. Azriel himself seemed also to dwindle, to fade into the shadows. His voice was soft and low. "This is the second time you rescued me. Why do you keep doing it?"

"I dunno. You grew on me, I reckon."

"Perhaps the original motivating factor was greed, but it seems unsound to rescue me against unspeakable odds. Did you ever do anything of the kind before?"

Edric scratched his chin and rumbled a chuckle. "That was a bold thing to do at that," he said, wiping at his suddenly clammy neck. "But…I dunno. I decided it needed to be done, is all."

"You could have been captured. What would they have done to you?"

He shivered. "Best not to think about that!"

"Yet you took the chance. For me."

"Don't get all whimpery over it." Edric yanked the cloak taut over his shoulders and hunkered closer to the fire. "Sometimes us 'little creatures' do stupid things what seem right at the time."

Azriel sat back and stared with somber eyes into the glowing coals. "I do not know that I would have done the same."

Edric inhaled deeply, also watching the lulling flicker. "Well…a man don't know what he's capable of until the moment, does he?"

"I am ashamed of myself."

"Don't be. You don't know me. Not really. Who am I to you, anyway? Who's anyone?"

"You should seek to be a good neighbor, like the Good Samaritan. But I, as an Angel…" His fingers reached his lips and softly drummed.

"Here," said Edric. "What's this Good Samaritan you all are talking about? What's so good about him?"

Azriel raised his head and stared with the faraway look Edric found so disturbing. "The Good Samaritan? You do not know the story?"

"I've heard the words but I'm not a churched man, Azriel."

"The Good Samaritan," he said slowly. "There was once a man who went traveling from Jerusalem to Jericho, when suddenly he was set upon by robbers. They stripped him of his finery, beat him, and stole all his goods, leaving him for dead. It happened that a Pharisee came down that road, but when he saw the man, he passed by on the opposite side without even examining him to see if he were still alive. At length, a priest came along, and when he too, saw him, he also passed him by, walking as far from him as he could get. But when a Samaritan traveler came upon him, he was moved with pity. Without pause, he approached the victim, cleansed his wounds with wine and precious oils, bandaged them, and helped him onto his own animal, taking him to an inn to care for him. The next day, the Samaritan needed to continue on his business, but he withdrew two silver coins, giving them to the innkeeper, saying, 'Take care of him. If you spend more than what I have given you, I shall repay you when I return.'"

Azriel's voice dwindled to silence while Edric considered the story. "And this Samaritan didn't know that poor bastard?" he asked gently.

"No. In fact, their people were enemies."

"Then why'd he go and do it?"

"Why did you?"

A rustling in the thickets allowed Edric the opportunity to consider the question. He stared blankly into the dark and shivered when the cold crept up his curved spine. He never could come up with a satisfactory answer.

⁂

After a dreamless night, they mounted up and rode silently.

Irritated, Edric often looked back at Azriel, who wore the same glassy stare mile after mile. "What you staring at?" he asked at last.

"I am staring at *you*," Azriel replied sluggishly, rolling with the horse's uneven stride. "You puzzle me. Your faith is turned so easily aside by the least little offense, and you lose all the foothold you gained. Is faith so fragile in you Little Creatures? Take you, for instance. When you were a child you say a prayer that is not immediately answered and it is all finished for you. There is no God, to your way of thinking. And Hugh Varney. He slowly dies from a tumor eating at his insides. He looks faith in the face, and sees a blank wall. You and Hugh Varney are very much alike."

Edric smirked. "I'm certain he'd be glad to hear that bit of news." Standing in the stirrups, Edric rubbed his rump before settling down again. "And what about you? What about your faith? Hasn't it been shaken?"

"*My* faith? But Edric, I have certainty."

He smiled at the absurdity of it all. "You're an angel…but you aren't an angel."

"I shall be again. You still do not believe it, do you? Hugh Varney believes. He wants to."

"Go on! Not him! He's too clever."

Azriel scowled. "What would it take, Edric? A miracle? Most of you Little Creatures will never experience a miracle but have faith nonetheless. 'Blessed are they who believe but have not seen.'"

Absently, Edric stroked the horse's thick mane between his fingers, leaning into its rocking motion. Most of the time he ignored Azriel's urging, but for the first time since childhood, Edric tried to contemplate faith, so distant from the reality of his life. Saints, angels, God. When he used to think of it, his mind would fill with those rare images of church when he and his fellow villagers would stand far in the back, shadowed by the vestibule's arch, well behind the bejeweled backs of the wealthier merchants and lords. He remembered the gleam of golden crosses, and the sparkle of a ring on the priest or bishop. The strange aroma of incense lingered like mist just above the heads of those before him.

It smelled of foreign places, spice merchants on sailing ships, and markets in alien cultures.

Once, he shouldered forward so he could see. There were acolytes in starched white vestments, boys his age, but certainly far above him in rank. Their faces were clean, their demeanors haughty. Strident bells chimed when the host was elevated and the assembly murmured their amens to the priest's Latin chant.

Those were the images he held of God, something far away and golden, far from him and all he was.

Yet Azriel insisted it was all different from that. Of course Azriel was a lunatic…but he was also a monk.

"It's all a lot to take, isn't it," Edric began slowly. "I mean… what does it all signify? I seen Jesus up there on a cross, but I don't know what it's all for."

The stiff lines on Azriel's face softened. "'No one has greater love than this,'" said Azriel softly, "'to lay down one's life for one's friends.'"

Edric scratched his head. "You mean Jesus?"

"Yes."

Edric contemplated the yellow rapeseed fields they passed and the blue sky opening before them. His eyes squinted. "Who's his friends?"

"*You* are, though you do not seem to realize it. Our Lord died as an example of obedience to God for the sake of his friends."

"Blind me! You mean God expects us to die for some other poor bastard?"

"As you say."

"Well!" Edric grasped the reins and shook his head. "I'm not going to die for no fool."

"What if God asked you to?"

"He hasn't done too much for me lately."

Azriel postured and almost lost his balance on the sway-backed mount. "He gave you life!"

"And I already told you what I think of that!"

"What of Margery?"

Edric's heart contracted, and he growled, "What about her?"

"He gave you her."

His laugh was more like a bark. "What was I to her, anyway? I haven't got her now, have I?"

"'Ask and it shall be given you.'"

He puffed a breath. "I just ask, eh? Will she fall out of the sky like you? Oh. I forgot. You're not a sarding angel. You're a sarding monk."

"Have you asked?"

"Devil take you, Azriel or Brother Peter, or whatever the hell you'd be called! I'm not asking for something I can't have. I may be a fool, but I'm no damned fool!"

"Edric," he sighed. "You are not listening to me."

"You haven't said naught worth listening to."

"God hears, Edric. God listens."

Azriel was out of reach of his fists, but not of his tongue. "What about *you*, then? Has he heard *you*? You've been whining since the day I met you. 'I speak, but God don't answer!' Preach to someone who gives a damn!"

The silence satisfied. Edric did not need to look back to know how his remarks struck a blow to Azriel. After a time, the silence began to wear thin, and Edric cursed himself before looking back.

Paler than before, Azriel hung over the saddle. One bump might knock him loose. "I realize now what a great gift it was being an Angel." Thin as tissue, his voice crackled above the rhythmic thud of heavy hoofs. "I did not appreciate it. I took it for granted. To be in God's presence, in His love for all time—no wonder it is unimaginable to you. You live in this crust of a body, deaf to everything except your own selfishness and sin. You do not listen to the longing wail of your soul waiting out this life. I see. I see it now." Limply, he dropped his head back, beard-stubbled throat exposed to the wind. "No. I do not hear His voice as I used to, but if I am very still and very patient his spirit still calls to me. I feel his presence. But I am still very far from him—as you are."

"I wish you would just leave that kind of talk," Edric grumbled uneasily.

"Edric, why do you find it so hard to believe I am an Angel?"

Edric heaved his shoulders. "And why is it so hard for *you* to believe that you're that mad monk?"

Edric rode several yards before noticing Azriel's horse was not beside him. When he looked back, the horse was grazing along the verge and Azriel hung limply, lips drawn downward and his eyes fixed glassily at the road. A twinge of guilt poked Edric's heart. "Ah now." Kicking the horse's flank, he ambled his beast back toward Azriel. From top to toe, Edric studied him, dirty like himself, disheveled, bruised. "It isn't as bad as all that, is it?"

"What is there for me? If this is all, then what is the use?"

"I've asked m'self that many a time." Pushing on the saddle pommel Edric adjusted his seat and sniffed the marshy air. Flushed from the thickets, a pair of mourning doves keened upward.

Though it was true that most of the time Edric made no plans beyond the day itself, at least his mind was whole even if his body was not. What must it be like, he wondered, to grasp at the simplest of concepts—like who one was—and not be able to divine the answers? Life was frightening enough. Azriel was in many ways like a child, fearful, lost, and too proud to ask. The image softened Edric's mood. "Maybe…you're to be a man now. Ever think of that?"

Azriel's red-rimmed eyes glossed. "But I do not understand the nature of Man."

Edric snorted and leaned back. "Welcome to humanity." Softening, Edric leaned forward. "What do *you* want to do, Azriel? Do you want to go home to a monastery? I'll…I'll take you to one if you want."

"I *do* want to go home." Suddenly, dreadfully, Azriel sobbed.

Holy Mother. "Shall I take you on to Pershore? I'll give you the horses and you can give them back to them monks. Does that satisfy?"

"You do not understand."

Over the rise a horseman clambered, hauling his frantic mount to a rearing halt. "Get out of the road!" he cried, wiping the sweat from his face with a sleeve.

"What's *your* hurry!" sneered Edric.

"Did you just come from Evesham?" asked the man. "I'm needing to know if Hugh Varney is still there."

Edric avoided glancing at Azriel. "We might have. But I don't know naught about a Hugh Varney." Azriel's disquieting lack of reaction to Edric's obvious lie lay like a stone in his belly.

"He's the bailiff hereabouts. We got a murderess back in Comberton. A man killed in his own stable. An innkeeper."

Edric tightened the reins when he felt the horse gather under him. He trotted it in a circle, relieving the piebald's tension. "The innkeeper in Comberton? I'll be damned." Glancing at Azriel, he beamed. "So prayers *are* answered!"

"They got the woman what did it, but they're still searching for her companion. Some cripple. He stole some horses and ran away, leaving her. That's a knave if ever I heard."

Edric's smile hung frozen. His heart stiffened, trying to deny the inconceivable. "What...what does the woman look like? Have you seen her?"

"Aye. It was me what caught her. She's a right comely lass. Bright ginger hair, green eyes. I don't mind saying I'd murder for her too, but I don't think I'd be such a fool as to leave her behind."

"Where've they got her?"

"Keeping her at the inn. Some monks keeping watch of her. When Sir Hugh arrives, I'm sure they'll hang her. A pity. A pretty lass, that." He waved and clucked to the horse. "I must be off. God keep you."

Edric clutched at his chest, pressing on it to force the air back in. "Blessed, blessed Mary, Azriel! That's Margery! What's the fool woman gone and done?"

Azriel's usual calm fluctuated. Pink spots appeared on his cheeks. "Do you accuse her so quickly?" he murmured. "Perhaps she did nothing. What did *you* do?"

"I didn't do naught!"

"I do not understand. What does he mean they will 'hang' her?"

"You *are* a lackwit, aren't you? They'll hang her! Kill her!"

"*Kill* her? But why?"

"Because murder is against the law, and they think she done it!"

"Did she?"

"How the hell would *I* know?" Wringing his hands, he rode along helplessly with the piebald that wandered toward the verge and began nibbling on sweet young stalks.

"Sir Hugh sang the same lament. I do not understand what is so bad about dying? Our Lord did it."

"Sometimes you're so stupid it makes me teeth hurt. Dying is…well…it's *dying* that's what it is! It's a terrible thing to die, especially for naught."

"Must one die for something? After all, death is the beginning of one's eternity. It should be a time of rejoicing."

Edric leaned over, grabbed Azriel's shirt, and dragged him forward perilously between the horses. "Harken to me, you stupid whoreson! No one wants to die, get me? Heaven or no. We don't like it. It scares us to our marrow!"

Azriel raised his hand to wipe the spittle from his cheek. "There is no need to—"

Shaking him, Edric curled his other hand to a trembling fist. "No one wants to die, least of all for someone else's crime."

"But our Lord did."

"And he's God, isn't he? Already knew what's what, didn't he? The rest of us…" He opened his fingers suddenly and released Azriel. "Bless me, Azriel. What are we going to do?"

Motionless, Azriel remained upright and stiff. For a long time he weighed Edric's words. "Then…we should rescue her," he said at last. "Should we not?"

Swinging his head in renewed panic, Edric's mind furiously worked, but nothing came of it. "I dunno! Azriel, I can't breathe!" He leaned over, inhaling the sharp tang of horseflesh. "I'm just a cripple beggar and you're a—oh hell!"

Azriel studied him curiously. He leaned over to be eye to eye with Edric. "Is this human love? This is very interesting."

Whipping his body upright, Edric slashed at the air uselessly. "Oh God!" He wailed. "Oh blessed Jesus! Someone's got to help her!"

"Is that a prayer?" Azriel asked, sitting back with a smug expression. "I did not think you believed in God."

"I dunno. I don't care. I just want her to be safe. But I got to do more than pray!"

"You can start by praying, and the rest will fall into place."

Azriel swelled with renewed confidence, but Edric only glared at him. "Why should I trust what you say? You're a lunatic."

Grinning, Azriel leaned back on the horse and crossed his arms over his chest. "You were the answer to *my* prayer. Surely you could also be the answer to hers."

Praying. That was only for monks and fools, Edric decided. It never did work for Edric himself. He stared up the lonely road, worrying at a hangnail with a crooked tooth. What was Margery to him, anyway? *A whore, that's what.* She admitted it.

A sickening feeling twisted his gut. He swallowed. "Well...do you think I should kneel, Azriel?"

Azriel leaned confidentially toward him. "It certainly would do no harm."

"Bless me." Grunting, Edric dismounted and dragged the horse to the verge. He tossed the reins to Azriel before looking up the road one way and then down the other. Awkwardly, Edric knelt in the quiet of the damp undergrowth. His eyes followed scudding clouds over a gray-edged sky. "Um...dear Lord...I'm not good at this." He turned to Azriel still on horseback who regarded him with a tender expression. "Ah Azriel! I feel like the world's biggest fool."

"Go on. It is all well."

Rolling his eyes, Edric looked upward again, sensing the almighty looking sternly down on him. "Well, Lord. You know how it is and all. I...I haven't been very good. I been doing a lot of sinning, I reckon, but…you aren't given me much to work with!

It's just that Margery...I know I'm not worth much and she's just a whore, but the truth of it is…" He slid his gaze toward Azriel who gestured encouragement with a brightening face. "I reckon…I love the silly cow." There was no chance to hold back an unexpected gush of tears, and they rushed down his cheeks faster than he could swat them away. "God Almighty," he gasped. "I love her! And I don't want to see no hurt come to her. I'm not asking for much. I'm not even asking for a miracle…unless you want to make one. I'm only asking that you help me save her, like I done for this lunatic of yours. That's all. I reckon I can do the rest. Er...amen."

"That was very well done, Edric."

Edric wiped the wet from a reddened cheek. "'Ask and it will be given you,' right Azriel? That's what them monks told me too."

"That is correct, Edric."

"Well I asked and it sarding well better be given. Come along." Azriel paused while Edric mounted and yanked on the reins. "What's amiss, Azriel?"

"You are obviously this cripple they seek. How can you simply show yourself? Will they not 'hang' you, too?"

Edric smacked his forehead. "And if Hugh Varney comes along, they'll take *you* again! Damn! I didn't think out me prayer enough. I hope God'll make it work anyway." He kicked the piebald's flanks sharply and hurried up the road ahead of the lazier gait of Azriel's horse.

CHAPTER TWENTY-THREE

Hugh crouched over the writing desk, scratching on the parchment by the weak light of a flickering candle. Afraid he would not survive the journey back, he decided to write out all in a will, making certain Madelina knew how loyal Sebastian had been. "He shall get his due," he muttered, laying the quill aside.

The ache was not so bad, probably due to a tincture Sebastian prepared, and he sat back, resting his head against the chair. A vague disturbance and flickering light filtered through the shutters. When the noises grew louder, he rose and walked to the window.

Sebastian suddenly burst through the door.

"My lord, forgive me for disturbing you—"

"What, by the saints, is going on, Sebastian?"

"A fire! There is a fire in the courtyard! But worse! That monk has escaped. Disappeared!"

"Disappeared…" Hugh sank to his chair. "How could he disappear? Simply walk out…"

"I do not know, my lord. It is being investigated. Perhaps the fire was a diversion."

"From whom? Who would help this madman? Who…but God Himself?"

"My lord—"

Pressing his hands against the table, Hugh grunted and rose. He jabbed a finger at Sebastian. "I want that man back!"

"No one knows where he is."

"Someone must know!" Wavering a moment, Hugh gleamed with renewed strength. "Saddle the horses. We are going after him."

"But my lord. You…you…"

Hugh smiled. "Sebastian. Whatever this man is…well…you must admit, there is more to him than we originally thought. If there is a chance, then I must take it."

Perplexed, Sebastian sidled up to Hugh and gently touched his arm. "My lord, you are not saying you truly believe this man to be an angel?"

Hugh raised his chin, searching the smoke-blurred rafters for the words, but found only dust and cobwebs. "I do not know. I am beginning to wonder."

Straining to stay mounted, Hugh dug into the horse's flanks with his thighs and gripped the saddle pommel, dismissing Sebastian's worried expression. What did it matter? What did it all matter? Miraculously, this strange man escaped, simply walked out the door. There must be more to this. Did Sebastian not see? Or was it only for those already under a death sentence who could see 'beyond the ether'?

He ran the conversations with Azriel through his mind, touching on each nuance and gesture. He gave himself new interpretations while mulling them, changing his mind and pulling the phrases apart until every word was analyzed and dissected.

If an angel, if *truly* an angel, then it was a remarkable exchange. He wanted to hear more, he wanted to ask, to discover…

With a sigh, he leaned back. How tired he was! Azriel said he would not see the end of the year, but was it to be sooner than that? *I have to know! So much depends upon it!* Sliding his glance toward Sebastian, he almost sobbed. To Sebastian go the spoils. All of it. His home, his wealth, his own flesh and blood. What would

Sebastian make of his new temporary dynasty? Could he be trusted? Could anyone? Mutely he shook his head. *I must not do this.* He must not begin to second guess his decisions. He did not have that luxury.

The countryside was a verdant blur of misty flat plain and hill, dark copse, and gnarled hedge. He blanked his mind and let it wander over the vista before him until the grim expression of the squire intruded. "Sebastian, do you write to Teffania?"

Sebastian's face blushed, and he ducked his head out of habit. "Yes, my lord. Often."

"What do you write of?"

The blush deepened, but he managed to raise his chin. "Of…love, my lord. And…mundane things."

"I have not written to Lady Madelina." Hugh rolled his shoulders in unexpected discomfort. "I meant to, but…" Azriel's appearance in his life, like the sword of doom and truth, seemed to prevent further subterfuge. The time for that was over. "I must tell her the truth, Sebastian. It has come to that. Should I be a coward and do it by letter?"

"No, my lord."

"I know, dammit." Rolling the smooth leather of the reins in his fingers, he stared down at them, feeling the horse beneath him with its wide belly and rocking tread. Vibrant. The horse, the landscape, the chapped-nosed squire, the grunting men-at-arms and archers behind, all proceeded with an undeniable vitality, a vitality that was seeping from him.

They made camp for the night and Hugh slept fitfully. In the morning his weariness disgruntled his mind. Could none of it make any sense? What could help?

A rickety spire rose from the lee side of a hill. Hugh's gray eyes watched it and he raised his hand to stop the little troupe. "I want to go to the church yonder to pray, Sebastian."

"Yes, my lord."

They veered off the road and over the meadowland. The horses clopped over the gravel courtyard of the small stone church.

Hugh's horse moved just up to the portico. Before them rose a wide rim of worn steps that skirted the church's arched door, smelling of wet stone. The beast stopped, nuzzling the bottom step and at the singular sprouts of grass shooting up from between the gray, chiseled granite.

Gritting his teeth, Hugh dismounted, and leaned against the horse to breathe. Drawing courage from the war-horse's musky vigor, he gripped the saddle and pushed off. Sebastian was instantly by his side. Hugh smiled at him, resisting the urge to lean on his shoulder.

The long shadows of the church stretched over them, cooling as they entered the nave. Looking within, Hugh noted pillars, crypt, and altar with its hint of sparkling gold, veiled by candle smoke. Drawing forward, his spurs clicked against the tiled floor. Echoes cascaded from arch to arch and whispered back with the tangy aroma of incense.

A shadow moved in the transept, startling Hugh, until it formed into the shape of the priest. Approaching with a blank expression, the priest bowed when he was no more than a few paces away. "Peace be with you," he said. His voice and skin were like old parchment.

Hugh only acknowledged the cleric's greeting with a nod. He turned swiftly to Sebastian and then back to the priest with a cautious air. "Father, I would speak with you."

Sebastian stepped back, allowing the shadows to enclose him.

"Do you desire to be shriven?" asked the priest.

"No, no," he answered distractedly. "But could we sit? I…I am not feeling well these days."

The priest led him to a small chapel filled with many tall, thin tapers, their waxy smoke a comforting fragrance. Hugh sat on a wooden bench that creaked under his weight and then the priest sat opposite him. Glancing over the priest's yellowed face and wispy white hair, Hugh sighed and wearily sat back. "Well…how to begin? Father, I believe…I believe…I have met an angel. What do you say to that?"

The priest's brows rose, but he said nothing, waiting for Hugh to continue.

"They say he is a madman, but I do not quite believe it. He knows things, he says things. How do you feel about Heaven?"

"I do not understand your meaning?"

"I mean, is it a place?"

"It is the joyous city of God, where the streets are paved with gold."

"So…it *is* a place, then, like this place—"

"Oh, not like *this* place, my lord. Even this humble church in all its beauty cannot compare to the city God prepares for us. 'In my Father's house there are many dwelling places.'"

Hugh frowned. "Are you certain, Father? It seems that God would not make Heaven like what we know here…"

"And why not? This is the familiar. Who has been telling you otherwise? This mad man who calls himself an angel?"

"He said that God pulls us out of ourselves, and leaves behind our old skin like laundry."

"Like *laundry*! Forgive me, my lord, but I cannot believe a man of your ilk would listen to such…such…tripe!"

Hugh shifted uneasily, now uncertain of his memory. "He was an exquisite speaker, I can assure you, and spoke eloquently of God's love and forgiveness. It all made perfect sense…at the time."

"You have been duped, my lord, and in the worst way. You did not pay this man, did you? Such charlatans prey on those who seek simple answers to God's complex universe."

Is that what he did? He stared at the waxy puffs and valleys in his own lined palms and wondered. Was his willingness to believe Azriel only his way of grasping at straws? Yet Azriel's words, his manner! "Do not angels roam the earth, Father? Do they not speak and instruct men?"

"That is so."

"Have *you* ever met an angel?"

"As pious a life as I live, *I* have not had the privilege. Few have."

The dubious lilt to his voice annoyed, and Hugh eyed him critically. "You do not believe me."

"It is not a matter of belief, my lord. It is more a matter of what God wills. Do you think God would send an angel to you?"

"Why *not* me?"

"It is just that *I* have never seen an angel."

"Maybe you are not as pious as you thought!"

"My lord!" Slowly, the priest rose. "There is no need to insult. You came to me for help and I have granted it. If you think you have seen and talked to an angel…well, it is not for me to…to…."

"Question my sanity? I see. Angels are only for pious clerics."

"My lord!"

"Thank you, Father, for your insight. I shall give it all the consideration it is due." He stomped away from the astonished priest and swept up Sebastian.

"Did you get the answers you sought, my lord?" Sebastian asked, rushing beside Hugh's invigorated steps.

"No," he grumbled.

"Then…where to now?"

Hugh stopped in the portico and looked out to the countryside. A mist had encroached, veiling the hills and vanishing the heavy-headed copses to vague spindles. He sighed out his frustration in a silky cloud of breath. "I do not know, Sebastian. Pershore, maybe. Yes. Let us back to Pershore, let the damned monks deal with it."

His boots mashed the wet gravel into the slush beneath while Sebastian struggled to keep pace with him.

The squire took the reins from one of the archers and held the horse steady while Hugh mounted. Stroking the horse's cheek, Sebastian gazed up at Hugh. "What did the priest say? May I know?"

Hugh gazed blankly ahead, his mustache frowning deeply. "He said do not be an arse, Sir Hugh. He said do not waste your time on fancies. He said die like a man and stop whining. That is what he said. Mount, Sebastian. Let us get back to Pershore."

Setting his jaw, the squire returned to his horse. Hugh did not wait to see him mounted before he urged his own horse forward. Soon, they regained the main road and, drooping in his saddle, Hugh rode silently.

The fog did not move, but sprawled lethargically along the plains, obscuring the stone walls and wattled fences that framed the road. Sounds smothered under the weight of the blue mist. Distant hoof beats, vague and removed, seemed further away, but when a rider appeared abruptly out of the fog, even Hugh's horse was startled.

The destrier reared, and Hugh, heart racing, yanked with all his might on the reins to bring the horse to heel. "Whoa!" he cried, sneering at the rider whose mount pulled up short.

Wet from the mist, the man's face dragged into worry. "My lord! I…I beg pardon. I did not see you."

"You should know better than to career down a road like this in a fog." He walked the horse in a nervous circle to calm him.

"Am I close to Evesham? I am looking for Sir Hugh Varney."

"Well you almost killed him."

"My lord…Sir Hugh? Again, my lord, I beg your mercy."

"Never mind that. What do you want?"

CHAPTER TWENTY-FOUR

Amused, Latimer watched the emergence of Herbert's assertiveness. First, Herbert supervised the woman's incarceration, keeping her in their inner room while they took the outer one. Then he read the psalms to her in hopes of drawing out a confession, and finally he left her alone when she proved immovable.

Latimer stepped aside to allow the exasperated Herbert to leave the room, this time supposedly in search of water. Latimer knew the young monk felt uncomfortable around the lovely woman. Dirty and stinking, she bristled with visceral femininity. Whatever her relationship to Edric in all his filth, it seemed wholly appropriate.

Latimer peered into the room and spied her sitting by the window. She slumped forward, ginger hair draped over her face in brilliant vermilions and rusts. "You say nothing," he said, startling her. She sat up, and pushed the heavy locks back over her forehead with dirt-darkened fingers. Her eyes followed him when he moved into the room. "He is not here," he said of Herbert. "He went downstairs." Stopping at the opposite end, he leaned against the damp wall, resting his hands in the small of his back. He studied her studying him. "Why do you say nothing?" he asked softly.

She frowned, the muscles wrinkling her chin. "What would I say?"

"What really happened. You know, do you not?"

She glared with a defiant lift of her chin. "What good would it do me to say?"

He chuckled, causing her to snort scornfully. "Quite so. You are clever."

"Not clever enough."

"They will hang you."

"And you'd let them? What sort of monk are you?"

"The cautious sort. There is far more at stake. More than I can explain to you."

"I happen to think my life is worth some explanation."

Latimer smiled, delighted. "You *are* a vivacious one! No wonder Edric wanted us to look for you."

The halo of her hair caught the meager light in bright pulsations, like a red welt. "What do you know of it? I know that isn't true."

"Oh, but you are wrong. He *asked* us to look for you." He studied her changing expressions. "Poor Edric. Did you know that wretched innkeeper beat him within an inch of his life just because of his lameness? I am certain the man would have killed him if I had not intervened."

At last, the protective sheath fell away from her face. "The innkeeper? Oh, God."

"Yes. While you were…*with* that man in the stable—and I assume you were—Edric was recovering here, in these rooms."

A tear, her first, rolled from an eye. "I didn't know…I swear…"

"I know." Almost he moved to comfort her, but changed his mind and turned away. "And now here you are."

"What will you do?"

He watched her wipe the wet from her round cheek with a hand. He could see how Edric or any man could be enamored of her, yet what was her connection to the cripple? "What will *I* do? What *is* there for me to do?"

"So you *would* let me hang?"

"Should *I* hang? Was he not the very stench of humanity? Is the world a poorer place without him?"

"'Thou shalt not kill'," she murmured.

Poised in mid-step, Latimer swiveled. "Do you presume to quote Scripture to *me*?"

"No." She shook her head and sat back against the wall. "I don't know. I don't care no more."

Sighing with a mixture of impatience and scorn, Latimer hastened across the room to the door. Pausing, he glared at her. She slumped forward again, allowing her abundant hair to shield her. What was this wretched woman to him? A spike of guilt prickled his spine. He knew they would hang her and enjoy it. It did not much matter to them her guilt or innocence. No wonder Brother Peter wallowed in fantasy, if for nothing else than to shield himself from man's inhumanity to his neighbor.

He quickly exited, closed the door, and leaned heavily against it on the other side. What would Peter do in these circumstances? He chuckled sardonically. Of course, Brother Peter would never have gotten himself into such a predicament.

Latimer slid down the wall and sat alone in the dimness of the outer room, clutching his knees. He had been truly carried away by the moment, afraid the innkeeper was going to say something, ruin all his plans. Was it worth a human life?

He recalled what those in the inn were doing to Edric. There was certainly nothing human in that. No. What Latimer did was inexcusable, but not unforgivable. He satisfied himself with that.

What was he to do about the woman? She was blameless, at least where the innkeeper's death was concerned. Should she hang for such a thing?

Latimer closed his eyes, shutting out the woman. He attempted to open his mind to God, but the long moments wriggled past, and the sobering thought that he could not concentrate on a prayer worried his brow. He opened his eyes. Every situation, every hurt in the past always opened itself to prayer. Why did it elude him this time? The notion of his own guilt rose again but he irritably dismissed it. "*Mea culpa, mea maxima culpa…*" Lips parted with the words, but only a whisper came forth. He could not let her die. Not on *his* account. No matter what other sin she committed, he could not allow it.

Tightening his embrace of his knees, Latimer considered. The fully formed thought spilled forth. He had already taken desperate measures. What was one more?

Rising, he grasped the cold door ring and pulled it open, standing under the lintel's shadow.

She looked up cautiously and narrowed her eyes.

Taking his time to carefully close the door, Latimer leaned against it, drawing his strength from the oak. "You are right. I cannot let you die. You must…escape."

"Escape? With that lot out there? They'd hang me themselves just for the sport of it!"

"It must be at night when all are asleep. If I tell you what to do, can you manage to do it?" The idea quickly wove itself in his mind. He was amazed at how swiftly the deceit formed. He remembered Brother Peter often cheerfully exhorted him on his artful mendacity, but Latimer always took offense, never believing it true. But now…

"Truly?" she asked, slowly rising.

"Yes."

The brilliantly verdant eyes traveled the length of him. "What kind of man are you?"

"Do you want your freedom or not?"

"How do I know I can trust you?"

Indignant at first, Latimer gradually mellowed. What was there truly for him to say? His vows seemed of little worth now. All was falling apart and trickling between his fingers. The only thing left to concentrate on was Brother Peter. He licked the salty moisture from his upper lip. "You will simply have to. You have no choice." Stepping forward he stood over her. "I want you to escape so that I may get on with my own business. That is all."

Her fingers curled around the tips of her brassy locks and wound round and round. A trembling lip showed the only hint of her fear. "I don't want to die," she whispered.

"And you shan't. Tonight when it is darkest, you will wear my extra cassock and escape easily. Do you understand? Go back to wherever you came from or disappear completely, but do not stop, talk to no one, and leave this parish."

"Aye," she said with an earnest nod. "At darkest night."

"Yes." Carefully opening the door, he peered out for Brother Herbert, but he was still below. Creeping forward he went to the small coffer of extra clothes and retrieved his old cassock. Running callused palms fondly over the age-thinned cloth his stomach turned. "An abomination," he muttered, thinking of the woman wearing it, yet surely he was guilty of a far greater abomination. He shook his head, trying not to think of it while returning to the inner room. He solemnly handed her the bundle. "Here. Sit on it, and then sleep on it to hide it. When we retire for the night, put it on. I will come later. Do not move from this spot until then."

Margery nodded, clutching the dark parcel before stuffing it beneath her.

He fought down his revulsion. It all seemed to be a good plan. Latimer breathed easier. When she was away, they could pursue Brother Peter again. If Hugh Varney captured him and actually came to judge this murder, he might bring the monk. Nothing was a certainty anymore. Not even God. Where was He? Latimer could not summon the sense of His presence, feeling a particular slice of coldness that God did not surround him like He used to.

No matter. This would pass. When everything was on its proper course again, all would be well.

He sat on a stool beside the window and waited silently for night to fall.

CHAPTER TWENTY-FIVE

Moon-washed trees and spiked hedges hid them. They dragged the horses through the woods above the village. "I still don't understand why we have to return the horses *now*," whispered Edric. "Can't we do it later when we're all safely away?"

"That will not do. I cannot continue to use them knowing they are stolen goods."

"Isn't there no way around them commandments?"

Azriel smiled. "I am afraid not."

Stopping at the edge of the wood, Edric gazed down. The greatest smoke came from the inn hidden behind a single row of houses and shops. The faint yellow glow of its great hearth diffused outward even through the closed shutters, painting the edges of thatched roofs and daubed walls with flickering amber.

"Edric, I have been lately thinking about sacrifice," whispered Azriel. "It seems to be something we are faced with at the moment. Me risking capture, and you risking death. Risking death," he chuckled. "That sounds rather silly. How can death be a risk! Our Lord sacrificed His life when on earth, but…I suppose it is harder for you Little Creatures to do the same, is it not?"

Why don't he shut it, already? thought Edric, glancing nervously into the dark blue undergrowth.

"I wonder…Would you die for *her*?"

Edric turned sharply toward the madman's shadowed face. "Here you are, spouting obedience and God's will, and you don't know naught about any of it. You're a piece of work, Azriel."

"But Edric, *would* you?"

Edric licked a dry crust from his lips, feeling a pang in his chest that would not cease since his hearing about Margery's predicament. "Aye," he answered softly. "I…I reckon I would."

"Why?" Azriel's eyes shone like ice in the darkness. He sidled closer, leaning over to be near Edric's shaded face. "But you said dying is a fearful thing. Why would you do it?" A sudden burst of inspiration glistened in his eyes. "Because you love her! Is that it?"

Edric sneered at Azriel. He wanted to curse him for making him feel his helplessness, but he choked on the reply. With reluctance, he nodded instead.

Azriel gazed down into the town, its flickering, smoky shadows hiding all its secrets. "Strange…"

Edric pointed down toward the inn. "That's it. What do we do now?"

"We must take the horses down and leave them. Then we can assess what best to do about the captive."

"Take the horses down *there*? Are you mad?"

Before Azriel could reply, Edric slammed his hand over the madman's mouth, feeling Azriel's exasperated breath on his knuckles. Motioning Azriel to silence, Edric listened deeply into the dense shadows.

Footsteps. Definitely footsteps, stealthy and slow. Was someone stalking them?

Releasing Azriel, Edric grabbed both leads, pulled them forward, and got behind the beasts to smack their rumps, sending them off. He tugged on Azriel's tunic and dragged him into the brush, pulling him down beside him into a crouch.

A figure appeared at the edge of the horizon and stopped to watch the horses trotting away toward the village. The form paused, listened, considered. It took a tentative step closer, stopped, and waited again.

Edric held his breath and tried to keep perfectly still, worrying that Azriel would give them away.

The figure tarried only a moment longer until suddenly breaking into a run. It rushed past their hiding place with the crack of snapping twigs. Edric leapt from the dark and tackled him to the soft duff. The stranger expelled a breath with a grunt. Edric drew his knife. He raised it, but Azriel grabbed his wrist and yanked it back. "Edric! No!"

"Edric?"

Abruptly releasing his hold, Edric tumbled backwards off the struggling figure. "*Margery*?"

"Edric! God be praised!"

"I told you prayer works," huffed Azriel smugly.

Margery sat up and rubbed the back of her head over the cowl. Momentarily stunned, Edric shook his head and knelt beside her. "Margery! What…what are you doing here? And dressed like that?"

"What are *you* doing here?"

He stood back, his knife a forgotten appendage to his hand. The sight of her again paralyzed him, and then the unfamiliar specter of her wearing the loosely fitting cassock puzzled further. "I come to rescue you."

She pushed back the hood, revealing a broad, silvered smile. "You did?"

"Greetings, Margery," said Azriel, quickly scanning their surroundings. "Hadn't we all best get to a safer place?"

Edric sheathed the knife and yanked her to her feet, but did not release her hand while he dragged her into the woods. He limped as much as always, but this time he moved with unmeasured swiftness. The blind path was suddenly no obstacle for him. Instead, he rambled easily over gnarled roots, shimmied through the most tangled growths, and skimmed effortlessly down steep inclines.

Finally, they all came to rest at a creek bed beside a waterfall.

Feeling the noise of the falls would shield them, they settled in a place with a clear starlit view of their surrounds.

Edric could not take his eyes off of her. Even when she settled down amid a soft pile of leaves and clutched her legs, he noted each position of every curl. "Are you well, Margery?"

"I am now. I see you found your friend. Why'd you come back?"

"I heard they was keeping you for a murder. You didn't do it, did you lass?"

"'Course not!"

"How'd you get free, lass? I know for a fact they've sent for Hugh Varney to judge you."

"I got away, is all," she said blankly, her face hidden by hair.

"Where'd you get the cassock?"

"Borrowed it."

Azriel yawned. "We will get a little rest, and before dawn move on," he said, finding his own comfortable spot in their cozy circle.

She lifted her face, eyes scouting the tangled darkness. "So Azriel, are you and Edric friends again?"

Azriel measured her. "I have never stopped being his friend. Simply because one disapproves of another's behavior does not invalidate the relationship."

She looked at Edric who shrugged. "I don't ken what he says half the time neither," he said in confidential tones.

"Humans!" Azriel muttered in disgust.

"Azriel," she said to him, shyly. "You're really a…an angel?"

Rolling his eyes, Azriel heaved his shoulder in a weary sigh. "Yes. Though you need not pretend you believe it. I know you Little Creatures cannot believe without some sort of miraculous display."

"It's only Edric said you were…that you thought…."

"I am a lunatic," he said with a grimace. "Let us just leave it at that." He rolled over with a frustrated sigh.

Margery stared with some regret at his back, until finally turning to Edric. Her smile spread across her cheeks. Sudden shyness made

Edric withdraw his gaze first. "I…never thought to see you again, Margery. I'm glad you're safe."

"Why *did* you come back, then?"

"I couldn't let them hang you."

"Hang a whore?"

He cringed and he nestled into a tight uneven mound. "Ah Margery. I reckon that isn't important now."

"Truly? Even if…if I… You made me angry, Edric! I might have done something foolish out of anger."

"Not murder?"

"No. I told you that. You believe me, don't you?"

Her cheeks appeared soft in the silvery light. He wanted so much to rub his own rough cheek against them. But even so, an ache in his heart forced him to assess her earnest expression. "You mean you whored again. After you left me."

"You made me so cross…" She lowered her face, but he saw it darken from a blush before the shadows hid all.

"Everything's different now, Margery. I don't think the same about naught no more. I'm even beginning to think that this here lunatic is an angel after all." Giddily, he laughed. What happened to him these last few days was unbelievable. Was it a dream? He should be angry with her, but he could not conjure it. Perhaps Azriel's presence made him feel forgiving.

They gazed at one another a long time. Margery's eyes narrowed, searching Edric's face with a scrutinizing eye. Gingerly, she reached out to stroke his bruise-puffed eye, but he pulled back. Scooting closer, she persisted, and touching him at last, stroked the cheek lengthily with a knuckle. "I…I heard what they done to you. Are you well, Edric? Were you hurt bad?"

"It wasn't naught," he said into his sleeve. "Just leave it, woman."

Her hand fell away, dropping into her lap. "Come morning, where will we go?"

"I dunno. I've not thought that far ahead." He scanned the dark woods, searching for movement or sounds. "I was using all me brain power to think of a way to save you. Seems you didn't need my help."

"Oh, I do. You don't know how much."

Glad she could not see him redden, he turned away. He eyed Azriel's slim profile laid out on the grass. His breath was deep. Probably asleep. *Look at him. Naught at all to worry about.* Slowly, he turned back toward Margery, measuring the round contours of her shadowy silhouette. The stars were brighter since the gibbous drifted behind the trees, painting only glimpses of her face. She told him she was nineteen but she looked older, much older in fact than the twenty-six he originally thought. *It's a hard life what ages a man…or a woman, I reckon.* Sometimes he felt far older himself. His life was one misery after another, but he had forged a life…of a sort. She did, too. He even dared imagine what life might have been like if he never stopped to help Azriel. To be sure, he would never have met Margery…or eaten well, or slept in a bed. But to not have met Margery, that would have been an immeasurable loss. The sight of her, the scent of her, quickened his soul.

"And so…." Licking his lips, he tried to think, to form words. "Where will you go off to?"

"I suppose it's back home for me. I reckon that's safe. Maybe…I'd best consider some of the lads there."

"What you mean 'consider'?"

"I want a husband and children, Edric. I can't be tumbling strangers for coins. It isn't a life."

"Oh." He tried to breathe but could not quite catch his breath. "Well. Then you'll be leaving us?"

Her brow arched. "What's to keep me here?"

He stared at her chin. He could not manage to look any higher. Her image was blurred anyway by a strangling panic that had sustained him during their frantic ride back toward the village. Even with her safe and sound beside him, the dread did not lessen.

For a long time he looked through her, thinking. It would all go on like it did before. Was that what life was for?

"Don't go, Margery," he rasped.

Softly, she asked, "Why?"

He scowled. "You know why."

"Do I?"

Her head tilted in an angle he found irritating, and he crouched forward, burrowing his cold hands under folded arms. "God's teeth, woman! Do I have to say?"

"Aye," she said with an impertinent nod to her head, making the wild curls bob. "You do."

It was too hard. He was not like other men. He could not just spout sweet things to women on command. Yet her eyes stared intently. He ducked his head, trying to swallow and soothe a helplessly roughened voice. "This is what I am, Margery. I'm just a crooked man with naught to his name." Shrugging filled the space, but it did not seem to offer enough explanation or clarify his position like he feebly hoped it might. "I'm just a wretched man…a lame man…who loves you like his soul was tearing out." He heaved a trembling sigh, grateful again that darkness blurred his features. *Well I said it. God help me.* The silence continued and he raised his eyes briefly just to see if she still sat there. He figured, knowing the circumstances, she might at least be kind about it. He hoped so.

Squirming under the pall of silence he finally rasped, "Say something, woman! If you'll mock me then be done with it."

"Mock you? You love me, but you still don't know me."

"Know you or not, it's not every day I tell a silly cow of a woman I love her."

"Do you want an answer?"

"Christ!" He ducked his head again, rubbing the back of his neck raw. "I don't! I just…"

Her throaty laughter made him cringe at first, but it never became a raucous guffaw or, worse, sniggering. It softened to a fine breath, and she gently shook her head from side to side. "Ah Edric. You silly fool. Can't a woman love two cripples in a lifetime?"

Looking up sharply, he stared at the gentle angle of her head and at the radiant curve of starlight limning a cheek. His heart grew warm with a furious rhythm. Scooting along his rump, he quickly enclosed her in his arms and took a kiss. When she surrendered to his embrace, any lingering doubts were cast aside. It seemed that it had been ages since he tasted her, and now he feasted, feeling suddenly he had a right to it.

"A most unusual show of affection," said Azriel, startling them. "Do you creatures truly find it appealing?"

Margery glared at Edric as if to ask whether she should answer, but Edric only sighed at her before turning to him and making an obscene gesture.

"I don't think I care to know what that means," Azriel flustered.

Edric waved a dismissive hand at him before gathering Margery up again. Her breasts felt soft against his chest, and the gentle bow of her back was perfect for his hands. To open his lips over hers and savor the sweetness from her mouth was almost unendurable.

Azriel wandered away back to his spot, and Edric laid Margery beside him in the grass. They kissed and stroked one another's faces, saying nothing. For the first time, life actually seemed worth living. He could imagine a future and even allowed himself the luxury of happiness, gathering it about him like a woolly cloak.

In the morning, the shock did not wear off. Turning to look at her in the gray light he was even more aware of what was offered him. He kissed her passion-swollen lips and prayed in his head a heart-felt thank you to God for his life, a formerly unimaginable offering.

"We had best move on," said Azriel, with unfamiliar urgency.

Edric's smile wore away. "You're right. It isn't safe here. Let's go on, Margery. We've got a lot of road to cover."

They quickly disappeared into the undergrowth, tangling on budding thistle. Azriel walked ahead while Edric valiantly struggled to clear the way for Margery. They kept silent, using their strength to move at a swift pace, trying to beat the sun before it rose. *Curse the sun!* thought Edric, eyeing the glowing horizon. *Of all mornings, there isn't no mist to be had!*

They reached the edge of the woods that fell away abruptly to the open brow of a hill, speckled by boulders and gouged by creeks. Beyond were more sheltering woods. Edric caught his breath while leaning against a tree. "We'll head to that brake."

Azriel nodded and glanced at Margery. "I don't suppose either of you have food?" she asked, but they both shook their heads.

"There's always food for an enterprising beggar," said Edric, winking to Azriel. "Or maybe…" Reaching toward Margery beside him, he caught her hand and gave it a squeeze. "Work for a baker. I reckon I can haul a cart if need be."

"Quaint," sniffed Azriel.

"We'd find a place for you, too, Azriel. I been through too much to let you on your own now."

"I am perfectly capable of being on my own."

"No you aren't. Look what happened to you the first time you tried it. No. You'd best come on with us, and no more fuss."

Startled, Azriel blinked at him. "Are you jesting?"

"I can't let a lunatic like you out and about. It's better than being locked up in a monastery, isn't it?"

"You assume I have nowhere else to go."

"Now look, Azriel—"

"You may be right, that is the humorous part," he sighed. "I thought I would be redeemed by now. That I would become an Angel again." Sourly he shook his head. "Perhaps…that is not to be."

Edric licked his lips, frowning at the large tears welling in Azriel's eyes. "Harken, Azriel. There's no use in doing that. You've got to face facts. Now Margery and me…we'll look after you. It isn't going to be easy, but at least it promises a roof over your head and food on the table. Bless me, that's more than I ever had! What do you say?"

Azriel ran his sleeve over his face, wiping most of the wet away. "That is very generous of you, Edric. Quite against your nature, in fact. But I see now it is becoming your nature." He heaved a hearty sigh and bobbed his head in a nod. "Yes. In the interest of friendship, I shall go with you. I am at your mercy at any rate, as you are perfectly right in all you said. I am *not* capable on my own. I see that now. I am completely dependent upon you and your beneficence."

"Don't worry yourself," he muttered, pulling up his sagging stockings and secretly measuring Azriel's strong legs to his own. "You'll work for it, never you fear."

"You offer so much," said Azriel, a look of disheveled gratitude brightening his face. "What have I given you?"

"I dunno. Maybe…something I've never had before, something I never dreamed of."

"What is that?"

He smiled crookedly. "Hope."

Azriel smiled. "Ah yes. That is the Divine Father's gift to all. You see that at last."

"He didn't give it me," he said shyly, glancing at Margery. "*You* did, you sarding lunatic."

"I am only the Divine Father's messenger."

"Aye. I reckon you are." Edric ran a finger under his nose and led them out across the slanted hillside, their focus on the dark woods ahead.

Edric's mind wandered, thinking about food and how he could steal his next meal. The lay of the land rambled in his mind, the Avon and a swineherd's hut just past the vale. He thought that a spicy piglet would taste good about now. Azriel was fast enough to tackle it, or maybe even Margery. He was too slow with his bad foot.

The thought of his lameness made him smile all the more at Margery. He hoped he could measure up to the memory of her sire, for he knew this is what she saw in him. *Maybe there is good in me.* Maybe there was good in everyone. Why was it so hard to believe before?

The shout threw every new thought into frayed shreds, flapping away like a pennon after a battle. He whipped his head up. The woods behind were now too far away, and the trees ahead still too distant for safety. As one, they broke into a run, even when the archers and Hugh Varney's footmen shouted again for them to stop.

CHAPTER TWENTY-SIX

I must look like death, thought Hugh, glancing again at Sebastian while they rode quietly to Comberton. Yet the curious thing was he felt better now than he had for weeks. No potions marred his thoughts or slowed his reflexes. He still felt a bloated discomfort, yet the stabbing pain seemed muffled within a deeper place. It could not be accounted for except for his personal conviction that it had to do, somehow, with Azriel.

Hugh made that point to Sebastian the other night when they hunkered over a brooding fire, warm bowls of porridge heating their cupped hands. Sebastian gave him that skeptical look which meant Hugh must be delirious from pain to imagine something so outrageous, and so Hugh had closed his lips. Where Sebastian was always a comfort, he appeared now to be a stranger. This man…this *boy* now doubted his veracity, his very mental faculties. Was this the child to whom he would leave his estates? And his precious daughter?

Hugh coiled the reins around his fingers and scowled. He had fought battles, killed, connived, and came close many times to dishonoring himself, yet always he persevered. When poor crops threatened, somehow he found food for himself and his serfs. There were threats to the land and those he loved, yet he fought them off himself. *And for what?* Narrowing his eyes at the horizon, he pointedly kept his gaze from Sebastian. *For this snip of a boy to take my wealth?* Worried he would die during one of his worse fits, he sent the letter to Madelina. He preferred she read of his illness from his own hand than hear of his death from some footman. In it, he made florid speeches regarding Sebastian; how he trusted him, how he felt akin to him. Now the words lay like festering bones on a discarded platter. He was treated like an invalid.

Brother Peter—strangely enigmatic in his dishevelment—held the key. Hugh felt better, he knew, because of Brother Peter…or was it Azriel? It was certainly not due to these physicians who gave up on him, nor these priests with their feeble encouragement, nor even Sebastian's condescension. He was certain there was more to Brother Peter than others suspected.

"I am tired of thinking!"

"My lord?"

Startled, Hugh blushed. Did he say that aloud? So many thoughts jousted for space, so many feelings squeezed his vitals. He glanced at the squire whose ashen cheeks and deeply smudged eyes bespoke concern, not mockery. Hugh suddenly felt deeply shamed. He rubbed his nose to hide his warmed cheeks. "Sebastian…there is so much to consider. You must be so weary of hearing me say this. I only ask for an open mind."

"Yes, my lord. Anything you wish."

"God's eyes! It is not a command."

Sighing, the squire gripped his saddle and shifted forward. "I…I want to understand you, your point of view. But *I* view this episode with some concern, my lord. Not only for your welfare but for your soul."

"My soul? What on earth are you talking about?"

"My lord, I worry that you pursue this man not out of obligation to Pershore Abbey, but because of some…some evil that has pervaded you."

"Evil? You think this monk evil?"

"His madness that curses all who know him? Yes. I think it *is* evil."

Hugh shook his head. "There is no evil here, Sebastian, except in the sense of a man dying before his time—"

"My lord, all men must die!"

The horse neighed piteously when Hugh hauled on the reins. The startled footmen and archers rattled to a halt clumsily behind them. "How *dare* you!" Hugh struggled at his scabbard, and with the hiss of steal on leather, yanked the blade free. It gleamed above his head. "You, whom I was to make my kin!"

Sebastian made no move except to fix his eyes on the deadly blade. Slowly, with a trusting expression, he turned his gaze toward Hugh's face and rested it there.

The longbows propped over the archers' shoulders clattered together when they huddled nervously.

The blade wavered, until Hugh's strength gave out and the sword fell, smarting his thigh with a slap. "Dear God in Heaven." His fingers loosened, and the heavy sword slipped from his hand, clanging to the ground.

Without taking his eyes from Hugh, Sebastian smoothly dismounted, retrieved the weapon, and gently held it forth to Hugh, hilt first.

Hugh's gloved hand covered his face, the sweat of his brow darkening the fingertips. For a long time he inhaled the unctuous leather, shutting his eyes from the unthinkable. What was the matter with him? Was he trying to *slay* the squire?

His lids were thick with emotion when he beheld Sebastian standing at his stirrup holding out the sword. A moan slipped from Hugh's lips when he shook his head. The squire urged the weapon upon him, raising it higher. Hugh's hand quivered, reaching forward and closing on the hilt. Without strength, Hugh lifted the sword and unsteadily sheathed it. "Forgive me, Sebastian," he whispered.

Sebastian mounted his horse. "There is nothing to forgive, my lord."

A mere few moments ago birds chirped from the sparse branches, and frogs interrupted the gurgle of the nearby Avon.

Hugh heard none of it now. Only his breathing filled his ears and the relentless pounding of blood resonating through his veins. "Forgive me, Sebastian. Perhaps you are right. There very well may be an evil coursing through me, the very same which kills me so slowly. Surely it is evil which turns me against your devotion."

"I had no right to say."

"Of course you did. I must sound like a child, whimpering constantly. Poor Sebastian. You must endure that too. Forgive me for ever doubting your loyalties."

"Doubting?"

"Never mind," he murmured. "Have I been foolish? Chasing after fancies?"

"I do not know, my lord. What is Man but a poor creature? How can we truly understand the divine?"

"You are kind to say that. More kind than I deserve." The lax jaws of the footmen caught his eye at last and he frowned at himself, kicking the horse's flanks to send it along. Sebastian followed. "We will get this murder business over in Comberton first and then resume our search. I feel damnably stupid for letting him escape."

"It is not your fault, my lord."

"It is my responsibility and I allowed my circumstances to dictate the affair. He is clever and used his wiles to deceive me." Hugh swallowed the sour taste of the words, running his tongue within his mouth. He did not feel that Brother Peter deceived him. He was certain to the very core of his being that the monk's words—or was it the angel's—were correct. Yet believing it did not make it so. He saw that much in Sebastian's eyes.

They rode in silence and camped before sundown. In the morning, they reached the town well after daybreak, but Hugh was vexed by the sudden commotion in the streets.

They reached the inn and entered the inn yard when all hell broke loose. Shouting people came from all directions, converging on him and his retinue. His charger's ears laid back and the heavy hoofs tamped the rutted yard. "Clear a path!" he shouted above them. Some heeded while others surged forward to fill the space. "Clear a path!" he yelled again, this time to the two footmen. They lowered their spears and thrust into the crowd, creating a fence in front of the destrier's chest. "Who is in charge here?" Hugh demanded above their heads, and then saw two cowled men approach.

"Sir Hugh!" cried one of them, pushing himself forward. "Where is Brother Peter?"

Hugh's sneer, a great leveler, stopped the monk. "Who are *you*?"

"Forgive me, Sir Hugh. I am Brother Latimer, and this Brother Herbert. From Pershore Abbey. We, too, have come in search of Brother Peter. Where is he?"

"He is not here."

"Not here? But I was told—"

"Must we do this in the inn yard?"

"No, of course not." Brother Latimer whisked aside, allowing the squire to take Hugh's horse when the knight dismounted. Sebastian threw the reins to several urchins' willing hands and then tossed coins to them. He followed Hugh into the inn.

Hugh strode into the warm, smoky room and sat in a large chair by the fire. Sebastian moved swiftly toward some men gathered in a corner and told them to leave.

"Leave?" said one. "We've paid our money, haven't we?"

"I do not wish to argue," Sebastian said, pulling his sword free.

The men stared at their own meager knives and moved all at once toward the door, skirting the monks. The squire assisted the men with a shove and then stood in front of the door, discouraging any other interruption.

Brother Latimer approached and Hugh studied his angular face, trying to decide about him. This was the spokesman, he was certain of it, the one Abbot Gervase sent out to do the spadework.

"Sir Hugh," Latimer said, clasping his hands inside his sleeves. "About Brother Peter?"

"Brother Peter…escaped."

"*What*?" The façade slipped and Latimer's countenance flared into uncontrolled outrage. Until he seemed to realize it. He relaxed with a long breath, and pulled at his scapular. "I thought you had safely captured our wayward brother," he said with strained composure. Brother Herbert said nothing, but the whiteness of his face told all.

"We did. It is a long story. But we will find him again, never fear that. Now. What of this murder business? Bring the cursed woman forth."

Latimer's eyes darted toward the unhelpful Herbert. "That is a strange coincidence, Sir Hugh. She, too, escaped."

Hugh slammed his palms on the chair arm. "What by the Blessed Virgin goes on here? Did you not send for me to judge a murderer and horse thief?"

"The horses have come back," offered Herbert unexpectedly.

Hugh looked from one flustered monk to the other. "The horses have returned but your prisoner escaped?"

Latimer took the reins again. "Um…yes, Sir Hugh."

"I see." Drumming his fingers, he stole a glance at Sebastian's stone face. "What do we do now?"

"I suggest we search for Brother Peter," Herbert interjected. Hugh caught the vestiges of frustration in Latimer's eyes before they were hidden away again. "And the woman, too, of course."

Hugh remained immobile, causing the composed Brother Latimer to grow in agitation. The monk squeezed his fingers so tightly that they whitened. "Tell me about Brother Peter," Hugh asked.

The question seemed to take Latimer by surprise, and he paused to collect himself. "What should I tell you of him, Sir Hugh?"

"Have you known him long?"

"Yes. Over twenty years."

"Oh." That was disappointing news. He somehow did not expect that. Or was it he did not want that? "Has he always been mad?"

"No, my lord. He was my dearest friend and as sane as you or I. It hurts me deeply that he is so ill. I only wish to help him."

This, too, was not what Hugh wanted to hear. He dared not look at Sebastian. Pressing his thumbnail into the chair arm instead, Hugh stamped several little crescents in a row. "And yet, he still seems to possess an unshakable mastery of the divine."

Latimer paused so long that Hugh raised his head. The monk struggled to speak, composing words in careful order. "Brother Peter…has never lost sight, no matter his sanity, of that which the Holy Ghost teaches. God granted him that. It is a blessing."

"He has a keen sense of it."

"Yes, Sir Hugh. How astute of you to have recognized it."

"Are we not going to look for him?" asked Herbert.

A log snapped in the hearth, spitting a glowing ember onto the floor. It ignited the end of a straw of old thresh, sending a harsh smell into the room like that of burning hair.

Hugh turned toward Herbert and bobbed his head. "Yes. Yes we are. The sooner the better, I think." He rose quickly and was unprepared for a sharp pain drilling into his side. It stopped him momentarily, but by applying his fist to his gut, he was able to move forward without assistance. He only hoped he could get to the horse unaided and stay mounted.

The noise of the inn yard was considerably more subdued from when they entered, and he glanced once at the footmen in appreciation before setting his foot in the stirrup and mounting. Pulling the horse about, he clattered over the hard crust of road. Out of the corner of his eye he watched the monks scramble for their own mounts, and smirked with feral delight at their inconvenience.

The squire's horse sidled up beside him. "Curious events, my lord," Sebastian offered, tightening his reins.

Hugh nodded. Something was odd about all of it. Each affair seemed tied to one another. It did not sit well with him. With a chill down his neck, he considered Sebastian's warning of evil. "String your bows," he said over his shoulder to the archers, and glanced with brooding brows out to the opening hills. He did not like the feeling rattling over him, as if something were looming quite close, something over which he had no control. His palm itched, hovering near the sword pommel. *Nothing is simple*, he lamented. Why could he not have died swiftly at the end of a lance instead of this drawing out? He further wished these monks could be more comforting, but they seemed too self-absorbed.

The bland hills with their scalps of trees held his drifting gaze, and he vaguely wondered if he possessed enough strength to see this thing through. Scanning the surrounding countryside, he saw nothing remarkable from one prominence to another. Even a distant band of three people—two men and a woman—did not at first garner any undue attention.

"My lord!" shouted one of his men, a short burly footman trotting alongside. The look on his face was enough to make Hugh pull on the reins.

"What is it?"

The footman gestured toward the trio hastening across the slanted hillside. "That's him! The cripple. I recognize him. He's the one what brung the Mad Monk his supper at the manor. I'm sure of it. I remember that walk."

"That's the woman!" shouted Herbert. His horse shouldered past the footman, shoving him aside.

Hugh squinted at the trio again. Then the *third* man… "It is a conspiracy," Hugh whispered. Grinding his jaw, his beard bristled. "Stop them all. Stop them now!"

Hugh's mind smoldered with thoughts racing one after the other, competing with the renewing pain in his side. He dug his fist deeper. The reprieve was over. The pain returned in full force.

He gripped the saddle horns and noticed from the edge of his eye that the bowmen had raised their weapons and fired.

"*No*!" cried Hugh, too late.

CHAPTER TWENTY-SEVEN

Margery stumbled. Edric lifted her, urging with desperate pleas. She was almost to her feet when Azriel shouted to them, "Hurry! I fear for your safety!"

"Sarding lunatic," Edric muttered, panic pounding his chest.

Margery was up and moving while Edric bent over for a moment to breathe, hands on his knees. "Edric!" cried Azriel, looking back.

"I'm coming," he wheezed, throwing his heavy foot forward. Looking up breathlessly at the madman, he saw an odd determined look on Azriel's face. *Fear not*, Edric thought. *We'll get you out of this, Azriel.*

Something whirred past Edric's head and all at once someone slammed into him, knocking the breath from his lungs. Tumbling endlessly, he finally crashed against a boulder. He swore and squinted back over his shoulder, ready to hurl a curse at Azriel. But his eyes rounded with horror at what he saw.

Azriel wavered, a peculiar expression of bewilderment and shock stretching his facial features. His body seemed to hang in mid-stride, twisted. Azriel looked down at the three arrows protruding from his abdomen.

Margery screamed and Azriel fell to his knees. Helplessly, Azriel held his arms outward, curiously fingering the stiff shafts.

"Christ!" cried Edric. "Holy Virgin! Azriel! You damn fool!"

Wide-eyed, Azriel stared first at the fletching, and then further at the blood streaming down his tunic. His open hands trembled, and he seemed not to be aware of Edric wailing over him. "This…is very interesting. How unexpected! It simply happened, Edric. I simply pushed you out of the way without thinking."

"Ah, Azriel! The bastards!"

"No," he said, looking at Edric at last. "You must forgive them."

"No! How can I ever do that?"

"Have you learned nothing from me?" Fascinated, Azriel stared again at the spectacle of arrows spiking from his body. "Blood…warm and rushing through me. I will miss the blood, I think."

"Azriel." Azriel leaned, falling limp into Edric's arms. The bruise on Azriel's temple had only just faded, but the others on his jaw from Edric's own fists had not. The dirty bandage on Azriel's arm was brown from old crusted blood.

"Forgive them, Edric."

Edric could not think. His chest blazed with panic. What was the fool saying? "Forgive? Anything. Just…stay quiet while I reckon this out."

The footmen and archers swarmed up the hill, coming closer. He stared at Margery, but her face was blurred with tears. Azriel grew paler and smaller lying in Edric's arms. "What can I do? Ah look at you!"

"Edric." Mouth trembling, his glossy eyes searched Edric's. "I think I understand your fear of death now. For one thing, it hurts." His eyes squinted momentarily with a twinge. "I do not like this feeling. It is so invasive, even if this body *is* only a shell. And the pain…it seems to grow."

"Hush, Azriel. Hush, man."

"So this is death…" His commentary was swallowed by an oncoming wave of panic, an expression Edric never before saw on the madman's face. "Oh, Edric!" the trembling lips whispered. He grabbed Edric's shirt at the yoke. "What will happen to me? What am I to do?"

"You aren't going to die," he said huskily. "We'll…we'll fix you up. Won't we, Margery?"

Margery scooted forward and delicately laid her hands on Azriel's face, easing the hair from his brow. "Don't you worry," she said. But the quiver in her voice did not reassure. "You'll be fixed up proper. Be still."

"Why do you lie to me?" he rasped. "I need your help, Edric. As I have always needed it. What am I to do?"

Edric licked parched lips, and nudged down the lump in his throat. "I won't lie to you, then. But God's truth, Azriel. I don't know the first thing about dying. I've been trying to avoid it all me life. I thought…didn't you say it was a time of rejoicing? That it's the beginning of eternity."

"For *you*! But…I am already supposed to *be* eternal! I do not know what it means now for me. Edric…I am frightened!" Azriel's face whitened, pronouncing the red rims of his eyes.

"Here now. Isn't it you what told me to have faith? Take a slice yourself, Azriel. Why, you've met the Almighty, haven't you? Face to face. You know what He's like. Forgiving and all. Everything will come out, won't it? Why don't you pray? I reckon praying's a good idea."

Azriel managed a smile before a wince of pain soured his mouth. "Of course. You are right. I am not thinking. I knew you would help me." Lids closing, his lips murmured a prayer.

Edric stole a quick glance over his shoulder. Soon the footmen would reach them. He thought of finding a weapon, but there was nothing. The meager knife he stole from the monk was poor protection. Finally, he raised his head to Margery. "You'd better run, lass. I can belay them long enough for you to get away."

Azriel's eyes opened slowly. "Yes. You can both get away now. Go on."

"Oh, you stupid whoreson! Is that why you done it?" His head swayed with misery. "Go on, Margery," Edric cried. "*You* go on!"

Her trembling lips curved upward for a flash, and her eyes smiled at him "That's that melted butter inside you, Edric. But I'm not going to leave you two."

"You can't do any good here, woman. Please, Margery…"

"Be still, will you." Shaking her head, she continued stroking Azriel's face.

Azriel's eyes snapped open with a gasp so sudden they both lurched back.

"Edric," Azriel said, a strange look of awe growing on his face. Azriel's eyes searched past him, gazing distantly. "You must not worry anymore about me. He has done it at last. The Divine Father. He…He is calling me home, Edric. Home, where I belong."

"That's right, Azriel." Gently he rocked him. "You're going home. You'll get your halo back, won't you?"

"Yes. Yes, I will get *myself* back. And I will serve the Lord again as He intended." A breath raised his chest and the arrows splayed and fell with the crumpling ribcage. "This is not 'good-bye', Edric. I will be here. I will ask to be your Guardian Angel, and I shall remain beside you."

"'Course you will. And I can still ask you for advice, eh? That'll do."

Azriel's blinking slowed. The lids seemed to become heavier to lift. "She loves you, Edric. I am glad of it. As for me…if it were not for you…" He tried to inhale a deep breath but couldn't. A crimson trickle parted his lips. "I understand now," he sputtered, "why He loves you Little Creatures so much."

Edric's grimace pooled his own tears around his mouth. He licked the saltiness from his lips. "God's toes, Azriel. What the hell am I to do with that?"

Azriel's eyes rolled back, gazing heavenward. "This is what You did for them, Lord," he whispered. "I did not know. I could not understand entirely before. But now I see."

Edric glanced at Margery, begging for help with his own

helpless eyes.

Azriel took a deep, strained breath, and then another, until his face suddenly opened into beatific wonder. Short, jerky breaths wrenched his ribcage. "Oh! Edric!" he rasped, his voice rattling hollowly. "I can hear them again! Oh glorious Angel voices! Oh my brothers! I hear you at last!" Arching his back he reached upward, eyes locked on the sky. Clawed fingers rose and gripped Edric's shoulders, squeezing. "O Divine Father! Thank you! Thank you!" Gulping a desperate breath it gurgled on the blood in his throat. "Edric…"

Like a cut thread, the tense fingers suddenly released, and he fell back. Limp, his body grew heavier and quiet in Edric's arms.

With great care, Edric laid him down and slid his arm out from under him. Margery's fingers grabbed Edric's just as several ominous shadows criss-crossed over them.

Edric shoved aside the sadness and replaced it with rage. He hurled himself forward, swinging his arms to force them back. "You killed him!" he screamed. "He didn't do naught! He was a good man! He never hurt no one!"

"Get out of the way, you!" said the short footman, prodding him with his spear.

Edric shoved the spear aside. "Leave him alone! Haven't you done enough?"

The footmen and archers were all around them. Edric's strength felt suddenly drained, and he looked up helplessly at Margery. How could he protect her now? He was nothing. No weapon, no strength…no Azriel.

A lordly-looking man stumped up the hill and stood behind the row of men. The two monks rushed forward but the footmen's spears stopped them. Edric's mind tried to take it all in, but his anger and confusion reigned. "He hasn't done naught and you killed him!" he cried to Hugh Varney, for he knew that this man must be the knight.

Sir Hugh shouldered past the footmen and gestured at Edric. "Take this one. You are charged with murder along with this woman."

"Murder? Me? It's you what should be charged. I haven't murdered nobody!"

"That we will discover," he answered grimly. "If you are innocent as you say then all will be well."

"It won't be well for him." Edric turned again to the crumpled, bloody body. Hugh measured Azriel with regret, his face paling and his brow furrowing into a stern line. "Poor little angel," Edric murmured. "I hope you got your halo, Azriel."

A hand gripped Edric's arm, but he ignored it. He expected the footman to drag him off, but when he looked down, it was not the footman's hand. "What did you call him?" asked Sir Hugh.

"That's what he called himself. Maybe he was and maybe he wasn't, but he gave me a helping hand when all I ever got were curses. It was the hand of God!"

"Damn this!" Sir Hugh stomped back and forth before the body. "Latimer!" he hissed at last. "Get up here and take your brother and let me make an end to this!"

The footmen parted and Latimer rushed forward. Pain aged his face and drew his eyes in glossy smears. He knelt beside Azriel and turned him.

Herbert stood solemnly above them, his hands encased in his scapular. But he offered no comfort, no benediction except to becross himself.

Latimer knelt a long time, his shoulders shaking gently at first, until the shaking grew more violent. Yet it was no sob wrenched from the monk's chest, but the sudden incongruous belch of laughter.

Horrified, Edric tried to draw closer, but a footman held him back.

Halfway down the hill, Sir Hugh turned and glared back at the monk. The squire stood flabbergasted beside him. "What ails you, man?" asked Hugh, but when he got no response from Latimer, he turned to the other. "Brother Herbert?"

"My lord," said Latimer, turning and rising. He carelessly wiped a tear from his eye, and gestured toward the corpse. "I have known Brother Peter for over twenty years. We were like brothers in the true sense of it."

"Yes, yes. We all know that."

Latimer chuckled again, shaking his head, and looked once more at the corpse. "But this, Sir Hugh, *this* is *not* Brother Peter."

"What?" Scrambling upward he pushed the men aside and glared at the monks. "Are you insane? Who have we been searching for all this time?"

"I know, my lord," Latimer said calmly. "To end it would please me also. But I tell you God's truth. This is not Brother Peter. I do not know *who* this is."

Hugh turned to the stunned Herbert and pushed forward to grab his shoulder. Herbert yelped. "Brother Herbert. Put an end to this insanity. Tell me. *Is* this Brother Peter?"

Herbert shrugged out from under Hugh's grip and shook his head. "M-my lord, I did not know Brother Peter. I never even knew his name until a sennight ago."

Edric wrenched free and stood over Azriel, searching all the confused faces surrounding them. "Are you saying this isn't the Mad Monk?" It was his turn to laugh. He stomped the ground and clapped his hands. "Ha! You've got the last laugh, Azriel!" he shouted to the sky. "Bless me if you *aren't* me guardian angel!"

"Silence!" Hugh's gloved hand fisted, trembling. "This is not a game. A man is dead. Two men. And *you,* friend," he said jabbing a finger at Edric, "are guilty of one at least."

"No!" All eyes suddenly turned toward Margery. She tossed the muddy hair from her face with a swipe of her hand. "It wasn't Edric! It wasn't me, neither. It's him!" Her finger pointed at Latimer.

Hugh threw his arms up in surrender. "This whole shire is mad!"

"I saw him," she went on. "In the stable. I heard him and the innkeeper—"

"Why didn't you say so before?" asked a dazed Herbert,

stepping forward.

"Would you have believed me?"

"I do not believe you now," said Hugh.

"But I saw him. I heard them. The innkeeper was drunk and prodding him. He pushed Brother Latimer down and threatened him. Said he'd tell the whole town how the monk lied, and then he demanded money to keep silent."

Edric breathed. The rusty smell of blood filled his nostrils, then the smell of sweat and fear. How he wanted to go to Margery, to comfort and to be comforted. It was a nightmare! Why did she not tell him she had seen the murder?

Unpleasant thoughts washed forward all at once, tumbling and spilling into the dank, hidden ripples of his mind. Why had she been in the stable? *Ah Margery. Why'd it have to be him?*

He gazed down at Azriel again. The face, so screwed up before in pain, was completely relaxed. Drained of all color, it now resembled a stone carving. Edric could well imagine these placid features to be the same as those stone angels he saw at the doors of cathedrals. The drooping lids, the arrogant slope of his lips, the patrician nose; it was not hard to envision this face with a radiant halo behind its head and huge feathered wings framing its body…even though Azriel told him angels did not have wings as such.

Edric knew he must forgive her. He knew Azriel would have wanted him to.

Hugh Varney stood still. His hand stroked his beard while he considered Margery's words. Edric wondered if the knight was beginning to believe her. Edric believed her, though he found it extraordinary that the monk was guilty. *The only monk what was ever kind to me. Don't that reckon.*

The knight thought in silence a long time, even looking to his squire, who shrugged imperceptibly. Finally, Hugh turned to Latimer. "Brother?"

But Latimer said nothing. He, too, did not move and barely breathed.

Maybe the whole shire is *mad*! thought Edric.

Even Herbert seemed agitated at Latimer's silence, and drew near to him, his face reddening. "Brother. Speak! This foul woman accuses you. Say something!"

"Brother Latimer?" urged Hugh.

Latimer sighed, releasing his hands from the haven of his scapular. They fell to his sides and a deeper sigh billowed from his body. "Brother Peter once told me," he said carefully, "that the sins we commit on earth are like pebbles upon a scale, each weighing a man's soul heavier and heavier. If his soul is too heavy, you see, it cannot soar aloft to God. But when we pray and atone, only then may we lift each pebble—one by one—free of this scale." Glancing at Hugh, Latimer smiled with a sad curl to his lips. "Slowly, my lord, I lift each pebble away from my own soul." He searched Hugh's face. "How much does the life of one miserable man weigh? How many pebbles will it take?"

Mortified, Hugh stared blankly at the monk. At last he said to the footmen, "Secure Brother Latimer and help Brother Herbert with this…this other."

Latimer walked meekly away to the horses while a footman grasped his arm. Herbert stood immobile, unable to help while several men lifted Azriel's body and carried it down the hill.

Edric wiped his face with a grimy hand. "My lord," he said to Hugh. "What of us? Margery and me?"

"You two…." Silently he assessed them, and all at once seemed to surrender something within. "You are free to go."

Eagerly, Edric took Margery's cold hand and crushed it to his chest. He followed the men who carried Azriel away, watching one of his limp hands sway. They stopped when Hugh called out to them.

"You…you seemed to have known this man," said Sir Hugh. "The one you call Azriel."

A warm lump in his throat threatened a sob again, but Edric swallowed hard, grasping Margery's hand tighter. "Only a little while."

Hugh dug his toe into the grass, kicking the stalks gently with his boot. "Brother Latimer claims he is not this monk. Perhaps he is not. Who is he, then, if not Brother Peter?"

Edric swallowed. He would not weep again, not in front of this man. He inhaled the scent of sweet, wet grass and the gentle perfume of nectared flowers. "Maybe…he was what he claimed to be."

Lowering his face, Hugh spoke almost into his own chest. "You do not truly believe that…do you?"

"My lord," he said, shaking his head with wonder. He cast a brief glance at Margery. "These last few days…I think I'd believe anything."

Clutching Margery's hand, Edric left Hugh, and descended the hill, keeping Azriel's lifeless body in his sights. The confusion and noise withdrew, growing softer as if going quietly to its rest, until a sound rustled in the trees of the nearby copse, and suddenly ascended into the hazy blue, wings flapping, fluttering, and struggling toward the sky. Edric raised his face toward the sound and a strained smile spread his lips.

Yes, he thought. At least they sounded *something* like wings.

AUTHOR'S AFTERWORD

What else but a parable could this be? Sometime in 1999, I got the idea to do my take on an angel story. This story never fit into any of the other molds of what one would call "historical fiction" and so never left the sanctuary of my office. Until now.

I have an old book about the abbeys of England. *Abbeys*, to be exact, by M. R. James from 1925, with photographs, floor plans, and illustrations of said abbeys, most of them merely ruins from Henry VIII's rampage through the monasteries. I came across the Pershore Abbey entry and the mention of the fire on St. Urban's Day in 1223. It got the wheels turning in my mind and inspired this tale. They had a very good library, apparently, and some of its books still survive. As Mr. James says, "Books from the Abbey library are rather rare. Those I have seen (in the British Museum and at Lambeth, principally) have "Parshar" written on their fly-leaves, and no other marks of ownership." Early on in the history of Pershore Abbey, Edward the Confessor conferred a good share of its lands to his new Westminster Abbey, far away near London. The abbey and church thrived throughout the Middle Ages despite this "honor" from Westminster, until the dissolution of the monasteries under Henry VIII. The abbey was destroyed as was the nave, leaving the choir and transepts. "Taking it all around," says the author M. R. James, "Pershore occupies a very high place indeed among our churches."

As for the characters themselves, there is only one actual person from history to be had in the lot, and that is the abbot of Pershore.

ABOUT THE AUTHOR

Los Angeles native and award-winning author **Jeri Westerson** writes the critically acclaimed Crispin Guest Medieval Noir mysteries and other novels. Her medieval mysteries have garnered nominations for the Shamus, the Macavity, the Agatha, Romantic Times Reviewer's Choice, and the Bruce Alexander Historical Mystery Award. When not writing, Jeri dabbles in beekeeping, gourmet cooking, fine wines, cheap chocolate, and swoons over anything British. **JeriWesterson.com**

Craig Westerson ©

CPSIA information can be obtained at www.ICGtesting.com
Printed in the USA
BVOW05s1812190515

401009BV00003B/73/P

9 781502 466280